Wal
Wall, Alan.
The lightning cage

$ 24.95

1st U.S. ed.

The Lightning Cage

The Lightning Cage

ALAN WALL

ST. MARTIN'S PRESS ⚏ NEW YORK

THOMAS DUNNE BOOKS.
An imprint of St. Martin's Press.

www.stmartins.com

Library of Congress Cataloging-in-Publication Data

Wall, Alan.
    The lightning cage / Alan Wall.—1st U.S. ed.
        p. cm.
    ISBN 0-312-28772-0
    1. Sales personnel—Fiction. 2. Literary historians—Fiction.
3. London (England)—Fiction. 4. Mentally ill—Fiction. 5. Poets—
Fiction. I. Title.

PR6073.A415 L54 2003
823'.914—dc21   2002035370

First published in Great Britain by Secker & Warburg
Random House UK Limited

First U.S. Edition: March 2003

10 9 8 7 6 5 4 3 2 1

To
John A. Canning
historian and teacher

Contents

Acknowledgements

I would like to thank the following for their help: Philip Byrne, Gill Coleridge, Ann Denham, Marius Kociejowski, Duncan Macpherson, Geoff Mulligan, Nathaniel and Anthony Rudolf, David Rees and Monsignor George Tancred.

I am very grateful to Professor Roy Porter for generously agreeing to read this book in typescript, and for his comments on it.

I would like to thank the staff of the London Library for their assistance.

Therefore Lord Chilford, having given surety for the person of Mr Richard Pelham, Lunatic, the latter shall be transported to Chilford Villa, Twickenham, from out of this Chelsea Asylum.

It is noted that, as a member of the Royal Society, Lord Chilford has shown a particular interest in the genesis of madness, its diagnosis, and what emollients and expedients may diminish, if not its existence, then perhaps its more terrible effects.

THOMAS PARKER, *The Chelsea Asylum*

For the coffin and the cradle and the purse are all against a man.

CHRISTOPHER SMART, *Jubilate Agno*

During the recent demolition work on Chilford Villa, human remains were discovered in the foundations. They showed evidence of medical experimentation. They appear to date from the time of Lord Chilford's occupancy in the eighteenth century. Police say the remains represent a mystery.

Richmond and Twickenham Times, 1935

Part One

Richard Pelham, Lunatic

Mad: (1) Disordered in the mind; broken in the understanding; distracted; delirious without a fever.

Johnson's *Dictionary*

I never had much time for Freud. Always in pursuit of devious normality, as it lurks and sniffs the wind inside its labyrinthine repressions. He didn't know what to do with madness; his talking cure was no help at all. And it is the madness of the poet Richard Pelham that has come finally to fascinate and hold me, for Pelham had demons. Real demons.

I first came across his work all those years ago in Leeds, when I needed a thesis to write. But perhaps I'm forgetting that the past has precedence over the present: before we can arrive here, we must first go there.

Richard Pelham lived in Grub Street when there was still a place in London bearing that name, before the specific location and its burden of humanity, the glory, jest and riddle of it all, were alchemised into a mere turn of phrase; before grass grew over the topography and turned it into metaphor.

He lived amongst the pimps and whores of his day, accepting all that the glittering squalor of the times afforded, including debts, evictions and disease. His own devotion to gin was legendary, and most people remember him now, if at all, as the subject of that famous encounter with Dr Johnson, recorded by Boswell. Pelham had met the great lexicographer years before at St John's Gate when they were both writing for the *Gentleman's Magazine*. On the occasion of the later encounter, the poet had managed to tumble drunkenly down a whole flight of stairs, despite the fact that the proportions of the staircase at Gough Square were generous by Georgian standards and that it was still only ten o'clock in the morning. Johnson had given Pelham a kindly admonition about the danger of liquors taken in promiscuous quantities, but his words had no noticeable effect, and after he'd generously handed the poet the money he had come to solicit in the first place, it was only a matter of hours before it had all been spent in the taverns around Fleet Street. Many years later, Boswell had asked Johnson what he thought Pelham might have been capable of had he remained sober all his life. Johnson replied, with a shake of his massive head so vigorous that his ill-fitting wig became even more skew-whiff: 'Why, for all we know, Sir, nothing at all. Perhaps intoxication was his only route to poetry, for his genius and his oddity do appear to have become increasingly inseparable.'

Richard Pelham. An accomplished poet in a certain Augustan manner, author of *Psalms of Solace* and *Silent Endearments*, both books highly praised in their day, though perhaps too resolutely coffined in convention to suit the temper of our own chaotic age. But the last part of the Clarendon *Collected Poems* of 1912 contained a substantial section entitled 'Drafts and Fragments', and there could be found printed all that remained of what Pelham himself had undoubtedly thought his magnum opus, *The Instruments of the Passion.* These extracts show a mind far removed from the stately rhyming couplets of the earlier verses, a mind which has undergone the torments of madness, or perhaps something worse, and yet has still survived to bring back news from that bleak kingdom. His text seems almost as problematical now as it did at the beginning of the century. What did it mean, and where was it written? I set out to answer these questions once, at the beginning of my quest, which is now at long last drawing to a close.

Pelham and I have one thing in common at least: financial ineptitude. Though it's true that for a while back there I gave the impression of being shrewd enough. In fact, for a while I appeared positively successful, even to myself. I held up my money to the world and the world bowed graciously and took it.

Pelham's father had been bankrupted after an unwise speculation concerning the importation of exotic fruit and had ended his days in the debtors' prison – an image that haunted the poet for the rest of his life. Pelham went on to become a sizar at Cambridge, scraping grease from the plates of more wealthy (and more foolish) undergraduates. But he was awarded many prizes for his highly formalised religious verse, and by the time he left for London fine things were already predicted for him. Pelham's genius for writing, though, was matched only by his genius for dissolution. Undistinguished journeyman-work provided him with enough money to survive, but in the process denied him the leisure out of which he might have fashioned some work of real distinction. A brief and disastrous marriage was unofficially dissolved when his wife fled back to Dublin, taking their six-month-old son with her. From then on, Pelham became notorious, but for all the wrong reasons. One day, in the church of St Mary Woolnoth, he had started weeping inconsolably during a morning service. He had been led away at last by a kindly verger, who had called a physician to attend him. And so began the first unofficial diagnoses of the man's distress. Hypochondria. Melancholy. Then lunacy. Pelham began to convene public meetings on the highways of London, where he would denounce the rotten and corrupted seed of man's greedy spirit, and throw himself on the mercy of the Lord:

An Angel with a cittern crouches outside a city tavern and asks me, What time is it Now? Time for celebrating the infinite goodness of Almighty God, I cried, and fell down in prayer beside him. And so we did remain enraptured, until the publican violently moved us on. They say that my mind is a lyre with all the strings undone.

Bedlam was only a short walk from Grub Street, a fact that both Pope and Swift made much of when they ridiculed the paltry scribblers of their day. It was no subject of humour for Pelham, though. He had visited the place many times and had stood for hours watching the inmates, chained and bawling as the spectators gaped. In some of his most harrowing lines he had imagined himself dying there, as his father had died years before in the debtors' prison, ranting at fate and God, or perhaps even stripped down to mute incomprehension, like Tom Rakewell in Hogarth's painting. From a safe distance, his wife pleaded and cajoled on his behalf and raised enough money from well-disposed spirits such as Johnson himself to have Pelham sent to the Chelsea Asylum, a private institution under the care of Dr Parker. And there, with no gin to console or distract him, and only his beloved *Psalms* for comfort, legend had it that he had begun to write *The Instruments of the Passion*.

I started research on Pelham over twenty years ago at Leeds University. I had no particular interest in him. In fact, I had barely heard of him before, but my strongest area of study was the eighteenth century, and after taking my First in English, I had been asked if I wanted to stay on to do research for a thesis. The truth – I can admit it now, though I suppose I couldn't then – was that I didn't particularly want to read any more books at all for a while. I had spent the better part of three years in Rome at the English College, discovering that I wasn't cut out to be a priest, and then I had left and gone to Leeds, where I had just completed another three years. Books, books, books. Despite all the climbing I had done on the Yorkshire outcrops, I still felt as though my mind had been overfed, and my body undernourished. And as for my soul, I had spent far too much time on that already, to no purpose at all that I could see. There were lots of things I wanted to do, but none I could imagine ever making much of a living at. So academic life beckoned to me, if a little wearily. I scanned the indexes, periodicals and ancient catalogues in search of a subject untouched by twentieth-century academia. Then one day, I bought an old copy of Stamford Tewk's *Eighteenth-Century Bibliography*, and discovered this curious entry:

If Blake created our idea of the modern poet, in the wildness of his brilliance, it was Coleridge who undoubtedly invented the idea of the imagination. It was not a mechanistic faculty, like the fancy, but the power which makes new all that it touches. In this sense the work of Richard Pelham may be divided into two: the published books, which were verbal artefacts of classic eighteenth-century fancy, brilliant and glittering fancy, but fancy nonetheless; and what we have of The Instruments of the Passion, *which is all imagination, however wayward and disjointed in some of its sudden transmutations. Like Christopher Smart's* Jubilate Agno, *or Blake's work fifty years later, this is what we have come to mean by poetry: reckless of decorum, finding a proper holiness at the heart of things rather than mere propriety, its language electric with longing and desire, its structure a syntax of hungry roots, not a symmetry of waving branches. Pelham paid his courtly dues in the measured couplets of* Psalms of Solace *and* Silent Endearments, *then he retired into a secrecy where his age was not invited to follow, where he was an agent of subversion, a prophet of the shadows enlightenment was casting about it even then. A correction: the age was briefly invited into this subterranean world where monsters were starting to yawn and stretch, in the person of Lord Chilford, Pelham's patron and keeper for some years, but the age quietly declined the invitation, and carried on about its scientific business. Pelham the man, uniquely, underwent the terrors of both star-machine and lightning cage. Pelham the poet at least managed to tell us something of the experience.*

There was an unexpected quality to this; it gave off a sinister glow like marshlight and it held me. When I then checked and found that nothing of any substance had been written about this man since the nineteenth century, I took him for my subject. And so it begins.

The Mad-Doctor

It was once my privilege to have in my care that remarkable though damaged man, Richard Pelham.

THOMAS PARKER, *The Chelsea Asylum*

The man who owned the Chelsea Asylum where Richard Pelham was incarcerated, Dr Thomas Parker, had been highly thought of in his time, though doubts have of late been cast upon both his competence and his integrity. He had been regarded for many years as at least a blessed alternative to the corrupt Monro family and their indifferent rule at Bethlehem Hospital, but scholars have recently begun to establish that Parker's own account of his private institution in Chelsea was perhaps somewhat under-motivated in its pursuit of the diamond edges of the truth.

To begin with, increasingly on the agenda nowadays is the character of Parker himself. He had no medical qualifications, unless you include his patent medicine, Parker's Liquid Panacea, an indigestible concoction whose sale and subsequent consumption led to the pharmacologist being violently thrown out of many towns and villages in the south-west of England. The substance, according to its inventor, could cure insomnia, gout, indigestion, impotence, infertility, insanity, scrofula, worms and baldness. But that was only what was printed on the bottle. It was reported that, in his roadside homilies, Parker made much heftier claims for his mysterious mixture. It was said that one child, having had half a bottle of the filthy brown elixir shaken down her throat by a mother desperate to quell her incessant wailing, had very nearly died. The mother did subsequently admit that the little girl was never to complain so intemperately again throughout the whole of her childhood, though modern interpreters are inclined to put this down to the irreparable damage caused to certain parts of her throat. There was also a man in Taunton who, having been assured that a large swig of the stuff each evening would undoubtedly alleviate the embarrassment of his detumescent state in bed with his much younger bride, chased Parker out of town while wielding a sabre, threatening that in the event of the quack's return, he'd cut the fellow's own instrument of passion off completely. Whatever the effect of Parker's medication, it was evidently not the one anticipated by its disgruntled purchaser.

Then there was the printing house in Exeter, which specialised in medical treatises. It was owned by Parker and was heavily in debt, until it burned to the ground one fine May evening, thereby absolving Parker of a multitude of responsibilities and commitments. Many local people were in no doubt who had borne the torch aloft through the streets that night.

So by the time he opened the Chelsea Asylum, Parker's provenance was hardly impeccable, but for the better part of two hundred years it had been assumed that his treatment of the mad and the supposedly mad had at least been superior to the other alternatives on offer. Yet even in the exiguous, extant text of *The Instruments of the Passion* there were passages which indicated a considerable degree of cruelty in Parker's treatment of his wards, and a remarkable degree of absenteeism on the part of the institution's presiding spirit – eleven and a half months out of every twelve, to be precise. And as for the famous lost invention, the star-machine, the discovery a few years back of the unpublished diary of Nathan Albert, around whom the original machine had been built, established that, far from being an early anticipation of the healing properties of nature as previously thought, this therapeutic contraption was an iron bed provided with vicious restraints of steel and leather, so that lunatics could be pushed out into the garden at night to gaze without blinking (that being one of the more precise and ingenious restraints) at what Parker supposed might still conceivably be the cause of their lunacy: namely, the moon. To gaze without interruption for hours at a time in the middle of the night, particularly in winter when the sky is so much clearer, at the source of the complaint, might bring about a reversal in the condition and thus facilitate enlightenment. Though, as in the case of Nathan Albert himself, pneumonia, lung collapse and a rapid death were considerably more likely, and claimed a number of victims. But nobody cared much, for only a few ever paid any attention to what went on behind the asylum walls.

Still, Pelham was relieved to find himself in Chelsea instead of Bedlam, despite the coded messages and cries for help embedded in his hermetic text. And he survived the star-machine, though the following lines exhibited the terror it had produced in him:

> *Eyes tied open while the heavens weep*
> *Laments for man on his cold bed*
> *Strapped to the contrivance of his exile.*

(One must assume that it had rained at some point during Pelham's therapeutic session.) Given the conditions that often obtained regarding the treatment of the mad in the eighteenth century, the greatest blessing bestowed upon the poet Richard Pelham was undoubtedly to be left alone for most of the time. Apart from his subjections to Parker's inventions, and the periods of what were called his 'sudden Insanities', he was usually shut up in a room by himself with pens and paper to write *The Instruments of the Passion*, and as the asylum records make plain, Parker himself only really remembered he was still there when that famous letter arrived from Lord Chilford.

To Thomas Parker Esq.,
The Chelsea Asylum.

Sir,
 It has been brought to my attention lately that you are responsible for the continuing supervision of one Richard Pelham, a poet of some distinction, afflicted I am informed with periodic bouts of derangement.
 I have been reading Pelham's Psalms of Solace *and also his* Silent Endearments *and have remarked constantly to myself a*

certain preternatural astuteness of mind in the observation and description of natural phenomena, & cetera.

Enquiring of a colleague at the Royal Society, who follows such matters of letters more closely than I, if he knew anything of the man, he informed me that – far from inhabiting some docile country living in a parsonage as I had assumed – this precocious observer of natural phenomena had spent ten years amongst the most insalubrious passages of London, and was now incarcerated under the aegis of your care, his wits having disintegrated some time before.

I have a particular interest in this matter. I daresay you may already be acquainted with the little treatise I wrote a while back, and which the Society published as a pamphlet last year, entitled 'An Aetiology of Insanity'.

I have for some time wished to examine a gifted man, and if possible a man of evident genius, afflicted with a severe distemper of the mind. Along with the Society itself, I have long regarded the repeated use of metaphor as in some way emblematic of many of the mind's disorders.

My informant, who I grant may well be ignorant of the present facts, has told me that the word on Pelham is that the poor wretch, while patently incompetent, is mostly neither violent nor malicious, and indeed continues to compose verses of sorts, despite his unhappy condition.

If this is truly the case, then he would make an ideal subject for my proposed inquiry. I would wish to take the fellow under my own care for some time and study his behaviour intently during that period. My findings would almost certainly be published as a longer essay by the Society. Obviously your assistance would be generously acknowledged. Equally obviously, any promised incomes to yourself from the anticipated clinical care of Pelham over the forthcoming years, would be made good.

I remain,

Yours,

Chilford,
Chilford Villa,
Twickenham

Parker did not see this letter for at least a month, such being the ramshackle nature of communications within his domain. He was in Birmingham at the time of its arrival, having recently founded a new asylum there, and had been busy soliciting potential inmates from disgruntled families, particularly ones where testaments were in dispute. When he finally had sight of the letter, he was so flattered by the scientific lord's condescension that he dashed off the following reply to him, delivered to Twickenham by a courier on horseback the next morning.

My gracious Lord,
Anything I might do to assist your study, which I have no doubt will come to be seen as of the greatest importance, shall assuredly be done. Perhaps we could meet to discuss the nicer points of Pelham's dilemma before I hand him over to you?

I am your obedient servant,

Thomas Parker

The log of the Chelsea Asylum, made out dutifully during those years by its chief keeper, Ezekiel Hague, records that upon Parker's return to the place the following Monday he shouted as soon as he was through the stout oak door,

'Remind me, will you, which one's Pelham? Didn't I machine him once?'

'Yes, sir,' replied the ever-dutiful Hague, 'and tried the other treatment too, during one of his visitations.'

As I read and re-read *The Chelsea Asylum* in the university library up in Leeds, I kept turning back to these remarks, which Parker had banished to a footnote: 'Pelham's wife returned to Dublin, and lived thereafter in the bosom of her Papist family. Her own attempted description of her husband's curious condition was, I concluded, typical of the medieval superstition that still characterises her religion, so I resolved to ignore it entirely, and proceed with Pelham's treatment as I would with any other of my wards.'

I looked up from the book. So Pelham's wife had been a Roman Catholic, even though he himself had belonged to the established Church: it was not unknown. But what was this 'attempted diagnosis' that made Parker think of the popish idolatries of the Middle Ages? I didn't like the sound of that. I felt a pull backwards, in a direction where I really didn't want to go. I had spent enough of my life kneeling in the darkness of ill-lit chapels in Rome, and I had resolved to be done with it, to live in the daylight from now on, in a region untouched either by the angels above or their opposite number below.

The Dangerous World

My mother groan'd, my father wept,
Into the dangerous world I leapt.

WILLIAM BLAKE, 'Infant Sorrow'

And so, little by little, after working my way through the available Pelham texts, and much surrounding material, I started to let the books sit closed on the table. The flat I rented was at the edge of Roundhay Park, where I went running every day. At weekends I was out on the crags climbing with the boys. I even started going up there during the week too sometimes. It was the nearest I ever came to total freedom, even in the wind and rain. When the only urgency is making the next move, or falling off a sheer face of granite, the mind achieves true clarity. But other urgencies were already pressing in on me.

Money had certainly started to seem urgent enough, largely because I never had any, and I was perhaps getting a bit long in the tooth to be shuffling by on a student grant. My thesis, as you've probably realised, was by now going nowhere in a hurry. It was called 'Decorum and Insanity: Eighteenth-Century Literary Convention and Revolt'. My supervisor, an obese and bearded man with a permanent snuffling air of disgruntlement, had forced me to open up the subject a little. He had no interest whatsoever in Pelham, whom I think he had barely read, and though he insisted I should bring in the careers and psychological disablements of Cowper and Smart, he was most insistent that this should not turn out to be a panegyric to derangement.

'There are enough idiots out there pitting madness against enlightenment without you joining in too,' he said, scowling. I don't think he liked me much and I didn't like him at all. We silently agreed to leave one another alone and gradually I came to leave my thesis alone too. Then I came back one day from my early morning run in the park, and found this telegram lying on the mat: *Father very ill. Please come quickly. Mother.*

By the time I arrived in Tooting, my father wasn't merely very ill: he was dying, and in the days that followed, as I sat for hours at his bedside, I had time to examine my feelings about him. I was surprised to discover that they were almost entirely retrospective: I didn't seem to have brought any feelings about him into the present at all. They were all historical, wrapped up in a filament of departed years. He was a tall, handsome man, in an understated English sort of way, a thin shingle of brown hair still raggedly in place above his reliable brown eyes. He was fifteen years my mother's senior, and a well-regarded chartered accountant. I stared at his face on the pillow, and unerased glimpses of my childhood flickered briefly through me.

Once I had thought my father the very perfection of man, but then I suppose that's a gift given by every son to his father, at least before he gets to know any better. By my early manhood I had begun to wonder a little. The strangest thing about him was his excessive normality. He seemed determined to eschew every idiosyncrasy. Each time a new Rover model appeared, my father would buy it, and this was I think the nearest thing to any extravagance of gesture I ever detected in him. He did love those Rovers, though he would never drive one above fifty miles an hour. I once asked him to show us what it would do flat out, and he pulled in at the nearest lay-by, where he gave me a lecture, a long one, on the subject of road safety. He had found himself incapable of speaking to me on the subject of my decision to go to Rome and become a priest. Whatever pleasure my vocation gave my mother, it undoubtedly gave my father at least as much pain. A man should take charge of his own affairs – I think that was his real religion. A man's savings are penance enough. It wasn't that he objected to priests; after all, the one down the road administered the sacraments to him each week. But that didn't mean that his own son actually had to *be* one. I think it embarrassed him. It was aberrant behaviour and it was financially inept.

I was actually out running around the common when he died. The next day, after the undertakers had carried him with all due ceremony out of the house, I crept around his study. Drawer after drawer of docked receipts and ticket stubs, all neatly classified. My mother reported that he had said one last thing to her: 'I've sorted everything out, Sylvia.'

'So typical of your father, that,' she said, with the handkerchief to her face.

The funeral made me uneasy. I was asked to give one of the readings, and standing up there in the pulpit declaiming sacred words to those in the pews beneath brought back a little too much of the beliefs and feelings that had once sent me out to Rome. When the priest read out the final exequies for Adam Bayliss, my mother started to cry. I didn't, though, and it struck me that I had never seen my father cry either. Two dry-eyed Baylisses then – at least we had that much in common. After the reception, when we were back home, my mother said, 'Just think, Chris, if you had continued with your studies in Rome, it might have been you there today conducting your father's funeral.' I looked at her without speaking for a moment. She had been a beautiful woman, my mother, there was no doubt about that. She was still beautiful, with her high cheekbones and hazel eyes, even though her hair had switched from blonde to silver. And I knew that I would never in the whole of my life be anything to her except a failed priest, whatever else I might manage to achieve. Her problem, not mine.

Two days later, my mother asked if I might perhaps stay at home with her for a while.

'You could work here,' she said. 'It's not as though you've any lectures or anything to go to. You spend half of your time out climbing, from what you say. It would be nice for me to have a little company, now that I don't have your father any more.' So I nodded and stayed. It seemed to be the least I could do.

And since I was in London, I thought I should check out the site of Chilford Villa, Pelham's next domicile after the

Chelsea Asylum. So I took my father's Rover from the garage, drove to Richmond and then walked down the river.

Along that stretch, you can watch the tufted heads of grebes dipping and twisting and gobbling about, and count plenty of coots. It was cold, a cold that seemed to lift right off the Thames and into my flesh. I stopped before Marble Hill, its confident Palladian proportions probably the nearest thing to Chilford Villa that the Thames still affords and, as I stared at its river frontage, I remembered Pelham's words: 'No place for the dark inside this luminous geometry.'

I walked past St Mary's, where they'd buried the crippled poet Pope – at evening as I recalled, so as not to upset any sensibilities, what with him being a papist and therefore more than a little suspect. Then I stood before that plot of land which had once been Chilford Villa.

For two whole days Pelham had been interviewed by Parker, who had even insisted that the poet read him sections from whatever this extended work was which, so Parker's employees said, Pelham scratched away at day and night. Pelham took out the large pile of sheets on which he was writing *The Instruments of the Passion*. He started to read, but warily, taking care to suppress any mention of the moon in the text in case he should find himself destined once more for the star-machine. Parker could make neither head nor tail of any of it, and nor could Pelham fathom this sudden aggressive beneficence, from a man whom he barely recognised and who had not initially recognised him at all. When Parker reckoned that he had enough information to make a good impression, he explained to Pelham that he was to be transferred to the care of Lord Chilford, who had a particular interest in his welfare. Parker described the location of Chilford's villa.

'An asylum by the river then,' Pelham said, almost smiling.

'Yes. You would like that, Richard, wouldn't you?'

The villa had been completed only two years before. It was in the neo-Palladian style, which had already been made popular at Chiswick House, Marble Hill and, in a more modest way, with Alexander Pope's own home. Lord Chilford had as a young man been sent off on his grand tour, and had sketched antiquities in Rome, along with the façades of Renaissance palaces. He had marvelled at churches and cathedrals in towns the length and breadth of Italy. But when he arrived at Vicenza, something changed. With his first sight of the Villa Rotunda, as he wrote excitedly in his journal, 'Classical antiquity ceased to be a curiosity in a dusty cellar, and became the purest spirit of beauty and proportion translated into the present. I resolved that upon my return to England I would create something in the style of that unparalleled genius, Palladio.' Chilford Villa was the result.

Parker took Pelham to Twickenham in his own carriage. Lord Chilford's letter to Blount describes the scene.

I had no real idea what to expect in terms of the physical appearance of Pelham, except that by prejudice and assumption we expect a man of great gifts or even great torment to bear some physical sign of distinction too. The slight and dishevelled figure who climbed down from the coach alongside Parker I at first assumed to be a man-servant. It was only when he was introduced to me that I realised I was beholding our poet. A little more than five and a half feet in height with a sallow face, a small nose, a slow-moving, slightly feminine mouth, but the eyes are extraordinary. They have about them a haunted intensity unlike anything I have ever before seen. There is also a scar across his forehead, quite severe, of which I made a note to enquire further regarding the causes. The man stared at me, but said nothing. He had if anything the look of something which has learnt over the years the manner of being hunted. Also his hands are extraordinarily slim and expressive – indeed they have an eloquence entirely their own, and sometimes when Pelham himself remains silent, it is as though the wordless shapings of his fingers would speak for him. I showed him the whole house, but he said nothing. It was as though his spirit sank with each fresh room we encountered. This is probably connected with his condition, as I hope to establish over the next months.

That evening, newly settled in his quarters on the rustic level, Pelham wrote the following lines:

> *A Goth made furious by Rome's luxury*
> *Smash't a household god and freed a spirit*
> *It had once inshrin'd . . .*

It took him a week to understand that he had the free run of the house and grounds; that he could come and go as he pleased; that he had access at all times to Chilford's library. This represented an extraordinary change after his previous confinement. It is hard to establish now what terrified him the more: the unimpeachable geometric perfection of the villa, or the hybrid garden statuary, like the black basalt sphinx, which Chilford had gathered on his travels. And then the following week Lord Chilford began the first of his experimental treatments using tincture of opium.

As I stared at the site where the villa once stood, and where now there was another unimpeachably geometric building, a block of flats, I suddenly knew that I would never go back to Leeds, and never return to my thesis. In truth, it had already ended six months before, but I hadn't been able to bring myself to admit it. Maybe I'd simply started on the wrong topic. I had certainly come to suspect that the unweeded data of the life and work of this man would resist rationalisation, and there was also perhaps something about him that I did not wish to get any closer to. There was no space in my mind where I could easily house him or the anarchy of his torments. I knew that my engagement with Mr Richard Pelham was now finished, for ever I thought at the time. But I was wrong.

Supply and Demand

O! may thy Virtue guard thee through the Roads
Of Drury's mazy Courts and dark Abodes,
The Harlots' guileful Paths, who nightly stand,
Where Catherine-street descends into the Strand.

RICHARD PELHAM, 'Temptation'

Gradually I edged up the speed of the Rover. It accelerated a little crossly, with a bad grace, but I kept pushing. Then one day I drove off down the A303 to Stonehenge, and I had my foot flat down for much of the way. When I arrived back and put the car in my father's garage, it wouldn't shut up. Its fan kept wheezing and there were angry scalding drips splashing down from the radiator. The car was breathing heavily in indignation at me, and for a moment I had the distinct and unsettling notion that some part of my father's identity had been incorporated into its rubber and steel. I certainly knew I was being told off, and that night I informed my mother I was going to look for a job, so I could buy my own car. I also informed her that I'd soon be taking a flat of my own. She looked at me and smiled serenely. We both knew what she wasn't saying: 'Priests don't have to go looking for flats. They live in big houses next to churches, and the car's provided at the Lord's discretion.'

'You're definitely not going back to Leeds?'

'No,' I said, 'I'm not.'

'Something else you've started and not finished then, Chris.'

I remember the late Richard Nixon once announcing to the nation, in that tone of hunched sincerity he had made his own, 'I am not a quitter.' I am, I suppose. I had quit on my training for the priesthood and now I was quitting on my thesis too. My mother was not slow in pointing out the connection. On both occasions, I felt nothing but a mild sense of exhilaration and relief. Perhaps freedom really did come from renouncing commitments, even though one wasn't permitted to mention the fact. I had also quit on Jane some time before, but I'll have to come back to that. I can't face talking about her just yet.

Anyway, I started supply teaching in schools around Streatham. As any teacher will tell you, you can always get supply work, and it doesn't take long to discover why. You're the maverick figure in the staff room, the Johnny-come-lately who'll soon be gone. I watched the faces of the teachers who'd made a lifetime's job of it. It was visible in their expressions how their early enthusiasm (for I was sure that most had had some) was changing into a merely competent professionalism, and how even that in some of the older ones was now sliding into an increasing weariness of spirit, a melancholy resignation imprisoned in a timetable. I started to pick up something of the same gloomy fatalism myself, though I had only been at it for a few months. The sound of a crowd of children bestirring themselves into mayhem, even from a long way off, caused bad, black weather to gather inside my mind. I never disliked them, don't get me wrong. One or two I would cheerfully have killed, like any other teacher, but on the whole I didn't dislike them. I simply could not see the point of throwing my words into that great thrashing pool, as they grew so quickly from shivering spawn into feeding sharks. To read them a poem felt at times like offering up a sacrifice before a particularly murderous sect. I recited one by Pelham, and they never cleared their heads of turmoil long enough to take in a single line. But I made enough money to buy myself a car on hire purchase, a second-hand convertible MG that didn't tell me off whenever I pressed it up to ninety miles an hour. Then I started scanning the Situations Vacant columns.

The ad spoke about a printing firm in Wandsworth, which was looking for someone well educated and presentable, who must also have a car and a clean driving licence. Previous experience in the business preferred but not essential. I posted my letter requesting an interview that evening. And the next Monday I drove over there.

As you make your way out of the centre of Wandsworth along Garratt Lane, there is a scatter of industrial buildings by the edge of the tiny River Wandle. One of these, built sometime in the 1920s in a parochial version of the International Style, was Shipley's Print Group. The whitewash on its walls had long turned to grey, and the yellow paint of its metal window frames was peeling at the same slow, consistent rate throughout. I parked my ageing green MG at the edge of the courtyard, and went in to be interviewed. Opposite the entrance area was a full-length mirror, and I stopped to examine myself. At five foot ten and a half, I was trim, muscly but trim, my black hair cropped to my temples, my chin blue from the scraping of the razor's edge, my face solid and serious, no hint of weakness about it. I had inherited my father's professional brown eyes, and square-set features. And my suit was neatly pressed, my black shoes brilliant with polish: I had always taken a certain pride in my appearance.

Andrew Cavendish-Porter was about my height, but his suit was a lot more expensive. His light brown hair was brushed back from his forehead and had started to thin. His jowls were dark and heavy and I could see the beginning of a paunch which even his expensive tailoring could not entirely disguise. But the scowl of care and concern on his face vanished suddenly as he treated me to his smile. It was a smile that suggested his bank account was in a lot better shape than mine. His wide grey eyes were almost unnerving in their unblinking calm. His voice was low and soothing and within minutes he was explaining that he was forming a new division within the company for a particular area of specialisation that he had in mind, and needed initially a sales rep who could probably soon be promoted to an account manager, assuming all worked out as he hoped. I wasn't at all sure of the difference between these job descriptions, but I nodded intelligently, showed enthusiasm and alacrity, expressed my particular interest in the world of printing. In short I played the applicant to perfection and was told the following week that I'd been given the job.

Outside on the tarmac forecourt, Andrew shook my hand and stared at my MG.

'That yours, is it?'

'Yes.'

'First car I ever had.'

I pointed in turn to the classic Jaguar parked some way off in the corner. 'Would that be yours?'

'Yes,' he said happily. 'One of them anyway.'

And so I became a sales rep for the Shipley Print Group, driving up and down motorways in my car, and taking great care to keep all my petrol receipts. I picked things up quickly. My patter about the particular benefits the company afforded was soon as impressive as anyone else's. And Andrew Cavendish-Porter was as good as his word. Within a year I was an account manager, and six months later my MG was replaced by a company car, a BMW. I bought a flat in Battersea along Prince of Wales Drive. This was at the very edge of the park and on the other side, across the river, was the house of Andrew Cavendish-Porter and his wife Helena. As for academic life, I didn't miss it much. After all, I had my books and my music, women who occasionally came and always went, and I was paid for things I had learnt how to do with some competence. I found the neatness of this satisfying, after the interminable open-endedness and scatter of energies up at Leeds University.

The area of specialisation on which Andrew and I were exercising our joint intelligence was art: art prints, art calendars, art diaries, art cards. I spent half of my time scouting around galleries of one sort or another, where, as we put it to the curators, the full potential of their exhibits was not being realised via their repro product line. I would turn up and explain the various packages we could arrange to print for them, and the irresistibly competitive prices we offered for the service. Andrew had taken the precaution of giving one of the major London galleries such exceptionally keen prices (he worked at a loss to hold the account) that he kept the business year in, year out. But it was certainly impressive when I pulled out their catalogues and calendars. You could almost see the publication manager's thoughts written right across his face as he considered: well, if it's good enough for *them* . . .

It wasn't a bad life by any means. I certainly preferred it to university, though I missed my climbing companions, but it was a relief simply to do a job and see it finished. Andrew and I got on well enough, but he was always anxious for more business, however much we had. Andrew was no small–time Charlie, as I soon realised. And he started to talk one day about going abroad to find the new accounts he was after. Then he discovered I lived in Prince of Wales Drive and said, 'But that's only ten minutes away from us. We're in Oakley Street over the other side of the river. You must come to dinner and we can start to talk about the future. We've already made a success of the present.'

That was how I began to visit the house of Andrew Cavendish–Porter and his wife Helena.

Helena was so gaunt that it almost stopped her being beautiful – almost, but not quite. She was a good inch taller than I was, and you could make out the shape of the bones in her face. Her eyes were such a dark shade of brown that in the candlelight they looked as black as her hair, which fell luxuriantly about her skinny shoulders. She never seemed to do more than peck at her food, though she provided a generous enough meal for her guests, while Andrew meanwhile set forth his views, whatever the topic of conversation might be. Andrew was undoubtedly afflicted with certainty. He never wavered in his profound conviction that if he believed something to be true, it must therefore be indisputable on any rational assessment.

I suppose I'd abandoned the last of my certainties when I abandoned Rome, so it's possible that Andrew filled a gap for me. And since he made me a director of the company, and doubled my salary, I wasn't complaining. I never could entirely understand the logic of his move into Europe, but I wasn't about to pass up the prospect of motoring through Italy and France and looking at some of the world's great paintings.

One day Andrew saw me staring at his other car, an Austin Healey 3000 he kept parked outside his house, and smiled.

'Do you want it?'

'Yes,' I said without hesitation. 'Why, can I have it?'

'It's yours. I'll sell it to the company next week. I'll take the BMW instead. Suit me better for the European trips.'

Andrew offered such sharp prices, including transportation, that some of the foreign museums simply couldn't refuse. In fact the prices weren't so much keen as positively anxious. I began to wonder what my role was during these trips, apart from being Andrew's companion, because his figures didn't add up to me, so I didn't have much to say to those foreign curators. I simply couldn't see how he could make any profit on these jobs, given the cost of shipping the stuff over from England. But he seemed happy enough with it all, so who was I to complain? And he introduced me to some of the clubs he frequented, scattered about the continent. These offered a somewhat specialised service. Along with the expensive drink and the expensive food, there was also expensive sex.

It must sound odd but, having given up the priesthood at least partly because of my inability to remain chaste, I now lived a largely celibate existence. There had been Jane in Leeds, of course, and occasionally these days I would see someone for a while, but never for very long, and none of them ever held the key to my flat. I always wanted to make sure I could retreat into my solitude at the end of the week, with everything in its place, exactly where I had left it. It was pleasant sometimes to have someone to share my weekend drives, particularly when the weather was fine in the summer and I could take the hood down on the Healey. One of these female companions of mine had said to me, smiling, but only just, 'You don't really need a girlfriend, Chris. Just something to fill up your passenger seat.' So perhaps Andrew's clubs suited me in my way as much as they evidently suited him in his. It was brief, hygienic and non-committal. Only once did I hear the echo in my mind of the words of my old confessor in Rome, who had looked at me sadly on a rainy Italian afternoon when I had gone to him to be shriven, and had said, 'Some men seek celibacy only through fear of female affection and fecundity, imagining that to be a vocation, when it is no more than a sin.' I could still hear the sound of the rain hammering on the window pane, and still see the infinite sadness of the old priest's expression. It was not long after that I had packed it all in and gone to Leeds.

These trips abroad involved Andrew and myself in mutual complicity. We were roped together now by our knowledge of one another. When anyone else asked us about our journeys overseas, an invisible wink would pass between us. We knew something the others couldn't know. And this knowledge that we shared also excluded Andrew's wife. In one sense I was closer to his heart than she was. I went over there to dinner more and more often.

Things between them were not as I had first supposed. Seeing her fragile, emaciated beauty, and the twitching unstillness of her hands and face, I had assumed that Andrew had taken her on in his life, much as he had taken me on, as though sprinkling his largesse like holy water over those about him. As though he had employed us both, in short. But as they relaxed in front of me, and grew ever more confident in their confidences, I began to realise how I had misconstrued it all.

For one thing, I started to realise that the impression Andrew gave of great wealth was insubstantial. He was in his own phrase, a bit levered at the present moment, or as anyone else would have put it, deeply in debt. Andrew presented this as a sign of his economic courage, what he called his spunk, but Helena had begun to see it all differently. In fact, I came to feel that Helena's physical gauntness was no more than an outward expression of the continual shrivelling of the spirit within. I had looked at the photographs of her on the mantelpiece when I was alone in the room, and that figure was a lot less thin and a lot more ready to smile than her current incarnation. Helena Cavendish-Porter had come to feel that she had not only married beneath herself, but had compounded the situation by marrying into financial insecurity as well.

The Norfolk branch of the Cavendish dynasty had been landowners for generations, and compared with them everything about Andrew was just a little too assertive and brash. It wasn't as if his wife's family could criticise him for speaking too loudly, for my brief meeting with Helena's relatives made it evident that they had been bawling at one another for generations, across open fields and croquet lawns, and vast oak tables laden with weighty meals; it was simply that he spoke too loudly at the wrong time, and about things his in-laws assumed one discussed in tones closer to a whisper, while locked in a room with one's professional advisers. He did not appear to understand the distinction between what was to be advertised and what should properly be kept quietly stored away with the family silver. His failure to respect this crucial demarcation signified a defect in the pattern of his breeding, which the Cavendishes knew very well was probably irremediable. And now their daughter had chosen to swim in the murk of the same mongrel gene pool. Andrew's apparent worldly success represented for them only the dimmest consolation for such a dynastic climbdown, but probably only Helena knew on what slender foundations that success itself rested and how easily it might all be undermined.

A certain sadness had started to shape itself into a permanent expression on Helena's angular and handsome face, perhaps echoing the distant disappointment of her family. And in his turn Andrew looked more and more at the immaculate pedigree of his wife with a respect which had about it a hint of weariness, much as one might look at a distinguished painting which has cost just a little too much to acquire, and which one is now growing bored with after all. Helena got on with raising their two children and organising the house, which appeared to have a ceaseless schedule of works and alterations all the year round, while Andrew got on with making money from his various enterprises. The way Helena would look at him sometimes implied her acute awareness that, whatever joys he had once shared with her between the sheets, he took most of his pleasure elsewhere these days, between different sheets, in other cities. The whole house, with its eighteenth-century hunting scenes and watercolour landscapes, its crystal glittering above polished mahogany, even with its two beautiful, dark-eyed children, seemed, in some manner that came finally to scar the heart, stained throughout with sadness and waste.

And I was Andrew's alibi. If he dropped me at some European airport and drove off alone in that BMW, I was the one who would call Helena when I arrived back and tell her that he had been detained over there. Urgent work to do. A big print job in the offing. She would fall silent and then say quietly, after a long pause, 'I see. So you have a few days to yourself then, Chris.'

One night at dinner she ate even less than usual, but took more of the wine, and then started smoking one cigarette after another. By the time the liqueurs were served, she was drunk and determined to have a good time, in that desolate way drunks have.

'When I first met Andrew Cavendish-Porter he wasn't Andrew Cavendish-Porter, of course,' she said and leaned forward. She never wore a bra. I suppose her slender figure didn't need that support, but the outline of her breasts was all too visible against her silk frock and I was not completely sober myself. 'Were you, Andy? He was just plain old Andrew Porter in those days. But Andy thought it might sound a bit common to go through life as nothing but a mere Porter. Like one of those chaps who carry boxes of fish on their shoulders, or that character in the John Osborne play, the one who plays a trumpet and gets inside everyone's knickers. So, anyway, Andrew just suggested we should hyphenate ourselves, didn't you, darling? He bypassed the College of Heralds and all that nonsense, and just cranked himself up the hierarchy solo. My parents were *appalled*. It was one thing when great families amalgamated, but another altogether to find themselves suddenly linked up to the Porters of Hemel Hempstead. But here we are, all these years later, still with a little dash of something between us.'

Helena poured herself another cognac, and I reached out and steadied her hand so that she didn't spill it. Andrew said nothing, his grey eyes never even blinking in the candlelight as he stared at his unhappy, high-born wife, then turned and looked at me as he started, very slowly, to smile, and I suppose what the smile said was, 'What does she know, eh Christopher? What does she know of our European nights together? We're the boys with the knowledge, aren't we, and she can't come in, however far her bloody pedigree goes back.'

That night I walked home from their house around

midnight and I stopped in the middle of Albert Bridge to gaze down into the darkness for twenty minutes or more. I watched the moving water and then found myself thinking how it was only a few miles upriver that Richard Pelham had occupied Chilford Villa two centuries before.

Bottled Lightning

Bring in the bottled lightning.

CHARLES DICKENS, *Nicholas Nickleby*

Harvey's discovery of the circulation of the blood should really have put an end to all talk of humours in the scientific community. But the humoral terms persisted, much as, four hundred years after Copernicus, we still talk merrily of sunrise and sunset, as though that ball of flame had never ceased spinning around us, while we remain motionless at the still heart of space. Lord Chilford had a particular interest in the melancholic type, which he deemed Pelham to be. He had in his library the rare third edition of Burton's *Anatomy of Melancholy*, which bore on its title page an engraving with various compartments. The illustrations represented Burton himself, Jealousy, Solitude, Inamerato, Hypochondriachus, Superstition and Madness. Chilford handed the book to Pelham.

'Do you know this work?'

'Yes.'

'I have my own theory regarding the melancholy disposi-

tion, Pelham, which is that an excessive hoard of images and
memories prevents the discharge of disagreeable sensations
from mind and body. This is one reason those engaged in
composition like yourself may be so prone to it. It is part of
your trade, I suppose, for it has always been part of the
scrivener's profession to make heaps of all you have known,
as Nennius had it.'

'And what do you propose to do with my heaps?' Pelham
asked with a wintry smile.

'Let's burn away one or two at least, shall we, and see what
happens.'

There was no pharmacological agreement at this time
regarding the effects of opium. John Jones in *The Mysteries of
Opium Reveal'd* simply stated that it caused a 'pleasant
Sensation'. Some thought that it heated and expanded the
blood. Chilford was widely enough read to know that both
Homer and Virgil had spoken of its healing powers. What it
heals, according to them, is the past still trapped inside a
human being, that dead chronology which corrodes the soul.
This idea dovetailed with Chilford's own notion of the
damaging retention of images, the overburdening of the
mind with lurid, superannuated information.

Paracelsus had invented laudanum, but he frisked up its
alchemical credentials by dropping unperforated pearls and
gold leaf into the mix. This added considerably both to its
mystique and its price, but the devotees who could afford the
concoction swore by it. It took a while for physicians to
establish that only the opium was necessary to achieve the
desired effect, all the rest being by way of a magus's window-
dressing. So there was nothing magical in the potion that

Lord Chilford administered to Pelham, merely a muddy mixture in a beaker. Alcoholic tincture of opium.

Half an hour later, Chilford dropped a pin into a brandy glass on the little table beside Pelham and the poet in his reverie heard a thousand church bells clanging with celebratory peels in a square the size of St Mark's in Venice. Pelham had by now overcome the extreme agitation that he had initially displayed. It was in fact the alcohol in the solution, not the opium, which distressed him, for he had decided that alcohol was an inferno in earthly form for him, and he had solemnly renounced any further use of it lest he should choose damnation and the road to hell of his own volition. But if Lord Chilford said it was to be taken, then he would take it. He had been placed under this man's authority. Chilford was his patron and worldly redeemer.

For the first hour or so Chilford observed that Pelham seemed happy to sit entirely motionless in a chair and gaze at the flames as they swayed and flickered in the fireplace of the study. Pelham wore a fixed smile as the rush of exaltation and well-being swept through him. In the later stages, Chilford would coax the poet to talk about his visions, and note down matters he thought worthy of record. Pelham had occasionally been given borage and hellebore at the Chelsea Asylum, and he had of course indulged himself on his own account with untold quantities of gin, but the effect of the opium was unprecedented: it released what Chilford called the deposit of images within Pelham, including one in particular which the poet had been at great pains for some time to suppress entirely, though even this at last appeared to be free of terror for him. For the moment anyway. Even this particular spirit

he could face now with equanimity, at times even a certain
flinty humour. Chilford confided to his journal:

*It seems to me that if Pelham displays the symptoms of insanity it is
in the form of hallucination and a species of religious mania. He talks
calmly and coherently about what he calls his visitations by spirits,
though informing me that these have largely ceased of late. The
opium brought back some of their vividness for a while. He described
them for me with remarkable precision, as though other figures were
indeed in the room. I begin to understand perhaps a little more the
source of the absurd claims made by Pelham's wife about his
condition, in the letter that Parker handed me. Also the nonsense in
Ezekiel Hague's hand from the asylum log, about the purported
goings on in Chelsea. Anything imaged so firmly and fiercely in the
mind is likely to convince not merely the principal but also the
spectators of its reality.*

*Pelham's obsession with the words of the Bible: this is surely the
source for many of his wilder images of angels and suchlike. A morbid
and extreme imagination fed such stuff incessantly will illuminate
them with all the strength of intellect of the man concerned. I have
encouraged him to read the classics more, though he still appears
determined to complete his version of the Psalms, in the Gothic mode
as he puts it. He read me some, which struck me as barbarous.*

*I wonder if the drug might indeed heighten particular faculties.
Yesterday Pelham informed me, in the latter part of his intoxication,
that he had heard the flutter of an eyelid in the chamber above him. I
went upstairs to discover that Lady Chilford had indeed recently
fallen asleep in a chair. And later he said with great confidence that
we had a little visitor next door. I went into the library and only after
a careful search found a tiny mouse in the wainscot.*

He asked me, Where does it come from, what you are giving me?

Poppies, I replied. Papaver somniferum. *Ah, he said, those little mouths of fire in the valleys. The elves' volcanoes. When I was a boy, we called them lightnings.*

It seems evident that whatever the nature of Pelham's condition it was largely in remission at the time of his entry into Chilford Villa. Lord Chilford, to his credit, soon realised this, and ceased administering opium. But he had brought intoxication back into Pelham's life, after its lengthy absence. Pelham was to remark in a letter that opium gummed up the wheels of time and held still all the machines of invention. He could hear the vegetation outside growing in whispers. A new hole had been created inside him that once more needed to be filled. And at the same time, an old one had perhaps been re-opened.

However chilly and sceptical Chilford's remarks about the reported manifestations in regard to Pelham, one cannot help but sense a certain disappointment at his not having the opportunity to see them at this point for himself. His ambition actively to cure a lunatic can be sensed in the account of the matter he finally wrote for the Royal Society.

Lord Chilford was more and more inclined to spend his weekends as well as his weeks in his large house on Piccadilly, with his young wife, and to take a greater part in the political life of the realm.

There were those who found King George II more acceptable as an English monarch than King George I, though Chilford's Twickenham neighbour Pope had not been one of them. He wrote, 'Still Dunce the Second reigns like Dunce the First.' The new king's grasp of English was considerably better than his father's, who could not understand his subjects at all and never expressed the slightest wish to. George II at least spoke English well enough to exclaim frequently how much he detested 'bainting and boetry'. Whatever Chilford's views on his monarch, and we don't precisely know them, he had obviously been itching for some time to return more fully to the life of the city. He decided to leave Pelham at the villa. Jacob had been instructed to keep a careful watch over Chilford's ward, and instruct his wife to do the same. They were told to report immediately any interesting symptoms, for his lordship had not yet altogether given up hope of a return of Pelham's full-blown dementia. He placed his partly-written paper on the subject in his desk drawer, as the poet, with the last dose of Chilford's laudanum inside him, went out to the house of easement and stood there askew from time, a colossus towering over the waterfall of his own golden urine.

Chimera #1

Let's all move one place on.

LEWIS CARROLL, *Alice in Wonderland*

The worst part of the day was the drive to work in the morning and the drive back in the evening. I was always mired in rush-hour traffic. My Healey was mostly throttling with frustration in neutral. I learnt a different route, up Trinity Road from the Wandsworth roundabout, which gave the chance of one serious flare of acceleration to full revs in third, before the traffic lights came up, and the lords of caution and inertia reasserted their domain.

So it was a pleasant change on this particular Sunday morning to set off towards my mother's house: the roads were empty and the engine of the car chortled with exhilaration to find itself at last with a little freedom. A Healey still has the recognisable sound of an engine, a real engine, while most modern cars sound more and more like over-tuned sewing machines. Mother was making me lunch. She looked out of the window at the car.

'Is that blue and white thing yours?' she said. 'It's very

pretty.'

'It's my company car, mother. I've told you before.'

'So does that mean it's yours or the company's?'

'Technically it belongs to the company.'

'So it's not yours?'

'But I'm now a director of the company.'

'Does that mean you own the company then?'

I sighed. 'No, but I do play an important role in deciding what the company does. One day soon I'll have my own shareholding, and then I will own the company. Or a part of it anyway.'

She looked at me sceptically.

'Anyway, you're obviously doing well for yourself, Chris. You have more in common with your father than I had imagined. I thought God had meant you to be a priest. I thought the way the world worked was a matter of indifference to you, that you were preoccupied only with things of the spirit. Your father would have been so pleased to see me proved wrong on that one. Had he lived, of course.'

As she finished preparing the food, I scanned the books that constituted our little household library. It was well stocked with Catholic items. The works of Chesterton, Christopher Dawson, Henri de Lubac, Ronald Knox on enthusiasm, Evelyn Waugh on Ronald Knox, and Graham Greene on the infinite varieties of worldly corruption. I couldn't help remembering how, although I was frequently enjoined to read Chesterton in my childhood for the brisk and combative Catholicism he propounded, I would more often find my father in his armchair with one of the darker works of Waugh, a look close to serenity on his face. Comedy could be made, it seemed, out of staring into the black pit of human motivation. There was a book there I didn't recognise, which my father must have bought in the last year of his life: a biography of Chesterton. I flipped through the pages. In the illustrations was a reproduction of one of his early manuscripts and in every margin there were doodled devils, vile creatures spitting malice, with nothing comic about them whatsoever.

I left soon after lunch and made my way over to North Kensington. After our fiery beginning in the museum and gallery print business, things had slowed down recently. Andrew spent half his time abroad and when he wasn't abroad he seemed to pass most of his days in places other than Shipley's, though I was never sure where. The numerous accounts we had picked up in France, Belgium and Italy didn't appear to have added much in the way of profit to the company. For four years we had been the fastest-growing sector of the group, but no more. And now we had started losing some of the British work too. Even with our London gallery, the loss-leader which we'd believed impregnable, we had been undercut by some company which had made an even better offer. Whether they too were working at a loss for promotion's sake we couldn't fathom, but we did register the fact that their offices and print works were in Cornwall, not London. I took comfort in the fact that we were an integral part of a much larger organisation. Safety in numbers. And we had done very well indeed for a good few years. All the same, we needed to crank up our turnover. And that was why I was devoting two hours of my Sunday afternoon to the West London College of Art, so that I could quote on a brochure reproducing works from their diploma exhibition. We had picked up a few of the colleges recently. It wasn't big money, but it was something; it kept the machines turning and everything helped.

The West London College was not dissimilar in appearance to Shipley's, except that it had been built forty years later in the 1960s and the progress of its dilapidation appeared swifter. I made my way through the rooms devoted to the students' work, quickly scribbling down notes for the estimate I would prepare the next day, but I stopped at the middle of the second wall in the final room. A single painting there made me put my pencil in my pocket and close my notepad.

I can't explain it precisely, but then I suppose you never can. It was a view of the sea and sky and in the foreground was a figure, sitting on the sand and staring out towards the horizon. The figure was painted in a manner that made it almost epicene, but I knew it was female. There was something about the acid blues and aquamarines and the way they shifted back and forth by way of blue-grey skylines and pathways that lifted this painting above everything else in the show. Almost the whole of it was blue, in one shade or another. There were a few tiny flecks of white and gold, but that was all. Even the seated woman, arching forward into her own blue prospect, was blue throughout, a darker grey-blue that seemed both melancholy and yearning at the same time. I leaned down to read the title: *Chimera #1* by Alice Ashe.

Two days later I arrived with a photographer and told him which pictures I wanted shooting. There was a minor altercation with some official when the tripod was set up, but my card was soon brandished at him, and I explained that I had been asked to submit quotations for a brochure and needed to take a few sample shots to make up a chromalyn. This was, in fact, not true, but I had decided to go in with a number of made-up pages – it would give us a much better chance of picking up the job. If I failed, then I'd have to write off the photographer's costs, but Shipley's could bear it. That was one advantage of being part of a large and successful organisation. My worries about our little part of it were always offset by the bigger picture. I had a certain autonomy, particularly since Andrew had started making himself scarce, so I told the photographer to concentrate on that painting by Alice Ashe, to make absolutely sure he got that one right.

I spent hours into the evening all that week putting a dummy brochure together. Then I made the quote so low that no one could have turned it down: another act of my recently found independence. I put *Chimera #1* on the cover. That was the only thing the principal balked at.

'I doubt we'd be wanting Alice Ashe on the cover,' he said. 'I admire her work myself, but I hardly think it represents the usual standards of the college. Perhaps a little . . . I don't know, retrospective.'

'I found it the most striking thing in your show, that's why I put it on the front.' He was a gaunt man in his fifties, in whom weariness had just got the edge over exasperation. He shrugged. 'You may be right. The actual *quality* of work, though, is not the only consideration in a place such as this.

Alice's piece must certainly be in the brochure somewhere, I agree, but I wouldn't have thought it should appear on the cover. It might give the wrong impression about our activities.'

'One thing I must do,' I said, 'is to have a written agreement from all the students whose work we are reproducing. We have a standard form, but we have been caught out that way before. If someone should start to get difficult . . .'

He sighed again. 'I can imagine, believe me. See my secretary next door. She'll give you all the addresses. You obviously know what you're doing. I find your prices astonishing, by the way.'

'Sharp, aren't they?'

'Very sharp indeed.'

I collected all the addresses from the principal's secretary. To the others I sent a standard letter and a permission form to be completed and returned. Only with Alice did I drive over to see for myself. There was something there I felt I needed to find out about. Hence, I suppose, the almost altruistic quotation I had given to the principal.

Where Notting Hill starts to blur into North Kensington, there are rows of Victorian houses, long ago split up into maisonettes and bedsits, their white, crumbling porticoes often depositing whole chunks of rotting plaster on to the pavement, and it was in the basement of one of these that Alice lived, five minutes' walk from Portobello Road. It took almost a minute for the shuffling within to stop and for her face finally to appear at the door.

Alice Ashe was the whitest woman I had ever seen. Not

blonde and not albino, but white, her hair as moon-blanched as her skin. Her eyes were grey like Andrew's, and a small constellation of ghost-freckles scattered drops of milk over the blank sheet of her face. It was as though, as an embryo, she had been wombed in bleach and the bleach had soaked right through her flesh. In a January field you'd have lost her. It was hard to believe she had ever seen sunlight.

'Alice Ashe?' She nodded slowly. I took out my card and showed it to her. She stared at it and said nothing, as I explained that I was preparing the brochure for the college and that her painting from the diploma show was to be reproduced in it, and could I please come in for a moment? As I stepped inside I picked up that mild reefer reek of rooms from so many years before in Leeds. I stopped in the middle of the floor and stared all around me. The room was filled with her chimera paintings, *Chimera #2*, *#3*, *#4*, *#5*, *#6*. They were all like the one in the show, and yet all different. In each one the figure had taken its colour from the surroundings, whether it was in a bath, before a television set, in front of a curtain, or lying in a field. I walked around staring at them.

'You could have called them chameleons instead of chimeras,' I said and Alice smiled. A smile of such composed distance and serenity that it stopped my thoughts entirely and I stood still looking at her. When her smile ceased suddenly, I followed the line of her gaze to the silky black back making its way across the floor.

'You have cockroaches.'

'Yes,' she said, still following the stately progress of the one on the floor with her undeviating gaze, 'a whole family of them. A very big family.' I had noticed that some of the pictures had been taken down and were leaning against the wall, leaving large rectangular gaps where they had hung.

'Are you rehanging?' I asked her.

'No. I have to be out of here by the end of the month. I still don't know where I'll be going.'

A month later Alice moved into my flat in Battersea, and brought her paintings with her. And her dope.

Ditto or Double

Some would spirit themselves away
With adieus to our lethal rabble
But when they returned, oftentimes the next day
Their dosage was ditto or double.

STAMFORD TEWK, *Soho Ledger*

Pelham detested being summoned to Lord Chilford's room in the rustic. On the table a wax figure of a flayed man stared out at him, his skin all hacked away to reveal the veins and arteries beneath, red and blue roadways of the soul. Lord Chilford had laughed when he had first seen the poet recoiling from it.

'Don't worry, Pelham,' he had said lightly, 'we'll not do that to you. The fate of Marsyas shan't be yours. Not for the moment anyway.'

The room glittered with its instruments, many of them for cutting, sawing and chamfering bones of varying sizes and thickness. A trepanning set lay with its lid of red velvet always open on the desk. Pelham had asked one day what the different instruments were called. That one? A trephine. And that one? A raspatory. And that? A lenticular. He learnt the

names of the catlings too, as they shone in sinister attendance
alongside daintier lancets. There was a small silver dish to
catch the blood during venesection. On the cabinet beside
the table were two skulls, one European and one African. At
times, in his distraction, Pelham could still hear the locked
voices mourning inside them. The brass microscope with its
large adjustment screws seemed inexplicably minatory, a
Cyclops of ravenous curiosity, a polished eye to swallow the
world in a single, meditative blink. On one wall hung an
engraving of a gravid uterus, the unborn child already heavy
and muscled inside it. It made him think always of the prints
he had seen of Michelangelo, his prisoners torsioned and
quick inside the stone, so desperate to free themselves into
the fluent air. On the other wall there was a watercolour of
the shrine of Asclepius at Epidaurus, where the patients slept
on couches inside the portico, and phalanxes of priests
arrived to elicit their dreams, seeking thus to riddle out the
origin and destination of their ominous pathologies. (It was
rumoured that opium had played no small part in this
process.) There were wax figures which his lordship had
acquired on his European journeyings, one of a man with
half his head peeled away to reveal the brain inside. The
expression on his pthisic features suggested a stoicism fit for
Dante's legions of lost souls.

'How is your mind today, Pelham?' Lord Chilford asked,
with a sideways smile as he looked through the window
down to the river. A lighter was beating slowly upstream. He
turned in his fingers a new medical implement Pelham didn't
recognise. A drill of some sort. Pelham looked again at the
skulls on the cabinet. He imagined the sharpened point

breaching the calcium walls, blood and ichor dribbling out. For many weeks now all had been calm inside, all tranquil, no raging spirit trespassing, no voices cursing and blaspheming, no lakes of black bile giving off their feculent vapours.

'I have nothing to complain of at present, my Lord,' Pelham said quietly.

'Perhaps my regime has had some small effect after all,' Chilford said, still with a fixed smile, but no apparent joy.

'Perhaps the spirit is presently bored with me,' Pelham said, staring at the microscope now as it caught the light at an unexpected angle and signalled a message to him. One he did not understand. 'Perhaps he has gone off in search of more toothsome meals.'

'No spirits, Pelham – there are no spirits. A troubled marriage between *soma* and *psyche*, a miscegenation between the body and the mind, but no spirits. We have left the realm of superstition behind us now.'

Pelham kept his eye fixed on the sunlight gesturing so wildly from the barrel of the microscope, then suddenly it was gone. A cloud had draped the sun's face. A vernicle across those hot and wounded features.

'When will your Lordship and my Lady travel back to town?'

'Tomorrow. I'll return each fortnight or so. You are sure that you are happy to remain here?'

'It seems to have represented a great benefit to my spirits.'

'Then stay. Jacob and Josephine will provide for you. They know all your particular requirements by now. Make use of my study while I'm gone – continue with your appraisal of the wisdom of antiquity for a while. I think it preferable, given your condition, to your Hebraic excesses. Studies I mean, forgive me. I had meant to say studies.'

'I have been reading the Aeschylus you lent me, and have been reflecting on those furies. How merciless the female spirit can be without the intervention of God's grace. I should have thought that a mind can be packed tight enough to explode, simply from the images that these works provide, without any Hebraic excesses whatsoever.'

'Try not to have your head explode, Pelham,' Lord Chilford said, rising, 'I've not properly finished writing my account of what goes on inside it yet. Already a source of some excited speculation at the Society.'

'Were it to explode,' Pelham said, bowing to his patron and taking a step backwards, 'I doubt the agencies concerned would seek my permission first.'

Once Lord Chilford had moved back to town, Pelham was alone in the house with the servants, who one by one completed their tasks and returned to Piccadilly, leaving only Jacob and Josephine. For a few days he shifted very tenderly about the place, as though the walls had been instructed to fall on top of him should he make a single sharp noise. The self-congratulatory symmetry of Chilford Villa oppressed him. He loved the perfection of crystals, but he knew that the only creatures preserved in crystalline shapes were invariably dead ones.

Jacob and Josephine were both kindly, but had a way of looking at him sometimes and then smiling broadly, one to another. He knew what that meant. For them he was one more inexplicable indulgence acquired by their curious employer. Certainly not the first, but undoubtedly the most peculiar so far. Chilford had left Jacob instructions to allow Pelham anything he requested and to give him the free run of the house. He had not entirely abandoned hope that Pelham's lengthy tranquillity might still be interrupted by one of the incalculable frenzies of which he had heard reports. Even his study, which he normally locked while he was away, was to be kept open to give Pelham access to his library. No feasible stimuli were to be excluded, including the contents of his cellar. He recalled how in Herodotus some had thought Cleomenes touched by the god in his madness, while Cleomenes's own countrymen had been quite sure that his fate was the result of spending altogether too much time with the Scythians, amongst whom he learned to take his wine both neat and in heroic quantities. The same, he strongly suspected, might well be the case with Pelham.

On the rear porch, set into a corner of the balustrade, was one of the objects of the house which filled the poet with genuine dread. It was a model made in serpentine of the sea snake seen by Hans Egede in 1734, just off the south coast of Greenland. Its mane of drenched coils and its leprous, thrashing, scaly tail had been well captured by the anonymous sculptor. Pelham loathed this effigy as though it were alive and actually menaced him with articulate hostility, yet still he was drawn back each day to stare at it. At night it came alive in his dreams, its fluent language of ferocity restored in full. In some of the dark passages of the house there stood other creatures. There was a Roman plaster cast of Artemis at Ephesus. The breasts proliferated wildly from her waist upwards as though she were a burgeoning tree, the fruit of her own sexuality. There was the lion-footed griffin in marble. And there was the skeleton, propped up inside an open coffin, with his jaw dangling in a hideous post-mortem howl of hilarity. The poet came to believe that this ghoulish glee must be directed at him entirely. And this was merely a portion of the bric-à-brac from Chilford's tour.

Often he would go out into the grounds to escape. There was a rookery among the high oaks. Those black creatures screamed inside their own feathered world. A kingdom of appetite, with nothing to halt it except for the weather. Their wide eyes assessed him in brief glints of suspicious intelligence. Then he would withdraw from both grounds and river and sit in silence in Lord Chilford's study. The medical implements there reminded him how much his mind and his flesh feared intrusion. And then he was off again around the house.

While their employer was in attendance, both Jacob and his wife Josephine were careful to keep their noise in the attic storey, where they had their bedroom, to a minimum. The house was an echo chamber. The regular creak of a bed was like a cumbersome piston movement advertising itself. When his lordship was not in attendance, however, and the other servants had gone back to Piccadilly with him, they made the best of the freedom afforded them. They were both dutiful and conscientious in carrying out their tasks, and they were strict with themselves in regard to the hours when they began and ended their work, for Jacob had been too long in service to doubt how swiftly a good position could be forfeited for ever. But once their day was done they felt free to fulfil their marital obligations to one another. Since the only other occupant of the house at that time was the licensed idiot on the rustic floor, they made no effort to contain their cries, though Jacob always kept close to hand the restraints which Thomas Parker had left behind when he deposited Pelham. You may yet need them, he had been told.

Pelham stood by the doorway in the *piano nobile* and listened as their voices swept and soared above him. How close the wails of ecstasy are to those of torture, he thought. His wife had left so suddenly with their young son, never giving him an opportunity to try to cajole her into staying. He would undoubtedly have made the attempt, given the chance, and used all the powers of rhetoric for which he had once won university prizes, but she would have gone all the same. He remembered the silk sway of her breasts in his hands, as her little cotton shift came away, and the motion of her thighs beneath him as she permitted him to sink inside. Susannah. And little Tom, the fruit of their love. He'd not seen either of them since the day she departed. The cries above him were reaching a crescendo. The frenzy of that coupling made him feel dizzy. Was that a sound from heaven or from hell? Angels' bodies could, he had once been taught, interpenetrate entirely. And demons were fallen angels, after all. He had once believed that lovers should be indistinguishable one from another, their identities merged to the outrage of property, like the phoenix and the turtle.

That was the first time he had gone down the spiral stone steps that led to the cellar. The room was a hexagon, all painted white. Lord Chilford's wines were kept in eight big casks there. Good claret was his chief requirement. Pelham held the pot against the barrel and knocked out the wooden bung with the small hammer that hung on a length of bristling string. And that was where Jacob found him sleeping the next morning, his lips and teeth still livid from the juice of the grape.

The Price of Alice

Weave a circle round him thrice
For he on honey-dew hath fed
And drunk the milk of Paradise.

SAMUEL TAYLOR COLERIDGE, 'Kubla Khan'

I suppose that if I had stopped to think about it at all, I wouldn't have done it. A whole lifetime spent in avoidance of sharing the same space day in day out with any one person, and now, within a month, I had invited Alice to join me in the fastness of my own retreat and bring all her worldly possessions with her. Not that there were too many of those.

I hadn't been the only one who went out there to those women while we were ordinands in Rome. We called them cousins. They had a particular fondness for priests and priests in training. I think they thought some magic still accrued to us, so they might kiss it from our skin, as though to make love to us was a kind of sacrament in itself. As though we could enter them as Christ had once entered Jerusalem. There were a few scattered here and there around the centre of the city, but I always travelled to the suburbs to meet mine.

'How tidily you sin,' my confessor had said to me one day, as with head bowed I told him of my latest journey by bus to the realm of the forbidden. 'How neatly you separate the sacred from the profane.'

Within a month of arriving in Leeds I had met Jane, and two months later we were sharing a flat. Just the two of us and her little boy. He was only four then, the solitary offspring of her disastrous marriage to Roger. I had grown fond of the little boy and I was more than fond of Jane. She seemed as intelligent in her body as in her mind. She had a flare of red hair that settled half-way down her back and covered her breasts when she was naked. Our lovemaking was better than anything I had ever known with any cousin in the Roman suburbs. At night when she slept I would lift up the sheets to look at her body. In the neon light that leaked through our scanty curtains from the street outside, her hair was flame and her skin milk. Uncovered, she looked like one of the creatures in Alma-Tadema's *Tepidarium*. I remember that picture – we reproduced it in one of our gallery brochures. Those Victorians were smart: they camouflaged their pornographic canvases as research into antiquity. Then one night, on the top rung of passion, a second before you step out into space and start falling, she had whispered in my ear, 'I want your baby,' and nothing had ever been the same again. I found myself watching Roger intently when he came on his weekly visits to see his son, and saw the look in the boy's eyes as he welcomed his daddy into the little space of his life.

I hadn't started all this around me, you see. I needed to plan things, to get them right. I couldn't just drop into the middle of the lives of so many other people and begin as though from the beginning. I hadn't yet got to the beginning, so how was I supposed to get started?

'I just need some time to think things through,' I said as I stood on the doorstep with my bags in my hand.

'I'm not expecting you back, Chris,' Jane said quietly. 'We'll miss you.' As I said, she was as intelligent in her mind as in her body. Didn't seem to need to divide things up between them. And she was right, of course: I didn't go back. I thought of her often, and of the boy too, but I never did go back.

After Jane, I watched myself. The minute anyone murmured between the sheets in a way that might end in a crescendo of 'I want to have your baby', I made sure I finished things quickly. The women who spent any time in my flat always remarked on its tidiness, impressed by how efficiently I conducted my domestic life. The cooking, the ironing, the cleaning, the pressed clothes hanging ready in the wardrobe.

'You don't need a wife. Unlike most men, you don't even need a housekeeper,' Sally Leiris said on the day of her departure. 'What do you need, Chris?' And now it seemed I had suddenly decided the answer to that question must be Alice. Except that I hadn't decided anything at all. For once, I had simply acted. Normally I only did that on my way out, not on my way in. But if I didn't need a housekeeper, she certainly did. I had handed her my other set of keys, and had set to work with hammer and hooks and tacks, hanging her pictures on my walls. And when she said on that first night,

'Do you want some spliff?' I had nodded and said, 'Why not?'

There had been plenty of the stuff around up in Leeds when I had been there, but I'd only smoked a few times. I didn't like tobacco for one thing and I was always particular about my physical health. We'd all get drunk from time to time, and that was enough. It turned out that I didn't have to worry about the tobacco, since Alice rolled her joints using some herbal mix. And as I breathed deeply and the music opened up the space inside my head, I looked across at Alice, sitting at the table by the window, and realised that she was even more beautiful than I had thought. Beethoven's Violin Concerto was playing and I was startled suddenly to hear the strings laughing and dancing one over another. Why had I never noticed that before?

Alice had already set her easel up by the window and placed a primed canvas on it. She sat silently and stared through the glass. My flat was on the fifth floor and you could look out of the window and see across Battersea Park to the Peace Pagoda and the river and rows of houses beyond, including the house of Andrew and Helena, which now seemed like another country, one in which people spoke a different language entirely. I would take Alice to see them all the same. I could hardly keep her to myself up there for ever.

Later that night Alice went to the fridge and left the door hanging open as she walked backwards away from it all.

'What's the matter?' I said.

'I can't live in a house with meat in it, I should have told you. I'll dream about it now. There'll be blood in my sleep.'

Half an hour later, I carried a large black bag containing all the meat in my fridge down the five flights of my block of flats, since there was no lift, and put them into the large bin at the back of the building. The price of Alice, I supposed.

I prepared that brochure lovingly. The principal specified some piece of flat abstraction for the cover. I said nothing. When I supervised the printing, I put Alice's picture back on the front where I had first placed it, then I told them to print the lot.

The principal shook his head when I laid it out before him.

'But I was quite explicit. I told you I wanted Edward Holt's abstract, not this picture by Alice Ashe.'

'I pasted up new instructions,' I said, 'but I suppose they must have been torn off. The old ones were still underneath. That's probably what happened. It's unfortunate. I can pulp the lot if you insist, but I'm afraid at the prices I'm holding I just can't afford to run it out again for you. It's your choice.'

And as I had suspected, he shrugged and sighed, and said he supposed he'd have to take them as they were. That night I went back to Battersea with a whole batch of the brochures in my car boot for Alice. I had assumed she would be delighted. She stared at them for a moment, apparently without interest, and then turned back to her canvas.

She had started painting the park. Or rather, she had started turning the park into *Chimera #7*, which was, perhaps, not the same thing at all. Later that night, two joints later to be precise, I told her how I had smuggled her on to the front cover. I was laughing as I told the tale.

'You shouldn't have done that,' she said, and through the

haze of my well-being I felt the sudden sting of her rebuke. It seemed as though her face was focused steadily on mine for the first time, though she didn't appear to be looking at me so much as straight through me.

Months went by and I almost grew used to Alice, even when I had to pick up her underclothes from the floor where she had let them drop, noting out of the corner of my eye as I flung them into the washing machine the small, mysterious, often indeterminate stains that would occasionally appear upon them. I was always cleaning up after Alice, for Alice left items in her wake wherever she went. I could never entirely understand how someone who possessed almost nothing could so consistently strew floors and chairs and beds with such an abundance of debris. Every day I laid fresh newspapers underneath her easel in the hope that the paint that she dripped in her abstraction would land there, not on my immaculate fitted carpet.

After the first week I gave up waiting for her to volunteer to do the washing up and simply got on with it. Once I suggested she might prepare a meal and we had half a banana and half a mango each, both sprinkled with sliced grapes. At least it meant fewer utensils to clean afterwards. Alice didn't seem interested in food. When I wasn't there I don't think she ate at all. If in doubt, Alice would roll another joint and sit there spliffing away by the window, midway between her vision of the park and the canvas before her. The same canvas. I began to wonder how Alice had ever managed to finish any of her paintings. This chimera kept disappearing back into whatever it had arisen out of. No sooner was some part of the park coloured in than it was coloured out again. It became part of the routine of our life together. I didn't resent it. Or at least I resented other things a lot more.

Then it was summer again, Austin Healey weather. Each Saturday I checked the oil level and the tyre pressures, gave her a quick clean and then took the hood down. I drove Alice to Hastings, Glastonbury, King's Lynn, Clacton, up through the Cotswolds, down across the Weald. She would sit silently in the passenger seat as we burned rubber, her head immobile as the world blurred by. If the sun came out, she covered her face with a scarf. Something about her skin, she said. I think those drives might have been the happiest moments in my life. Our last trip was to the Black Mountains. I enjoyed picking the small hotels and buying her meals. I made sure we were always within range of a museum or gallery of some sort. I would take a few photographs and collect their printed material. That way all our trips were on expenses. I had been planning a drive to St Ives when she said, 'Do you mind if we don't go anywhere this weekend, Chris?' I shook my head and shrugged.

'Not if you don't want to,' I said. 'I thought you enjoyed it.'

'I'd just like to be still for a while.'

So that weekend we went nowhere. I continued my study of vegetarian cookery, occasionally looking out of the window and lamenting the waste of such glorious motoring weather, while Alice sat in front of her canvas over by the window. As I said, that painting of hers seemed to go on for ever. I stood behind her, taking a drag of the joint she had just passed back to me. Sometimes there were railings and a pond and grass and swings. There had been a rainbow there the day before, but now that too was gone.

'Why did you paint over the rainbow? I really liked the rainbow – I thought it gave a shape to everything.' I looked down at Alice. The white clock of her face was measuring out its own slow time. She said nothing as I handed her back the joint.

And on she went, painting in and painting out, blackening the sky or brightening the grass, adding a red van, or deleting the same, only stopping from time to time to roll and smoke some more of her herbal spliff. The music from the hi-fi system swelled and coasted, and for a while there were no hard edges at all in that flat with Alice. All geometry was abolished, as the straight lines and right angles slowly distorted and the ragged scrolls of smoke rose to the ceiling.

The following Monday Andrew made one of his rare appearances at Shipley's. He handed me the invoice for the work at the West London College. That was going back a bit.

'I hadn't realised we'd started working for charity,' he said. Andrew still had his smile in place, but it had thinned out somehow.

'Just to get the work,' I said.

'Hardly seems worth it for five thousand brochures a year, does it? You weren't even quoting at cost. By the way, from now on use CP Transport for all freight and deliveries, all right? I have asked you before.'

'It was only the other side of London, Andrew. I drove over with the stuff myself.'

'Thereby giving something else away free. Well done. As I said, from now on use CP for everything. No exceptions.'

'But they're in Bristol. Surely you don't want me to bring them up here for local deliveries?'

'For the third time, Chris' – Andrew's voice was now quiet and low, and there was even a hint of menace in it, the first time I'd ever heard it – 'use CP for everything.' I felt the need to change the subject quickly.

'By the way, I'm no longer alone.'

'Did you find Jesus?'

'No. Alice. She's moved in with me.' Andrew's full smile returned.

'Alice. Not a dog or a budgie, I take it? A girl?'

'A girl.'

'A grown-up one?'

'A woman, in fact.'

'Well, how exciting. Bring her over for dinner on Friday. I'm sure Helena will be thrilled. She kept asking where you'd suddenly disappeared to. I told her it must be either sex or religion.'

I don't know how much Alice smoked on an average day. I didn't even know who or where her supplier was, though I had a suspicion. It made her serene, perhaps even a little distant. Occasionally she seemed actually disconnected from everything around her; immersed entirely in the world of her own preoccupations. There were minute time lags between her eyes and her words. What she said often seemed unsynchronised with what she was thinking. At a guess, I would say that she'd already had a good few joints by the time I arrived back that Friday. So when she suggested we share one last one before setting out, I suggested we didn't.

'There'll be wine,' I said. 'Let's take it easy. We can have one when we get back.' Alice was clothed as she always was. As casually as I could, I wondered out loud whether she might perhaps consider putting a dress on. I knew that she had one because I had ironed it the day before. She gave me that look of hers, which could appear so serene sometimes, but at others could be perilously close to vacancy. Then she went off to the bedroom without saying a word. When she came back, she had put on the short green dress. Over the top of her blue jeans. And she still retained the constructor's boots on her feet. But then, she was a painter, after all. I didn't have the strength to argue.

We walked across the bridge and stopped there awhile to watch the river. When we arrived at the house, it was Andrew who opened the door. He was in his suit, but then he usually was. He looked at Alice, and there was a momentary flicker, no more than that, but enough to register his surprise. Then Helena appeared in a full-length red velvet dress, and I realised they had decided this was a ceremonial occasion. Helena looked Alice up and down, from the mop of her white bedraggled hair to her building-site boots, and simply said, 'Well.'

I fumbled my way through the introductions as we entered and were given our glasses of wine.

'And what do you do?' Andrew asked.

'I paint. I did a diploma at the West London College of Art.' Andrew swung his eyes towards the ceiling in his characteristic gesture of concentration and recollection. I noticed the small tuft of hair growing out of his nostrils.

'West London College of Art,' he said finally, 'but now, didn't we just do a job for them?'

'Yes,' I said. 'Quite a while back actually. The brochure, remember. That's Alice's painting on the front.' Andrew looked at me in silence, as though in the middle of a calculation, and then started to nod his head slowly as the facts sank in.

I had forgotten, of course. I had omitted entirely to mention Alice's dietary exclusions, which in fact were now my dietary exclusions too. I had taken her pledge. The subject of meat had been banished from our lives. When both our hosts were out of the room for a moment, I spoke quietly and hurriedly to Alice.

'I'm sorry. I forgot all about asking for a vegetarian meal. Slipped my mind completely. You're amongst serious carnivores here. Let's not make a fuss about it. If there's meat on your plate, I'll eat it for you.'

'I thought you'd given it up.'

'I have,' I said. 'But, just tonight.' I had begun to wish I had agreed to that pre-dinner joint after all.

So it was that when the Parma ham and melon were served, I managed somehow to scoop all the ham from Alice's plate while no one else was looking. And then, when the medallions of lamb appeared, I forked those from her plate too, leaving her with the vegetables. She took out a paper handkerchief from her jeans pocket and carefully wiped the traces of blood from the porcelain. Then she dropped the soiled paper on to her side plate. I picked it up quickly and stuffed it into my pocket. Thus did we survive dinner, perilously.

Alice had never demonstrated much of an appetite for sustained conversation, but it had not seemed to matter overmuch while the two of us were alone together in my flat across the river. That evening, around the table, her lack of interest in the content of questions addressed to her started to feel like more of a liability. Andrew and Helena finally gave up, and spoke exclusively to me, as though she weren't there at all. If they wanted to find out something about Alice, they asked me instead. Helena occasionally glanced in her direction and then back, reproachfully I began to think, towards me, as though to say, 'What on earth do you think you're about here? There must be the better part of fifteen years between you, and you have nothing in common, apart from the one obvious thing. The girl not only doesn't know how to dress; she's barely capable of coherent speech. Can sex *really* be so important, Chris?'

After dinner we wandered about, sipping coffee. Andrew decided to show off the Cavendish-Porter collection of paintings, what with Alice being in that line of business. He seemed particularly interested in her view of the hunting scenes.

'A wedding present, actually. What do you think of them?' Andrew was well oiled by now, and affable again.

Alice looked at them only for a matter of seconds and said, 'I think they're quite disgusting.'

'Disgusting?' Andrew echoed, evidently taken aback.

'They're all so formulaic,' Alice said, 'and the formula is only there to remind everyone what a lovely time you can have tearing other creatures to pieces.' Andrew stared at her, as though for the first time fully taking her in, as he considered the implications of this, which was by far her longest statement of the evening.

'Oh God, you're not one of *those* are you? Never heard such bloody nonsense in my life, frankly. Helena spent most of her childhood on top of a horse, didn't you, darling?' He shouted this last phrase through the open door, but Helena had started to wash up. Noisily. With each clanging lid and clattering plate I felt I heard an instruction to be gone.

That night, for the first time since she had moved in, Alice and I did not make love.

'You're full of meat,' she said. 'There's an animals' graveyard inside you.'

I lay there and reflected on the evening. Alice had already started snoring, very gently. It struck me that I had never before seen Andrew and Helena bonding; they had even started confirming one another's opinions, nodding at one another's pronouncements. Alice had managed to bring them together in a surge of shared hostility.

I pulled the sheets gently from her so that I could stare at her small boyish body, and I marvelled to see how dark the hair between her legs appeared in the gloom. I looked again at the hair on her head, but it was entirely white, and every single straggle of it seemed a different length from all the others. How could that be? Then I lay and listened to the sound of her, the little unexpected mountains that breached the mist of her breathing. It was warm in the room and I didn't cover her again. I kept looking her up and down, from the charcoal furrow between her legs to the firm, small pointings of her breasts. Then at last my head sank back on to the pillow, and we lay there, the two of us, like a couple of Spartan soldiers sprawled on the hillside together after battle.

His Sudden Fits

I'm sipping at a distillation of the crystal-fountain, an alchemical pot-full glows translucent in its clarity here on the table, and its bright and esoteric metal has begun once again to illuminate my veins. Gin: ardent spirit of Geneva, the stringent logic of the heart, the machinery that snares a creature used to soaring.

RICHARD PELHAM, *Letters*

Jacob did not at first know what to make of it, but his lordship had been most specific in demanding of him that whatever Pelham required should be provided. So he found a small table and chair and moved them down to the cellar, as the poet had requested, and Pelham started to pass his days between Chilford's study and the white hexagonal room underground, where he would take the books he had chosen, while helping himself to liberal potions from the casks. And he covered sheet after sheet of paper with his scribbles. Some days he did nothing else. Once, while the poet slept in an untidy heap, Jacob had picked one up and started to read:

Shall charity at least permit the adder his venom?

He had gone out and searched the grounds for adders, but had found none. That night as he lay in his bed with his hand on his wife's stiffening nipple, he said, 'He's a sot as well as a madman. Still, why should we complain? I daresay it's easier than entertaining princes.'

'Some princes are sots and madmen too, my love.'

Pelham refilled his glass. What, he was asking himself, do the teeth of desire finally close on? An apple or a grape? If a grape, then by drinking the juice from the grape the need for mastication can be avoided. Then wine could take the teeth out of desire, and all the sharpness from the heart's affections. Surely some ancient source had somewhere noted this down? Surely somewhere in Lord Chilford's library there must be an account of this? He took himself back up the stairs to search.

Inside the study, he stopped momentarily at the curious transparent effigy mounted on its own little plinth by the door. Two figures, one kneeling, one supine, the hands of the one plunged into the torso of the other. His lordship had informed him it was a present from his wife and was meant to signify love, but for the poet it looked closer to surgery.

'It's a whimsy-glass, Pelham, a frigger, no more,' Lord Chilford had called one day, as he saw him eyeing it defensively.

Many of the books from antiquity which Chilford had acquired Pelham had already examined. After a half-hour, it suddenly struck him that his lordship might himself have penned some thoughts on the subject, so he did what he had never done before: he turned the key to Lord Chilford's desk drawer and started rustling through the papers inside. He found nothing on the teeth of desire, but he did find a pile of sheets with this title: *Mr Richard Pelham, Lunatic.* And with his back against the wall, and his haunches on the cold floor, he began to read.

Mr Richard Pelham was brought to my home at Twickenham in May of this year from the Chelsea Asylum, with the full co-operation of Dr Thomas Parker.

As will probably be known to the Society's members, Pelham had made a name for himself with some volumes of verse, whose skill and aptitude were matched by a most acute observation of the minutiae of Nature. Pelham was thought to be destined for a life of literary accomplishment, but this was not to be.

Instead the progress of his years has evidenced acute debauchery followed by a descent into madness. At present the lunacy itself is in remission, though signs of it re-emerge frequently, not in noisome exhibitions, or physical tantrums, but in a kind of waking delirium which seems frequently to afflict him. His writings these days consist of little more than a glossography of this delirium. While his mind has lost none of its acuteness in local and specific observation, it appears governed entirely, if governed at all, by incoherent passions. In his writings, fantasies of religious victimhood are often expressed as identification with the Messiah. The expressions of religious belief which I have gleaned from him would make even the wildest Enthusiasts on makeshift outdoor pulpits sound like epiphanies of the Rational Mind. Wit at its most facetious has overrun judgement entirely.

In pursuit of my own theories regarding the retention of memories by the melancholic type, I administered opium to Pelham over a number of weeks. His ravings were lyrical and of some interest. There was also, unless I'm mistaken, a heightened sensibility in regard to sound. There was not, however, the disembarkation of clotted remembrance; I was disappointed in the hoped-for effect of alleviating this pressure of congealed chronology upon the normal mental functions. The same patterns of over-excitement followed by paralysing sloth are also observable, though much less pronounced than previously.

We have so far been treated to none of the 'sudden fits of insanity' noted by others. I had hoped to distil the essence of this phenomenon from the superstitious dross which has surrounded it. I shall not tire the patience of other members with some of the cant of darker and earlier ages to which I have been treated on this subject.

Pelham, despite his considerable gifts, is evidently in a state of intellectual incompetence, exacerbated by scriptural and theological obsession. It is hard to envisage him ever making a full enough recovery to take much part in life, public or otherwise, in any rewarding manner.

THIS PAPER TO BE CONTINUED

Pelham read this document twice and then he went to his room, where he collected some of the money that he still had in his possession, despite the bribes he had given weekly to the keepers at the Chelsea Asylum, and walked out of the house and the grounds. There were no instructions to say that he should not do this, but it was the first time that he had, all the same. He walked up the road to where Strawberry Hill was being Gothicised, and he slipped in unnoticed through the gate. Walpole had already finished feeding his birds and squirrels for that day and had set out for the House of Commons. And Pelham stared about him at what Lord Chilford once described as 'that fop's gimcrack castle, spirited out of the ghost of a past that never even existed in the first place'. With his dusty clothes and the buttons missing from his waistcoat, Pelham had about him the look of a cultivated foreman, and he simply stepped through the open door. The library was being completed. The famous pierced Gothic arches of the bookshelves had not yet received any volumes, but the borrowings from Westminster Abbey and old St Paul's were obvious enough to Pelham's eye and he saw what was going on immediately, with his first brief glance at the fake groinings above him. Gothic had been turned into a pretty confection for some fellow's private amusement. It was altogether too delicate, with its traceries and fretwork, and nothing else grand enough to offset the delicacy. An environment for priests, but without any priests to put inside it, either to consecrate or shrive. It lacked the awesome proportions of belief. It was devoid of reverence or terror. As he was leaving, he said to a workman, 'Don't trust this building, it's telling you lies.' Both Ruskin and Pugin were to say more or less the same thing when they arrived for their own visits a century later.

The Thames had always been a living thing for Pelham, from its source somewhere in Gloucestershire, not far from where he had been born, all the way to Gravesend, where, as he once wrote, fresh water and salt engaged in tidal dalliance, and the river opened its mouth on the sea, like a long, coiling fish. He watched its changing moods, and the joy or displeasure with which it allowed the boats to ride its back, or froze to virgin linen for ice-fairs. Now he walked along the towpath, noting the occasional didapper and asking the good Lord to spare him the cup he sensed was about to be offered.

And offered it was, at the first gin shop he came to in Teddington. Without hesitation he took it. The liquor burned away his guilt and increased his anger. That was to begin with, then he took more, until his anger had disappeared too, along with his guilt, until his mind became one with the gin and his thoughts translucent fish that moved about inside the sea of it, luminous spirits silently swerving this way then that inside the great cold aquarium of intoxication. He slept the first night on a pallet in the back of a tavern, and the second in a ditch beside the river, where he was terrified by a gang of lobcocks braying at some little local victory or outrage.

(Pelham's appetite for gin is at least worth a footnote here. It was not a gentleman's drink, but then Pelham was not really a gentleman. And even if he had been, the marks of derangement upon him would have meant that the normal rules did not apply. Gin was the drink of the poor. It was lethally powerful, and its effects troubled the government of the day so much that it introduced not one, but two, acts in rapid succession in an attempt to limit its sale. In Hogarth's prints, *Beer Street* and *Gin Lane*, the effects of traditional English ale are contrasted with this novel concoction, so potent it swiftly makes mothers sodden with oblivion, oblivious enough, indeed, to allow their own infants to fall to their deaths in the stairwells below. It is the poison of skeletal apparitions. Pelham had started to drink it in his days of penury on Grub Street. And just as, many years later, the Paris painter Utrillo would refuse a fine vintage, for he could take pleasure only in cheap, harsh wine drunk in great quantities, so it seems that the damaging intoxication supplied by gin provided Pelham with a sensation nothing else could match. Lord Chilford's wine had merely served by way of a prelude before the return of this darker theme.)

By the time he returned to the villa, he was ill, sick in his body as well as his mind. Jacob saw his ragged figure coming across the grass and led him gently to his room, where he put him to bed. At some point over the next twelve hours the symptoms which others had described, but neither Jacob himself nor his master had ever witnessed, returned in full. The sound of the crashing and yelling below woke Jacob and he rushed down the stairs to find Pelham surrounded by wreckage and yelling obscenities in a manner he would never have expected, given his knowledge of this deranged but gentle man. The newly acquired strength of the raging figure astonished him too, and it was only with the greatest difficulty that he managed to subdue him. So alarmed was he at the unexpected power confronting him in the shape of the diminutive poet that he shouted to Josephine to bring in the restraints that Thomas Parker had brought with him from the asylum. With these devices he chained and clamped Pelham to the bed, telling his wife to leave them so that she should not be tainted by the filth spewing from the man's mouth. Only when he was sure Pelham could not escape his restraints did he go out and saddle his horse. Then he rode at full speed to Lord Chilford's house on Piccadilly.

By the time his lordship arrived at Twickenham in the early hours of the morning, Pelham's fit had ceased. Although not asleep, he seemed to be drained of all energy, emotion or even capacity for speech. He lay in a state of tremulous vacuity. Josephine stood in silence at the edge of the room, staring at his supine shape on the bed.

Chilford walked over quietly to his side.

'How do you feel, Richard?' There was no reply. Chilford took his hand, and noted how cold it felt. The room too seemed icy. 'You have had one of your seizures, you poor man. Can you remember anything of it?' Still there was no reply. Chilford placed the palm of his hand upon the poet's forehead. The sweat had dried now, and the flesh felt as chilly as that of a corpse. Pelham appeared to be in some kind of trance. His lordship turned to go, but Josephine had started to point at Pelham's chest.

'What is it?' asked Jacob. But she said nothing, only carried on pointing. Chilford walked to the bed once more and pulled back the sheet. He stood staring at the marks on Pelham's flesh. He turned back towards Jacob and Josephine.

'Has he had access to any implement?' They both shook their heads. 'And you are sure these marks were not here when you undressed him, Jacob?' In silence, Jacob nodded his head slowly to show that they had not been. Chilford asked Jacob to go to his study, and bring back a quill, ink and paper, then he carefully copied what he saw, reproducing it as exactly as he could.

Later, sitting alone at his desk, he stared at the page before him, and finally said to himself out loud, 'Now how on earth did you do that?' Then he called to Jacob to bring him some of Pelham's manuscript papers for *The Instruments of the Passion*. He studied a number of these carefully and held them against the sheet upon which he had just written. He was no graphologist, but he could not help but notice an unmistakable similarity. For several hours, Lord Chilford wrote out his notes. When he was finished he walked to the window and stared down at the river. Only then did he at last start to smile.

The next day he spoke separately to Jacob and Josephine. He wanted to make absolutely sure that there had been no connivance between them, though he could not imagine why there should have been. At the end of his interview with Josephine, she faltered before leaving.

'What is it?' he had asked, alerted suddenly by her discomfort, for she was obviously distressed. 'Come along Josephine, I need to be apprised of all that occurred.'

'When I was alone in the house with him, after Jacob had gone to fetch your lordship, his voice suddenly changed. I was standing outside the room and I heard something different. I went inside.'

'And?'

'He spoke to me private words, words that only Jacob and I share. In the privacy of our bed.' Lord Chilford thought for a moment.

'He could have overheard them. He has been here in the house alone with you both.'

'But it was Jacob's voice doing the talking, not his. That's the only reason I stepped back inside. Whatever could have made that room so cold?'

'A window had probably been left open,' Chilford said impatiently. He was staring distractedly down towards the Thames, his smile now gone entirely.

'Everything was closed, my Lord. Jacob made sure before he left that everything was locked up tight.'

Later, Chilford summoned Jacob back to his study.

'Is there anything else Pelham said that you didn't tell me?' Jacob looked uncomfortable.

'There were many things he said. He was shouting all sorts of things, most of which are best forgotten.' Chilford walked round the table and laid his hand on Jacob's shoulder.

'What did he say that you are so anxious to spare me?' Jacob looked up finally, always the obedient servant; it was too late now for him to change that.

'He said my Lady would die, though it didn't seem to be him speaking. He said she would die in childbirth, my Lord.'

Chimera #2

The great post-natal myth: that we get born all at once.

HERMANN SIEGFRIED, *Chimera*

I had decided to surprise Alice, though in one sense perhaps I surprised her all the time. That's to say that, since she never made any decisions herself, I took them all for her. Almost all: let's not forget her weekly trip to the Siegfried Group in North Kensington, where I presumed she also collected her dope, which I'd developed a taste for, so I wasn't complaining. I planned the holiday in secret. I had booked two weeks in Tenby, in a house at the very edge of the harbour. I could imagine her sitting there drawing. I didn't tell her until the night before that we were going, and even then I only said 'A trip to Tenby' – I didn't say for how long. I had already packed spare clothes for her, not that she'd have noticed. She looked at me in silence for a moment.

'Where's Tenby?' she said finally. She was cutting her hair with a pair of nail scissors. There was no mirror in front of her during this operation, and that presumably explained why every strand was always a different length. I hurriedly dropped some sheets of paper on the floor about her chair.

'In Pembrokeshire. You can take your sketchbook and do some drawing.'

'I don't have a sketchbook,' she said, 'and I don't draw.'

The next day I rose early, took a shower and went to sort out the car. Tyre pressures. Oil. Petrol. I took the hood down. The sun was already bright in the autumn sky. When I finally came back into the bedroom with a coffee in my hand, I stared at Alice tangled in the bedclothes. Her flesh looked even whiter than the sheets. Finally she uncoiled from her sleep and stumbled into the living room, and as she sat at the table rolling a supply of joints in preparation for our journey, I plotted the route. Four and a half hours later we were driving along the twisting road that riddles its way down to the Pembrokeshire coast.

As we let ourselves into the blue house on the harbour front, Alice said, 'I didn't think you could rent places like this just for the weekend.' I said nothing.

From the wide, low window sill you could stare out at the boats bobbing on the swell, and this was where Alice almost immediately positioned herself, her arms locked around her knees. She had placed *Chimera* by Hermann Siegfried on the table, and it lay there like a Gideon's Bible in a hotel room. I knew she had put it there for me to read, for she had asked me to look at it a number of times before. I'd always managed to evade the invitation. It seemed to be the only book she possessed, and the members of the group she visited every Wednesday evening were, as far as I could understand, entirely devoted to the wisdom it contained. As she studied the metronome masts of Tenby's tiny fleet, slapping wave-time back one way then the other, I opened it and looked at a chapter title: 'Character as Signature'. Then I closed it again. I put the book down and walked over to Alice at the window. I dropped my hand gently on to her shoulder.

'Let's take a walk outside.' Without nodding or speaking, she simply stood up in physical acquiescence and I found myself reflecting how often she did that. I suppose that's what she'd done when I had invited her to join me in my flat in Battersea.

If you walk to the very top of the High Street, Tenby Bay suddenly opens out beneath you. You are on the same level now as the swooping, shrieking gulls. And here we sat on one of the benches gazing into the sky and sea before us. I had taken her hand, but she had not taken mine back, simply accepted my grasp, as usual. It did occur to me from time to time that I never had the faintest notion what was going on inside her head. I sometimes wondered if anything was going on in there at all. Could it really be possible simply to absorb life, instead of arguing with it all the time the way that I mostly did? Though I'd been arguing less of late. Whether you put it down to Alice or her spliff, or maybe the mixture of both, I had been calming down. I wasn't even cross with God any more.

'Beautiful, isn't it?' I said.

'Yes,' she said quietly. 'A pity we won't be here more than a few days.' That was going to be the biggest surprise of all.

I suppose people go to the seaside to be inside the weather, to crouch inside the season's heart. For the whole of that weekend it was a delight to be there, to be included in the early autumn sunshine and breezes. We walked the beaches, we found the places that served vegetarian food, we made love. Alice even started to ask me questions. I had fed her plenty of information about myself during the time we had spent together, but she never seemed to respond to any of it. I had often wondered if she even heard. But now she started to surprise me. Her questions showed that nothing I had said had ever been lost on her.

'Why did you leave Rome, Chris? Why did you decide not to become a priest?' We were lying in bed together. The window was slightly open and an early evening breeze was arriving, laced with the cries of the gulls.

'Fornication,' I said, but even as I said it I knew I was lying.

'There's no love in that word, is there? None of the sweetness people really find. The word spits on all of that.'

What she had said was true, and it was also true that my truant couplings had not dislodged my faith; they were, after all, by way of weakness rather than contradiction. The tragedy of them was probably that they simply did not affect me enough soon enough. That might have been what my old confessor in Rome had meant when he gave me the most mysterious of all his many puzzling penances: 'Pray that your sins may at last start to communicate to you the nature of your dilemma, since you always leave it to them to do the talking.'

No, what finally dislodged my faith was the way Jesus was disappearing back into the original text of his time, leaving me only dubious translations to read. Does the book recount the event or create it? 'Perhaps you are pushing the book

further and further away from your mind and your soul –
perhaps *that* is why the text is receding,' my confessor had
said, but I didn't think it was quite so simple.

'You didn't just abandon the priesthood when you left
Rome, though,' Alice said, 'from what you told me you
abandoned the Church too. Everything you ever believed.
How could you do that?'

It was true that I had attended mass when I had first landed
in Leeds, but I soon stopped. Jane had her own makeshift
religion, with a greater emphasis on charity than faith, and I
didn't feel like confessing her as a sin to anyone. But there
was something else as well: I couldn't bear to think of myself
as a spoiled priest. I knew some, hanging around at the edges
of the Church, and I found them a sad lot. If you catch them
off guard you can see them hunched over themselves in
fateful concentration, as though trying to spot what it is they
lost when they quit. And so some, like me, leave not only the
priesthood behind, but the Church too. We don't go to that
house any more. The trouble is that the Church never
entirely leaves us. It tracks along a few thoughts behind,
perhaps at times even a few thoughts ahead. And it's always
there when the silence gets started. I took Alice's hand again.

'I suppose that if I couldn't be the priestly representative of
Christ on this earth, I must have decided to have nothing to
do with him at all. If I couldn't administer his sacraments, I'd
leave them alone – except even that's not possible, since
baptism and confirmation are already lodged irrevocably
inside me. Penance and eucharist I can avoid. Holy orders
have already risen up and gone down the tube. As for
extreme unction, I probably won't be in a position to refuse

it by the time it's called for. These days they call it the sacrament of the sick, you know, but it will always be extreme unction for me. We all need some unction, don't we, some balm, whether we're in Gilead or Tooting? And that only leaves marriage.' I paused. 'Will you marry me, Alice?' This last question took me aback, almost as much as it evidently did her. She turned and looked at me.

'Why?'

'Because I love you. I know I love you because, for the first time in my life, I want someone to have my baby.' Her eyes never blinked, her stone-grey scrutiny continued uninterrupted, then she got up from the bed and walked over to the window. The gauze curtain flicked gently against her bare belly.

'No,' she said at last. 'Don't try to make embryos from embryos.' After that, she put on her clothes in silence and walked downstairs. I heard the door close: she had gone out. So there I had it, the summation of the wisdom of Hermann Siegfried: don't make embryos from embryos. I lay there in silence. I was living with a woman who'd never been born. That's why she was so white, such a consumptive mirage – the blood hadn't even started pumping through her veins yet. There was nothing inside her but the thin milk of possibility.

On Monday the weather changed. It turned to a black, growling smear of rage, spitting chilly venom at the clifftops and slapping the harbour with icy storms. This wasn't autumn any more, this was a premonition of what was to come. It was as though we were in a different place entirely. Everything felt damp now, even the bed. We drove to Pembroke, but that was damp and miserable too. The Healey was not the best car in heavy rain. The little restaurant we'd visited at the weekend was now deserted, and the vegetarian dishes had somehow lost their savour. All the salt was now in the wind. We were housebound, fingering the condensation on the windows, counting hours.

'We'll be going back tomorrow,' Alice said to the storm outside.

'No,' I said, not looking up. 'I booked this place for a fortnight.' She was silent for a while, then spoke again quietly.

'I have to be back by Wednesday, Chris, for the Siegfried Group, but I'll go by train if you want to stay.' My voice rose unintentionally.

'Surely you can miss that thing this once, can't you? What use is it if all it does is to turn into another form of dependence, if it's just something else you can't do without, like your bloody spliff?'

Alice took her coat from the hook and stepped outside into the rain. I stood by the window and watched as her shape disappeared into the murky howl of the evening. Then I went and bought a bottle of whisky. I needed something with more of a hard kick than Alice's herbal mixture. When I came back from the off-licence, I poured myself half a glass of straight Scotch and then sat down by the window with Siegfried's *Chimera* in my hand. What was the big deal with this man that I seemed to have ended up in competition with him? I started flicking through the pages. My eye landed on a quote:

Chimera #2

Nothing so true as what you once let fall:
Most women have no characters at all.

I knew this. This was my old territory. This was Alexander Pope's 'Epistle to a Lady'. And as I read on, I found that the words produced a curious panic in me. By now I already felt jagged inside. If you ask someone to marry you and you're turned down, you're not back where you were before you asked. You're in some different region, some hillside limbo where the mists reign. I poured out more whisky and drank it quickly, then poured some more again, trapped in my broken window of a mood. There was no sign of Alice, and now there were memories catching up on me, shipped in, it seemed, by the shifting shapes of that unending storm outside. When she finally came back, she was soaked. I offered her whisky, but she shook her head and took herself off to the bedroom.

It was as though she was moving further away from me with each minute. There had always been something strange about our lovemaking. It wasn't that Alice didn't make love, for she did; it's just that I was never sure she was making love to *me*. Without my being there, it would have been harder, or at least different, but all the same I never felt like its necessary subject – I felt temporarily sufficient but not necessary, and I started to think again about how easily Alice had moved in with me. I wasn't sure that she had ever made a single decision in all the time I had known her. And now she was more anxious to get back to the Siegfried Group than to stay here. It was desperation and anxiety that made me push and hammer so hard, pinioning her arms against the mattress and thrashing away in my swerving whisky haze. After we were finished, the sweat on our bodies turned acid and cold, and finally she said, 'That hurt.'

I went out to buy the newspaper the next day so that I could be alone for a while, even in the rain. I left her sleeping. I didn't want her to wake. I didn't want those grey eyes opening on me. I hacked up the hill through a visor of rain, and stood at the top exactly where I had first stood with Alice, looking out over the bay. A single gull dropped and veered in the air, no longer serenely riding the weather, but seeming to be imprisoned by it now, tangled in its darkening bluster and conflict. I went to the newsagent's at the top of the hill and looked out briefly over that bay which had seemed so idyllic when we arrived, and now was nothing but a squall of rain and vacancy. Then I went into the café nearby, and after only a twitch of hesitation as I looked at the menu, I ordered egg and bacon and sausage. I'd left one vegetarian behind in the blue house and maybe the ghost of another too. I flicked through the pages and I only registered the obituary because of the photograph. Mick Tiller. We had climbed together on the Yorkshire outcrops years before. But Mick was a rising star and I wasn't even a falling one, even when I fell. I could only follow on behind him, helping with belays and brewing the tea. Mick was our golden boy. He trained almost every day on the Don Robinson climbing wall at the university. He was the most supple and gymnastic human being I have ever seen, and when he turned his strength and grace and courage towards a new gritstone line, crowds would form at the foot of the rock to watch him.

That's when there were any people around. Often it was just us, in bleak moorland rain, with the grey fields beneath us stretching away to the horizon. I liked it best of all then.

I can still see him putting up his own route on Almscliffe, the one he named Axle-Grip, upside down on the overhang, with only one nut twenty-five feet below him for protection. It would have ripped out if he'd fallen, he knew that as well as we did. But he didn't fall. Instead he ended up on the cover of *Climbing World*. I still have my grainy black-and-white photographs somewhere, of Mick in his dirty sweater and jeans and his battered EBs, standing proud of the rock with his curly black hair flowing wildly in the wind, as he overcame one more impossibility. He put all his new routes down as 'Very Severe', but they're classified a lot higher than that in the Yorkshire gritstone guidebooks these days. E5, E6. Warning signs to the uninitiated: don't try climbing these, if you have any sense at all. Most of them I couldn't even make the first swooping moves on – they were so demanding, I simply couldn't get off the ground.

Then we all used to drink together, either up on the crags when the weather was fine, or back in town when it wasn't. Whatever he'd done the night before never seemed to affect him when he started climbing the next morning. Until he tore his hand trying to open a can of beer with a serrated knife at some midnight party. The major tendons in two fingers were severed. At first we didn't think it was so bad. He told us he'd be roped up again within a month. He didn't even bother to find any medical help for a while, but when he did, it suddenly became apparent how serious the injury was. He never fully recovered, and although he could still climb better than most people would ever dream of doing, he'd lost that mysterious edge the top boys had. Too much of his grip had gone. He couldn't do the fresh routes that make the headlines any more, though he would still solo old ones from time to time with astonishing speed. Then gradually he dropped out of sight altogether.

I had heard accounts of him now and then; that he lived in a caravan somewhere in North Yorkshire; that he drank a lot, and had become morose and bitter, but now I was reading his obituary, and seeing that young god's face stare out at me from twelve years before. Apparently he had climbed alone to the top of Malham Cove, taking with him in his bag nothing but a bottle of tequila, and when the bottle was empty, he'd jumped. They found his body all smashed up down there the next morning.

'Mick Tiller,' I said, very quietly when I was back in the little blue house. I held the obit page in front of her. 'He's dead,' I went on, 'my old friend. We climbed together, and now he's dead.' Alice looked briefly at the column. I felt I couldn't touch her, though I wanted to.

'Following the route of denial,' she said, after scanning the page, 'acting as though he'd never needed the womb in the first place.' This I presumed was once more the wisdom of Hermann Siegfried. It was the wrong thing to say, and for some reason I felt that Alice knew it was the wrong thing to say, and that was why she was saying it. Each word put more distance between us.

'Yes, well anyway he's dead,' I said, growing angry, 'and he was braver than your Mr Siegfried and your Miss Orley put together. And funny with it. I shouldn't think you spend too much time laughing at those therapy gigs of yours up in North Kensington, do you?'

'I was wondering when the contempt would finally come out, Chris,' she said, with a curious air of satisfaction as though she had at last been proven right. 'Contempt and what often passes for humour are more often than not disguises for fear, you know.'

That afternoon she took the train to London. I drove her to the station and stood on the platform as she climbed aboard.

'I'll see you back here on Thursday,' I said, trying to disguise the urgency in my voice. 'Remember I've rented this place for a fortnight.' Alice looked out of the carriage window and said quietly, 'How long did you rent me for, Chris?'

'What?' I said, but the train was already pulling out. 'Thursday night then,' I shouted.

Back at the little blue house I looked around and realised that Siegfried's book had gone along with Alice. Why hadn't she left that behind for me to read? But then, perhaps she needed it for her meeting. That was probably it. I remembered how I would drive her up to that group of hers, and how one evening I'd even managed to peer down into the basement where it all took place, and caught a glimpse of the brisk and busy lady who ran the affair, Miss Orley. Very professional looking in her wire-rimmed spectacles, with her salt and pepper hair pushed back seriously from her face, and tied up with a black silk ribbon. I had felt envious of her intimacy with Alice, but not envious enough to want to attend the meeting, as Alice had once suggested I should. I'd left one church and didn't feel like joining another just yet. Or could it be that I'd never entirely left the first?

The rain let up, but the cold remained. I drove along the coast and walked about here and there, and when Thursday night came I prepared a vegetarian feast. I bought a bottle of expensive wine to go with it. But Alice never came back that night, so I drank the Margaux myself. Then I started on what was left of the whisky bottle. At midnight I emptied the last of the whisky into my glass as I sat in the little alcove by the window with Mick Tiller's obituary in my lap as his face stared up at me from the crumpled newspaper.

And then the rain came back.

Thunder

What is the cause of thunder?

WILLIAM SHAKESPEARE, *King Lear*

To the great irritation of his wife, Lord Chilford remained at Twickenham. He decided to lessen her annoyance by arranging a surprise ball for her at the villa that Friday evening. Her pregnancy was still in its early stages, long before any confinement would be required, and she did take a particular delight in dancing. Jacob and Josephine were set to work with the preparations. Meanwhile, each day Chilford interviewed Pelham for hours at a time, in an attempt to arrive at an objective account of his condition.

LORD CHILFORD: Do you know what happened to you, Richard?
RICHARD PELHAM: I was taken again.
LC: What was it took you?
RP: Agarith.
LC: Is Agarith a spirit?
RP: An angel.

LC: A fallen one?

RP: One who sometimes needs a home. A condition I understand. Perhaps that's how he acquired my address.

LC: You had been drinking.

RP: In preparation for his return, yes.

LC: How did you know he was coming?

RP: I was sent a letter.

LC: By whom?

RP: By you, my Lord.

LC: Where did you find this letter?

RP: In the drawer of your desk.

LC: What did it say?

RP: When the unclean spirit is gone out of a man, he walketh through dry places, seeking rest; and finding none, he saith, I will return unto my house whence I came out. And when he cometh he findeth it swept and garnished. Then goeth he, and taketh to him seven other spirits more wicked than himself; and they enter in, and dwell there: and the last state of that man is worse than the first.

LC: I did not write those words, Richard. They are from scripture, I think.

RP: Maybe a man's a window pane, however much the glass of his soul has been stained.

LC: I do not understand.

RP: I cannot be merely seen through, even Richard Pelham in his confinement can't. I am flesh too.

LC: You are referring to my attempt to analyse your condition?

RP: Your trek over my mind.

LC: I merely believe that the mind and the body are

interconnected, Richard, so much so that the torments of the one must aggravate a torment in the other. An imbalance in the mind provokes disquiet in the body, and vice versa. I believe an excess of alcohol in the body might so affect the mind that it even believes itself to have visited hell.

RP: You cannot see the spirit that comes upon me with your enlarging lenses, so for you it is unreal. By your own confession you are a natural philosopher of the visible.

LC: And what are you, Richard?

RP: A sinful fellow, with my lusts and gluttonies on my head, visited at intervals by a spirit in need of a shelter for the night, in an age without words to welcome such visitations. Even in one of your palaces of healing, all they could do the last time that spirit arrived, was to hoist me up.

LC: Hoist you up?

RP: Fasten me to the tongue of the storm. That's when they burned the mark into my brow.

LC: Do you know what it was that wrote on the skin of your chest, Richard?

RP: Agarith. If he was there inside me again.

LC: The writing was in your hand.

RP: The writer was in my body.

LC: Do you have anything to tell me about my wife, Richard?

RP: Only that she is a very beautiful woman, my Lord, but then you already know that. And now I believe you are to have a child. My congratulations.

Chilford was impatient with the centuries of superstition, for he could still hear the whispering clamour of all that liturgy behind him. He had, in fact, thought a great deal about bodies and the language in which they utter their imbalances, their trials, their queered and quirky messages. Too premature in the calculus to ponder the writing all over Queequeg's body, and how it announces that he is a visitation from another world, Chilford could see all the same that the writing on Richard Pelham's body seemed to proclaim that this man had been touched by a region elsewhere, but he could only remain unmoved by the utter lack of co-ordinates to establish such a world's location, using any compass reason might tolerate, let alone confirm or ratify. He was inclined therefore to situate the world inside the turbulence of his subject's mind, not outside in any grid of latitude and longitude.

As for Pelham's own great obsession, namely what it was that was written on the body of Jesus himself during the course of that passion which ended with his death on the cross (for that was the true theme of *The Instruments of the Passion*), Chilford had also thought this subject through methodically enough:

1 That his hands, which had been said to transmit such an electric charge of love to the sick and the maimed as to heal them instantly with a single touch, should have nails driven through them so that they might touch no more.

2 That his feet, which had trodden the earth already created through him, or so orthodoxy maintained, in whatever species of ontological singularity, should walk no further upon it, fixed one upon the other now unto death. (Chilford had no reason to doubt the fact of the crucifixion, and could therefore only conclude that Jesus of Nazareth was

at this point drowning inside himself, his breath a diminishing torrent of protest at the forces about it, as they pressed ineluctably inwards, his body both uninhabitable and inescapable at the same time.)

3 And that, finally, his heart, which was said to have at its centre an unending upswelling of the love of the Father, should now contain merely a lance of the imperial soldiery, courtesy of one Longinus.

He who had abrogated the law of condemnation in pity's name, thus to redeem all those who truly sought redemption, hung there writhing at last on the nails of the law, unable even to write in the dust with his finger, as he had done once (according to record, anyway) so as to repel the dread agents of righteousness. When he opened his mouth, only blood came out. Thus, thought Chilford, did the Redeemer's body spout its omega.

Chilford was not alone in his intellectual encroachments on belief. As the universe became more and more of a mechanism, governed by laws whose force was acknowledged to be universal, the requirement for a God to keep the planets turning and the hours moving had seemed to lessen. This age's deity was no longer the passionate and jealous God of Abraham and Isaac, nor the *Abba* of Jesus's prayers and anguished cries; instead he became the *primum mobile*, an intelligence large enough to fashion those laws in the first place, but whose presence was thereafter largely unrequired. For rational and ordered men, this represented something of a comfort, indeed an undoubted progression; but of course, for those still tormented by forces which rationality could neither encompass nor subdue, the age of reason was an age of terror, perhaps a terror even greater than those in the ages which had preceded it. Richard Pelham in the time of his tribulation could find no minister who was even aware of the vocabulary of the powers that visited him, let alone one who could speak their language fluently enough to order them to be gone, assuming he wished them gone, for he never said any such thing. Such talk had after all been dispensed with, along with papish superstitions, and the incense and holy-water stoups of more primitive times. Things were looking up. There was deemed to be – it is not putting the matter too strongly – a heliotropic tendency in even the obscurest matter, for everything now yearned towards the light, the light at the centre of the word enlightenment. The black sun of Pelham's *Instruments* was an absurd trick of the imagination, a jest in bad taste, the product of a diseased mind, though it's worth remembering that in 1714 Tobias Swinden produced a paper for the Royal Society entitled *An Enquiry into the Nature and Place of Hell*, in which he established the sun as the only logical, scientific site of hell. Such a combination of size and unrelenting flame was required to roast the vast quantity of damned souls for eternity. But scientific accounts of eschatology like this were not to last much longer.

Chilford read and wrote into the early hours of the morning. He was trying hard to clarify terms.

So Pelham has a demon, does he? he thought. All right, if that's the common usage, then let's go along with it. He turned the pages of his Plato. The word had corrupted into demon now, but the *daimon* that accompanied Socrates was his spiritual guide, not some tormenting and degraded angel. It represented all that was best in the man's spirit. The narrative of how Satan, the wily adversary of Job, had become the foul fiend, the father of lies, the emperor of malignant spirits, was for Chilford the history of a shadow, the shadow any man can study when he turns away from the source of light and looks too studiously in the opposite direction. If you stare long enough into the darkness, your pupils contract. And ultimately your mind does too.

So, he thought, let us accept the demon, and even speculate that an earlier age might have called it *daimon* instead. Now, let us see what we might make of it.

If a demon has come on a visit, then where has it come from? Whose energy has it tapped into? Whose voice does it speak with? Whose eyes does it look through? Whose flesh does it use, whether to write upon or prod with torments? And should it offer delights, where is the source of the delight? Chilford formulated these questions, but he had no doubt as to the answer in each case: the mind and body of the one afflicted. They were signatures, but distorted signatures, out of the dark part of the mind. Lord Chilford took out the sheet of paper on which he had copied down the lettering on Pelham's chest, and studied it again. He started writing swiftly. Shortly before dawn he finished his narrative thus:

Pelham seems to be telling me that the country inside himself has been invaded, but not so much by Agarith as by those in the Chelsea Asylum, and then by me. He says he has been forced to translate the topography of his soul into a foreign language, and now is confused as to location and locution. When I asked him finally if there was anything he required, he replied, 'I should be grateful for a little peace now. Could I have some more of the lightning from the bottle?' – this is how he refers to the laudanum, so I woke Jacob and instructed him to make up the tincture, according to my instructions. It appears to render him calm; appears even to afford him some kind of protection, given that he is at times oblivious to the greatest personal discomfort, and at other times so fly-skinned with vulnerability that even a breeze could break his defences.

And then he went to bed, hoping for a deep sleep, though a short one, since the ball he had arranged for Lady Chilford was planned for later that day.

Pelham felt stained from his bingeing and his visitation. He did not know in what precise manner he would be punished, but he had little doubt that punishment of some sort must come. He had been tested with his liberty, and had shown himself unworthy to take hold of it. The preparations for Lord Chilford's party went on noisily, not that Pelham knew anything at all about that. Why, after all, should anyone have told him, even if he had been in a fit condition to be informed? They had already cleared the floor of the *piano nobile*, and Lady Chilford was already on her way from London. She had become very bored during the course of the week as she posed for her portrait in a fashionable studio in Covent Garden. She had even chosen the image of the oak tree which the artist would paint in as a backdrop for the final picture, with her listless, slightly cross expression upstaging the immemorial form. The artist's assistant was at that moment filling in the azure blue of her silk skirt, and the watery rivulets of its creases.

'Good afternoon, Mr Pelham,' Jacob had said, as he called in on him. That was all he had said, but he had said it with what struck Pelham as a minatory smile. Something was going on, though he had no idea what.

Lord Chilford had based Chilford Villa somewhat loosely upon the Villa Rotunda at Vicenza. Perfect proportions were achieved only by forfeiting practicality and comfort. Pelham's room was small and draughty, and had never been intended as a space for accommodation in any case. When Lord Chilford visited him there around five o'clock, he seemed if anything cheered by the slightly wild demeanour of the poet. This return of the *furor* had meant that his paper on insanity was now being completed to his satisfaction. It might effect Pelham's eventual cure, and the cure of many others too. The poet had always found Chilford's perfunctory bonhomie distressing, but in the light of his own recent drunkenness and loss of self-possession, he now found it truly alarming. What could be his lordship's intentions? Then the carriages started rolling down the drive, one, two, three, four, and Pelham looked quickly about him, as though the walls might contain a mute stony wisdom as to his new predicament. He fell upon his knees once more and began to pray.

Pelham could not imagine why so many people had come to the house, unless it was to discuss his fate. He had stolen wine from the cellar in considerable quantities and had absconded without permission from the villa for two days. Then he had become once more the home for the unhoused spirit. Jacob had obviously reported all this to his master, and his master had even come to see some of it for himself. And then the thunder above his head began, a relentless rolling crash and hammer, and he ran to the window to look out. Sure enough, a full moon was riding the few swift clouds, but there was no sign of any storm. He needed no further sign. Whatever the Lord wanted, He most certainly did not want to see any of his creatures ever again strapped to the star-machine, with grinning faces floating in the sky above them. He collected his few belongings and crept into Chilford's study to steal only two things: the bottle of laudanum and a small lancet engraved with the monogram EA. Then he fled from the house, never even turning back to see the shapes of the dancers in the windows on the floor above his room, as they ceremoniously marched and stamped and twirled to the lyric geometry of the music.

Pelham walked through the night. He was no athlete and it took him six hours and more to reach the edges of town, though he often rested so that he might lie in a ditch and sip some of the opium. Then he would stay awhile. Once again, infernal rats had started to scurry, with their little scratching feet, across his brain. Lady Chilford. He had caught sight of her before he left, as she shimmied down a corridor, bejewelled in billowing folds, the warm breath of her perfume engulfing everyone about her in brief clouds. How could anybody smell so sweet? Had Susannah too once smelt as sweet as that? His nose, in its lengthy exile, had forgotten. Pressing her sumptuous breasts so tightly into her bodice that the flesh appeared ready to explode into a man's hands. Just as Eve had once handed the fruit of damnation to Adam. Her gaze had lighted on him in the corridor, but only en route to somewhere else, as she turned her long neck first this way and then that, sometimes with the imperious bemusement of an ostrich, and at others with the white perfection of a swan. *Our Father, which art in heaven* ... It was only as he approached the fields of Wandsworth on his pilgrim's journey east, that he realised his papers for *The Instruments of the Passion* were still in Lord Chilford's study, where Jacob said he had taken them for his lordship's perusal. He stopped still under the troubled moon for ten minutes while he considered this, which felt like the final catastrophe of all. He knew, of course, that he could not go back. He felt that everything had now been taken from him at last, precisely as he deserved.

Pelham was fortunate not to be robbed and beaten senseless, for there were many travellers in the night whose business was menace and thieving along the highways, but his ungentlemanly appearance, remarked upon more than once by Chilford in his letters, most likely protected him. He didn't look as though he possessed anything much worth taking. His clothes were now in such a state of deterioration that even a vagabond might have thought twice before troubling to strip him of them. As he edged into London from the west, the last yawning link-boys ignored him, extinguishing their lights and heading home.

The city rose early in those days, and Pelham was soon walking through the shouting streets. He found an inn and met a woolstapler on his way to Halifax, with whom he shared a pleasant drink and some ragged conversation. Then he walked until he knew his ground again, and by the time he entered the area around Grub Street the place was ripe with noise and bustle, as some set out to work and others, in the unbuttoned uniforms of their debauchery, came home again. A cheeseman with a £7 Cheddar trotted past him. He breathed in the feculent air and felt free for the first time in years. Street criers were practising their hoarse crow notes outside the Strangers' Tavern, which boasted that it was never closed to thirsty travellers. Pelham knew of nowhere else he could be sure of a welcome, and so he made his way there, and once inside he knew he had returned at last to his true asylum.

Accounts

Account: A computation of debts or expenses.

Johnson's *Dictionary*

I started phoning the flat, but there was no reply. By that Saturday I couldn't stand it any longer, so I cut short my holiday and drove to London. That was the first long drive in the Healey I'd ever hated. When I arrived back I ran up the five flights of stairs and as I opened the door I heard the little jingle on the floor that I had been dreading: Alice's keys. She had put them through the letter box after leaving. She had taken all her things, except for her unfinished canvas. There was a sheet of paper on the table, and on it she had written:

We both need time. Not the same sort.
Alice

As I stood later by the window I looked at that canvas she'd spent so many months painting over, and suddenly realised something that I should have noticed the first day: it differed from all the other *Chimeras*. The colours were the same and the way the objects blended one into another, but there was no figure in the foreground. It was all background.

Now time itself was going backwards. In my mind I had compiled, it seemed, without even noticing, an Alice Diary, and now I knew that not a single entry could ever be annulled. I couldn't get her out of my mind. I contacted the West London College, but they had no forwarding address for her. Well, in fact, they did have one, but I lived there. A month after she'd gone, I drove up to the Siegfried Group one Wednesday evening. All the pre-natal figures appeared except for Alice. Maybe she would be late. I went into the pub opposite, a seedy place, the sort I'd normally avoid. I walked through the door and tasted the nicotine breath of its air as it exhaled a Jim Reeves dirge, the three or four notes of the bass line booming like a huge, fretful heart. And as I sat there with a pint in front of me, gradually giving up hope of ever seeing Alice again, I started to watch the sorry saga at the bar, as a rough-looking drunk refused to remove himself as requested by the barman. The requests grew more peremptory and finally the unwanted drinker turned and looked at the bottle a few inches to his left, and then he made the slightest feint of a gesture, but the barman saw it, saw exactly the same thing that I saw forming in the delinquent's sodden mind: the edge of the broken glass finding his face and twisting backwards and forwards as the flesh came apart.

'Out,' said the barman, any hint of diplomacy now gone from his Irish voice. His hand had moved up to a horizontal plane in line with the man's throat, and the fingers were curled tightly into the karate attack position. 'Out now, before I fucking deck you.' And the man had gone.

Somehow, after that, the acrid despair of the place seeped right through my skin. Alice hadn't arrived, so I finished my drink and went home, where I lay on my bed until something like sleep finally stretched a great, black, itching wing across my face.

I couldn't remember the last time I'd had a dream that had intruded on my daytime memory. Dreams were for the darkness and once I rose I had no interest in them. But now they started to take over. Dreams and memories became hard to separate. The whiteness of Alice's body, its sparseness, its curious frugality. Her flesh was somehow extreme in its understatement, and as I reached out I would be back up on the moors again, entering a chapel in the dark with a snowstorm blowing. In one dream she calmly peeled the skin away to reveal her heart, and that too was white, framed in the Gothic tautness of her ribcage. All white, except for the hair between her legs. I came across the shellac sheen of an Iroquois squaw hiding in a winter valley. A little warm wet cave of secrecy and delight. From such dreams I woke, incoherent with longing. It seemed that my body had its own memories, rooted firmly in torment and desire.

Then one day at dawn, stumbling from bed to escape from those dreams that pursued me, I looked about the flat. On the table were dirty cups and plates, knives and forks gluey with mouldering food; books were strewn across the floor, and clothes bedraggled the furniture. There were newspapers everywhere. In the kitchen the sink was so full I couldn't reach the taps. Later that day I spent an hour scrubbing frantically at the blurs of blue on the carpet by the window where Alice used to paint. I was suddenly desperate to clean things up again.

By this time I hardly saw Andrew from one month to the next. So it was a surprise when Mr Henry popped his head round the door five minutes after I'd arrived one Monday morning and asked me to accompany him to the boardroom.

I should explain that I had gradually come to realise the significance of the fact that Andrew was a director of only one sector of Shipley's, and I wasn't entirely sure how much of the share capital he held. There were obviously other people he was answerable to, but I had assumed all this would become clearer when I was myself given the shareholding he kept promising me. My directorship was a preliminary to acquiring a financial stake in the company. So I wasn't too sure what was happening when I walked into the boardroom and realised that all the directors of the company were seated around the table. All except one, that is: Andrew.

They made an impressive sight in their well-tailored suits and neatly knotted ties. Most were considerably older than Andrew and their grey hair and balding heads gave them a final touch of gravitas. The managing director was Mr Fairbrother, whom I seldom spoke to more than once a year, and that was during the company outing, when we all sipped drinks together and ate from paper plates, and carefully said nothing of any importance. There was something grave and considered about Fairbrother that I liked. He gestured for me to sit down at the end of the table, and as I did so he coughed and then started to speak.

'You must forgive us for asking you in here at such short

notice, Christopher, but we have a matter of some importance to sort out, and given the sudden difficulty of locating
Andrew Cavendish-Porter, we are left with yourself as our
primary source of information. We suspect this might take
the better part of the morning, so perhaps you would like a
coffee?' I nodded, and Fairbrother motioned to one of his
junior directors to go and arrange the refreshments. Then he
started.

At first, I simply couldn't work out what was happening.
What seems so clear in retrospect didn't seem at all clear at
the time. It was only as the interrogation drove relentlessly
on and I occasionally caught the looks of the other members
of the board as they paused from taking notes, or took a sip
of their coffee, that I began to realise what it was I was in the
middle of.

'How much do you know about the company called
CPT?' Mr Fairbrother was asking.

'That's Andrew's chosen freighting company.'

'And you know where they are based, of course.'

'Bristol.'

'So you didn't find it in any way odd that they should be
summoned from the West Country to London to pick up
packages in Wandsworth and deliver them to Ealing or
Dulwich or North Kensington, for example?'

I paused for a moment at this. 'Andrew had told me they
were to be used for any movement of goods, whatever it
was.'

'And you always do whatever Andrew Cavendish-Porter
tells you, evidently.' There was an uncharacteristic edge of
contempt in the tone of this remark.

'He is my boss,' I said.

'He is your senior director. You yourself are a director, of course, and not a mere employee. You have responsibilities beyond simply taking orders. You do acknowledge that?' I nodded uneasily. 'We have no access, as I'm sure you know, to the books of CP Transport, but we suspect that you do.'

'Well, you're wrong,' I said. 'I don't know anything about the company and I've never met any of its directors. All I know is that Andrew wished me to use it for all freight movements from Shipley's.'

'And I suppose you don't even know what the CP in CP Transport stands for?' said Tim Hollis, with his perennial smile. Tim was a small man with a flock of ginger hair and wire-rimmed glasses that perched precisely on his freckled nose. He was said to have married money. He lived in an Elizabethan farmhouse somewhere in Somerset, and a few years back at one of those company events he had asked about my background. On being told that I had once been in training to be a priest, he had turned and looked at me severely.

'If one of my daughters were to come home and tell me she was marrying a Roman Catholic, I would know I had failed somewhere,' he had said. I didn't make a habit of defending my long-dead priestly ambitions, but this sally had its effect.

'If your daughters look anything like you,' I had said, grinning unpleasantly, 'I shouldn't think you have much cause to worry.' And from that point on we had avoided one another. But, unlike me, Tim Hollis was a senior director and a shareholder too, facts that were gaining in importance with each minute that went by.

'Are you seriously telling us you don't know what CPT stands for?' he said again.

I had never even thought about the freighting company's name, though the initials did suddenly seem significant.

'It never occurred to me,' I said, feeling guilty even though all I had been guilty of was stupidity. 'Is it Andrew's company?' Fairbrother leaned forward and started to speak again.

'Yes, I think we can safely assume that the CP in CPT stands for Cavendish-Porter, don't you? There are no accounts lodged as yet at Companies House, though I daresay the police can establish the facts quickly enough, should that prove necessary.' This last statement was evidently designed to intimidate me, which it did.

'My involvement with CP Transport began and ended with me giving them transportation jobs.'

'Have you any idea what they were charging for those jobs?'

'No. Andrew handled all the invoicing.'

'And did it never occur to you, as a director, that offering cut-price work to galleries in France and Italy, and then providing the transport *gratis* was a little extraordinary?'

'I couldn't understand the economics of it. I told Andrew that.'

'Perhaps you understood the economics of these expenses, all the same.' Fairbrother held up a pile of receipts. 'I think we must assume you noticed at the, let me see,' he put on his glasses and slowly read the one at the top of the pile, 'Belle

Nuit in Nice, for example, how expensive the champagne was, particularly since it appears that you were not buying it merely for yourselves but also for your companions for the night. Ditto at the Cabaret Noir in Toulouse.'

'And there's plenty more where they came from, Chris,' Hollis said, his smile now even broader than usual. Why is it that people who shorten your name in conversation are so often the ones you would prefer to call you sir? 'I trust they were all good Catholic girls you were consorting with, or perhaps you were engaged on a missionary trip of some kind?'

'You became very close to Andrew Cavendish-Porter, so we are told,' Fairbrother continued quickly. I had the sudden feeling he disliked Hollis as much as I did. 'Going to dinner with him and his wife, sometimes every week. He even sold his old sports car to the company, at a very good price indeed to himself, so that you could have it as a company car. The only convertible company car in the history of Shipley's, I think I'm right in saying. I'm afraid it's very hard indeed to believe, Christopher, that the pair of you hadn't set out to milk this company dry. Given that Andrew was no more than a minority shareholder in one sector, but with access to considerable funds, and given our trusting, I now think perhaps in some ways even lax, attitude to accountability, I suppose the agreement between you was that you could take pretty much what you wanted as long as you agreed to keep mum about the amount of cash being shunted into CP Transport.'

'No,' I said, understanding fully for the first time where all this was leading. 'It wasn't like that. If that's what he's been doing, I knew nothing about it.'

'There must surely have been a nod and a wink somewhere. You yourelf have made nine journeys in the last six months, each one involving expenses for yourself and your wife. None of us actually knew you were married by the way, Christopher, we only found out from these accommodation receipts. Hotel expenses. Restaurant expenses. Entertainment expenses. Petrol expenses. How busy your company credit card has been. And unless I'm very much mistaken, not one of these trips has as yet brought to this company a single penny. In fact, the last job we can discover which you brought in over the last eighteen months was for' – here he pondered his notes – 'the West London College of Art. And according to the estimator, whom you mysteriously did not consult at the time, we worked on that one at a loss. Why, out of interest?'

'It was a way of bringing in new business,' I said unsteadily.

'Like all the European jobs, yes, I see. I see very clearly, I think.' Fairbrother took off his glasses now and stared at me with a look I remembered from somewhere, but I couldn't think where. It was only later I realised it was the same look my old confessor in Rome had given me that rainy afternoon. He now spoke with great deliberation. 'We haven't decided yet whether to make this a legal matter. In the circumstances, I suppose you might wish to go home and consider your resignation. For us to dismiss you would certainly require an explanation, and the explanation might not reflect well upon your behaviour here.'

And that was it. Except that Hollis accompanied me to my office, where I picked up a few things. I was about to take some of my papers from the desk when he waved me off.

'Leave the papers, Chris. We'll need them for the full investigation.' I looked at Hollis's unanswerable smile, and thought briefly of slapping the smugness from his features, but then I simply stepped outside and climbed into the Healey. I stopped the car a quarter of a mile along the road, and took down the hood. It was a clear autumn day, but there was the hint of a chill in the air. I didn't go straight back home, but drove to the A3, and when the road cleared, I floored the accelerator. You'll read in the old specifications that a 3000 will go up to 120, but mine wouldn't. Somewhere around 115, its power gave out. I wondered if it had always been like that, or if it was beginning to feel its age. All the same, the wind blew and the engine roared and the earth beneath me seemed to spin at the speed dictated by the pressure of my right foot on the pedals. So by the time I arrived back in Battersea, I felt as though some at least of my discontent had been blown away. Though it did seem that my future had too. First Alice and then my job. A week later I received the request for the Healey to be returned to the company within ten days, or the bailiffs would come and collect it.

The Pleasures of Delirium

25 drops and a pint of Gin is Paradise.

RICHARD PELHAM, *Letters*

The Strangers' Tavern was presided over by Ann Wigley. She had many years before married the landlord, Tobias Wigley, and had lived happily enough with him until he died of a medley of over-indulgences. She had known Pelham a long time back and remembered serving him drinks while he spouted so cleverly among the ever-changing host of his scribbling friends. Now she stared at him. He had lost weight since she had last seen him all those years before, when she had watched him at the table talking his wild, brilliant talk. Now his eyes seemed to blaze with some brightness that she couldn't fathom, some occult fire that simultaneously captured and repelled her. He had made a lengthy journey, she could see that much, anyway, and he seemed to gleam in the strangeness of its afterglow. Master Richard must have dived deep indeed in search of his pearl. She wondered if he'd found it. Her own cheeks were now chapped red and she had gained as many inches around the middle as he had lost.

He asked for gin and she told him he'd have to go elsewhere for that, but she served him brandy instead, and as she filled his glass a second time she watched him sip the glowing liquid and saw his face uncrease a little. How he had once impressed her with his talk. She wondered how he had acquired the scar across his forehead.

'You have nowhere to go, I suppose.' He shook his head. 'And it looks as though you have been out all night. I shan't ask why, but you had better have some sleep anyway. Come with me.' And she took him upstairs and put him in the little room next to hers, where she lit the fire for him and helped him climb into bed. Then she walked around the rooms to make sure everything was in order, and went down to the cellar to finish preparing the day's ale. When she called back half an hour later, he was sound asleep.

So Richard Pelham became a guest at the Strangers' Tavern. The habitués of the place were far from sure that Ann Wigley's relationship with him was entirely that of a hostess, but he paid for his keep in any case by writing and even performing entertainments. In one he actually appeared as Old Mother Fox, dressed up in Mistress Wigley's worn-out clothes for the purpose. He wrote the oratory and the songs, all long-since vanished. Music was played on the Jew's harp and the salt box. Dogs and monkeys cavorted dementedly, to the great delight of the inebriated crowd. To this period we must presumably ascribe the satire published on Pelham in the *Gentleman's Magazine*:

> *But see this gentle Lamb whom God hath chosen*
> *His Fleece shrived both of Blasphemy and Treason*

The Pleasures of Delirium

Even as his Wits are sheared of Sense —
All travelling, after his Virtue, hence.

So long as he stayed indoors under the aegis of Ann Wigley, he was safe, but it was probably inevitable that he would before long set out to explore the city's streets once more.

The place had been changing, though perhaps not as much as it would have liked. It was still guarded in those days by the watch, made up of unpaid parishioners, often old and close to infirmity. Horace Walpole was shot at in Hyde Park by a highwayman and later complained that 'one is forced to travel, even at noon, as if one was going to battle'. But beneath the smoking chimneys and the endless smuts, new and different buildings were sprouting up. After the Great Fire, the city had not been reshaped according to some magisterial design, but had flourished once more on the old, crooked street plan. Dirty yards and foul shambles jostled next to the houses of the wealthy. Curricles and phaetons trundled before tall, at times magnificent, new houses, rising on their narrow sites. The great squares were shaping little villages for wealthy eyes to look down on, piazzas of greenery in the sea-coal fog. The painted lintels were soon enough furred and smeared, and men from further east were paid to come and clean them. Pelham walked about examining all this, as though he were Gulliver on one of his travels. Then he went in search once more of the life of the spirit.

As the official Church had started on its long, slow rapprochement with Reason, dispensing with the apparatus of supernaturalism as much as possible, other sects had risen up to fill the vacuum, and one fine summer's day Pelham chanced upon George Whitefield preaching outdoors in Upper Moorfields. The year was probably 1753. The scene had become a common one. A man sold nuts from a barrow. Dogs scurried about the place barking. A fair number of the drunk and destitute lay raggedly about. A blind man walked listlessly along, while women in flat bonnets smiled this way and that, and a naval officer in a tricorn hat walked around rather grandly, his fiancée balanced on his arm. A small boy in vast baggy breeches made a manikin with a negro head jig and shudder and call out ribald blasphemies at Whitefield, who preached in the shade of an oak tree. But nothing could divert him: he called all within shouting distance to true repentance, so that the spirit might descend and fill the soul with a joy unimaginable. Two ancient-looking Jewish merchants stood still, arm in arm, and attended to these words in silence. But Pelham that day was one of those who fell to the ground and writhed in either torment or ecstasy; one who came to believe that the spirit *had* come upon him once more. And for a while Pelham dutifully attended every Methodist meeting that he could. But it soon became evident to his fellow enthusiasts that the Holy Spirit wasn't the only spirit providing him with intoxication, and he was instructed either to change his habits or to stay away. John Wesley was at that time preaching forcibly about the evils of gin.

Two things then happened. First, he added laudanum to the gin he was now drinking in quantity, and second he came upon the Children of Bethany. Then a third thing happened, presumably as a result of the other two: he was thrown out of his accommodation at the Strangers' Tavern.

Ann Wigley could no longer be doing with his gin drinking, or his self-dosing with opium, but she tired even more quickly of his sermons. There were even rumours that there had been odd goings on too, yells and crashes in the night. No one was ever entirely sure why Richard Pelham left the place in such a hurry, but now begins the outpouring of letters that constitute the larger part of his correspondence, at first from a scatter of insalubrious addresses, then finally from no address at all.

Pelham had fallen silent on the subject of religion since his incarceration in the Chelsea Asylum. He had written *The Instruments of the Passion*, it is true, and if called upon had read parts of it out, but always tentatively, always under instruction. Otherwise his religion and his insanity had been so closely identified by those in power over him that he feared any mention of the one would immediately imply the other. Even his naming of Agarith to Lord Chilford had only been by command. He was merely obeying the worldly power, as St Paul had advised. And after he had fled Chilford Villa he had expected with each day that passed to see Jacob at the head of a crowd of watchmen, come to collect him.

But now the length and breadth of England was astir with enthusiasm. The soporific Sabbath day attendance of conformity was being loudly subverted in the open-air prayer meetings, the evangelical calling upon the Lord, of Wesley and George Whitefield. A little scholarly group, the Bible Moths of Oxford, had already flourished into what came in time to be called the Methodist Revival. As we know, Pelham attended more than one of these love feasts, and felt, as he said in his letters, that he too was struck by the Spirit. In his own words, it smote him fiercely at the top of his ribcage, and laid him out on the ground, seemingly unconscious, while the Holy Ghost performed its ministry. The wailing and the moaning all about him were, he later said, the sounds of imprisoned souls being released at last from the chains of bondage. Egypt's tomb opened in Moorfields. He seems to have zigzagged haphazardly in and out of various conventicles until he came upon the Children of Bethany, in one of the tiny and untidy streets that ran off the Tottenham Court Road.

The work of religious scholars has remained inconclusive here, for there is scant documentation, but they are all agreed on one point: no creed had ever been promoted or adhered to by this church, which was not in any case a church, with all that implies of structure, authority and a tribe of ecclesiastical entrepreneurs, but a congregation, a huddled gathering of the brethren upon the shores of time. There was a certain creative fluency in regard to doctrine, and crucial ambiguities in regard to personal morality, in particular sexuality. The one thing resolutely affirmed was that the merits of the Passion of Our Lord are imputed to us. Thus are we saved, though sinners all. We should not intrude our own infinitesimal and opaquely depraved persons in the way of the action of grace. We must each one of us avoid all shalling and willing.

So deeply did these beliefs go that any large decision required the use of the holy lottery to elicit the expression of God's will for the congregation. A chalice was the receptacle, containing small pieces of wood from tent pegs, with a cross engraved upon only one. And here they accepted Pelham, with or without his addictions. Here, with an admiration verging on reverence, the poet came to look upon the features of Prince Zabrenus, the tall, black-bearded magus of this sect, who stood no higher than they did, for physical platforms led to spiritual ones, and called out in the ramshackle assembly hall of Bethany House, 'Think of me, my brothers and sisters, as no more than a self-proclaimed Galilean fool, for mine is truly an idiocy of Nazarene proportions.'

Driven

To drive away the heavy thought of care.

WILLIAM SHAKESPEARE, *Richard II*

My father, Adam Bayliss, accountant, had one great friend, Victor Cray, solicitor. He would come to our house every month for dinner, and I would clamber over his vast belly, and pull from his waistcoat pocket his golden watch, which, after he had turned a tiny wheel on it, would chime to announce each quarter hour. I would sit on his lap and stare in silence as the big hand made its way round, and then shout with joy when the chimes began. How many years ago was that? I didn't want to think about it as I made my way to his office in Morden. He met me at the door and I looked at him in wonder.

'You're a thin man,' I said. 'You didn't used to be.' He smiled an old man's weary smile. He looked as though he had lost not only his weight but most of his vigour since the last time I had seen him, at my father's funeral.

'Had no choice,' he said. 'Health.' Now where his great chin had had once hung and throbbed like a croaking toad's there was only a sheaf of lizard folds. And the belly that had ballooned inside his waistcoat had shrunk so that his suit flapped about him.

'Sit down,' he said, 'and tell me about this little difficulty of yours.'

I explained about Andrew and CPT, and how it certainly appeared that he had deliberately siphoned money out of Shipley's to fund the setting up of his own transport company; explained how it was assumed I had colluded in this manoeuvre, when in fact I had done no such thing, though I had been less than attentive in my directorial responsibilities.

'I would say you are being treated unfairly and a case could certainly be brought to that effect.' There was a pause, as Victor looked at me intently. I almost thought he was going to ask me to climb back up on to his knee. 'That's assuming you've told me the whole story.'

'There are a few more elements to it.' He motioned with his hands that I should inform him of these other elements. So I started, with some difficulty, to talk about my relationship with Andrew. I described the unusual arrangement regarding the car and explained how, in his increasingly lengthy absences, I had made decisions which in retrospect were perhaps unwise. How I had disposed of funds on my company credit card as though I were answerable to no one but myself. How I had used it to finance trips for myself and Alice which in truth had nothing to do with the company at all. How I had taken on at least one job for less than cost for private reasons. Then I swallowed and said, 'Then there were some irregular expenses in Europe.'

'What sort of expenses?' Victor asked. It had been a mistake to visit all this upon an old family friend, I realised that now. I should have just picked a solicitor out of Yellow Pages.

'What sort of expenses, Christopher?'

'Night clubs. Hostesses. Champagne.'

'You paid for sex on your company expenses?' No flies on Victor then, we could drop the euphemisms. After only a slight pause, I said, 'Yes.'

'Did you pay on your expense account, or did your friend Cavendish-Porter pay on his?'

'At first it was all on his. Then . . .'

'Then?'

'He told me to pick up a few of the bills.'

'And you did?'

'Yes.'

'Not in cash?'

'On the card.'

'So there are company records of it?'

'Yes.'

'How did you account for these nights of yours on the documentation?'

'Entertainment. We were meeting a lot of potential foreign clients. It would have seemed like no more than hotel and restaurant bills. Someone must have made it their business to contact these places and find out what services they actually provided.'

'But all this goes back over a number of years?'

'Yes.'

'So why bring it up now? Is it simply because of this Cavendish-Porter and his transport company?'

'I've been thinking about that over the last few days. I suppose the truth is, we were fine as long as we were bringing in the money. They'd probably have forgiven us anything. But for the last two years it's been dropping away. For the last nine months we've probably been running at a loss. Andrew was never there, I had my mind on other things. So they started paying attention to us, which they never did as long as we were in profit.'

Victor looked at me in silence for a moment. It was that look again – I thought I'd left that look behind in Rome, but it seemed to be following me around the world. Finally he spoke.

'This is personal advice, for which there is no charge, because if you were to proceed with this business, I shouldn't wish to be involved. If I were you, I'd accept that you have behaved recklessly and laid yourself open to charges of defrauding the company. If you were an employee merely, there could be grounds for saying that you had been led on by your director. But as it stands, I think you might cut a sorry figure if it came to court. It would all seem so . . . seedy. You're too young to need to buy sex with other people's money, Christopher. That's an old man's game.'

Victor had now risen.

'The car?' I said.

'Either give it back or go abroad in it for a very long time. And do give my love to your mother.'

★

My running had slowed down with Alice around. I think it might have had something to do with the marijuana. My circuits around Battersea Park had become meditations, I had even stopped now and then to stare at the river, but when I came back from seeing Victor that day I ran as hard as I ever had. I ran as though I wanted to hurt myself, and only as I came round the railings by the zoo did I stop. Helena was walking towards me as her Irish setter dashed and then dithered and sniffed over the grass. She carried on approaching me as I heaved for breath. It was the first time I'd ever seen her without her make-up, and her bony face and thin lips now looked pale and ghostly in the morning light.

'Hello, Chris.' I said nothing, but simply stared at her for a moment as I got my breath back. 'How are you?'

'Out of a job,' I said finally, 'otherwise fine.' There was a flicker across her face, but no more than that.

'Yes, it's all a bit awkward isn't it?'

'Where's Andrew, then?'

'Down in Bristol most of the time. Well, going between there and Bath – we've just found a new house. We're moving down there. It's lovely, actually.'

'Nice for you.'

Helena suddenly moved forward and put her hand on my arm. 'Andrew's sorry he's not been in touch. He was hoping you'd be kept on at Shipley's, but we heard it hadn't worked out that way. He'd be happy to take you on at CPT, you know.'

'Big of him,' I said. She let go of my arm and stepped backwards. The setter was still cavorting jerkily about the place.

'You know they let him down? You know they'd always

promised him a directorship and a shareholding in the main company as soon as he'd raised your turnover to half a million?' I shook my head.

'Then they changed their minds and made it a million. He decided it was all my eye and Betty Martin, and decided he'd best start looking out for himself. And us, of course.'

'Maybe he'll have to start doing it from the inside of a prison,' I said, but she shook her head and smiled briefly.

'They won't do that,' she said. 'If that's your worry, you can forget it. You'd like it down in the west, Chris. Think about it.' Then she turned her head and looked up towards my flat.

'Is Goldilocks still with you?'

Now it was time for me to shake my head. 'No. I eat my porridge alone these days.'

Her smile became fuller. 'I always thought you might drop by one of those evenings after you'd left Andrew abroad.' I suppose she saw the mild commotion of shock as I looked at her. 'Well, come on,' she said, 'you didn't really think I sat at home grieving for my darling Andy while he screwed his way across Europe, did you? I'll drop you a line with our new address, anyway. Andrew would have contacted you himself, but even a hint of connivance at this stage could be risky. Let's give it a few months, shall we, till it's all quietened down.'

Then she kissed me, shouted for her dog and set off swiftly towards the bridge. And by the time I was back in the flat standing in the shower with the scald of the water on my face, I thought: Alice and Helena, Helena and Alice. And I could feel my soul crouching down in preparation for some serious woman-hating.

With only a few days left before that car had to be returned, I thought I might as well put it through its paces. I had never cornered so hard, never accelerated so hard, never braked so hard. I probably took more rubber off those tyres in three days than I had in the previous three years, and every time I turned to look at the empty passenger seat, I pressed my foot down a little harder. So I suppose I can't really blame the man in the white Sierra. I accelerated too hard and he followed me, then when I braked hard as the lights changed he really wasn't expecting it. And I wasn't expecting the hammer blow that seemed to hit me on the neck. I climbed out rubbing the back of my head and walked round to look at the mangled chrome of the bumper, and the sheet of buckled blue steel that two minutes before had been the boot. I think the middle-aged Indian in the clapped-out Ford, with his grey cardigan hanging down below his grey jacket, was expecting me to be angry at the damage he had inflicted on my beautiful sports car, and was a little surprised as we exchanged details to see me starting to laugh, despite my physical discomfort.

I drove the car back to Shipley's and left the keys with the secretary.

'It needs a bit of attention, I'm afraid,' I said as I walked out. It was their car and their insurance policy, so they could sort it out. But by the time I'd walked home I realised that I needed some attention too. I went to the doctor the next day, and the day after that I was at the hospital. The bruising and soreness constituted a classic whiplash injury, which I was at first told might well turn out to be temporary, but by the third week of visits and X-rays and examinations, it began to seem that it might not turn out to be so temporary after all. I shan't bore you with the details of all those medicals, though there are some giddy-sounding words involved: spondylosis, radicalopathy, osteophytes. My frozen shoulder and neck showed no signs of thawing. And the pain wouldn't go away, despite the ibuprofen and the Neproxen. They offered me an epidural, but did explain to me that it's a bit awkward up there around the neck, what with the gaps for the needle being so small. Should there be a mistake while doing it, you end up paralysed. I decided to say no to that one. For a while I wore a brace, a soft white plastic one around my neck that looked like part of a urinal. Even with my new machine, my TENS (transcutaneous electrical nerve stimulation) blipping little bolts of lightning from one patch of flesh to another when I hooked myself up and switched on – even with this, I couldn't bend, couldn't lift, couldn't turn my head without thinking it through beforehand. Sometimes I could barely move at all, my neck was so solid that I was immobilised. I felt like Humpty Dumpty, with a ridiculous, vast egg on my shoulders, and a bird's neck far too delicate to support it.

Just as well I no longer had the car, since I couldn't have driven it, being barely able to move or see what was going on behind me for days at a time. I soon learned to stop and consider the implications of bending down to pick anything up. More often than not I would leave it where it fell.

And that's how, within a couple of months, I ceased to be a promising junior executive in a printing company, and became instead a stiff, disabled figure edging about in a flat eighty feet above Battersea Park, seldom going out except to buy food and walk up the road once a week to collect my state benefit.

I certainly missed Alice. And her dope.

Madmen's Epistles

A madman's Epistles are no Gospels.

WILLIAM SHAKESPEARE, *Twelfth Night*

Much of the early part of Pelham's addiction, like anyone
else's, was sheer delight. A number of the letters from this
period, which were collected in the Clarendon edition,
testify to that. It is worth remarking that Pelham must rank as
one of the most unrequited correspondents in the history of
the language. Of his letters to his wife, all went unanswered.
Of those to Samuel Johnson, a few were answered with a
little note and a little money. Of those to Ferdinand
Lowndes, an old and wealthy friend from Cambridge, an
occasional reply was forthcoming, when Lowndes, away on
his family estate outside Norwich, was not himself so
debauched that he was incapable of lifting a pen. To be fair,
when one examines these letters, it is often hard to see what
precisely their recipients were meant to say in reply. They
could be extremely short, like this one:

The elephant-shrew bathes in a dew drop.

Or this:

A schism in the weather. The mist that hovered and clung about everything with its creeping infection is gone. The sun's disc has hit the river with a wintry clang.

Others were more discursive, clearly reflecting the messianic vegetarianism of Prince Zabrenus and the Children of Bethany:

I have seen the oil-lamps burning in the windows and thought of the poor vast whales, harpooned by men in their Nantuckets, so that oil might pour from those great insides. I have looked on carp, salmon, trout, even the lobster, and wondered at their watery pleasures of the day before. Blood stuff'd in Skins is British Christians' Food? And eating hearts roasted? And why do so many souls lie sprawled among the ashes of a glass-house, so the heat of its daytime fires might leach into their flesh? Are they cooking too? For whose grand table? Only once, my friend, did I eat swan pie. And the pain that later developed was a white ghost in my intestines, yearning to fly.

To some extent one can observe the classic pattern of an opium addiction. In the early stages the mind achieves an unimagined fluency and scope, and thought expands to fill the million new universes provided for it. A fly crossing a curtain emits such a clamour of sound, such an intricate weave of noise, as to absorb the thinker for hours in the visualisation of all the worlds that surround him in a room, each one infinite, and each a source of ceaseless wonder. There are extraordinary mutations of time and space, with colours grown utterly spectacular, spectrums everywhere to rainbow the light. Astonishing undiscovered cities. Rivers that run with liquid gold. Every addict in the early stages is a traveller bearing exotic knowledge:

> *Have you ever seen the egg of a peregrine falcon? The texture of its skin is Mars, all clotted blood and sullen anger. Portents. An inflammation in the eye of war. Put your ear to it close enough, you'll catch the trigger of the claw and the spear of the beak beneath it. But then a second later pick up the swallow's egg and look at the scatter of stars there. Heaven shrunk to the size of a fingernail. This day our only angelus is the scavenger's bell. A gleaner of time's detritus.*

Then the other symptoms begin. We have an eloquent testimony of this from De Quincey: '*I had done a deed, they said, which the ibis and the crocodile trembled at . . . I was kissed with cancerous kisses, by crocodiles, and was laid, confounded with all unutterable abortions, amongst reeds and Nilotic mud.*' Or this letter about the unnameable and unsustainable terrors, written by Coleridge to Poole in 1796: '*It came on . . . several times on Thursday . . . but I took between sixty and seventy drops of laudanum, and stopped the Cerberus . . . But this morning he returned in full force, and his name is Legion.*'

Whatever Pelham's psychological symptoms from the drug, his physical state was made incalculably worse by the pints of gin which now accompanied his morphine intake. When he wrote to Lowndes, 'I fear my entrails are rotting', he was telling no more than a literal truth. The deterioration of his mind was for him a decline of the soul itself, which he had decided was leaking, dripping out of his pores in unaccountable torrents of cold sweat, and falling from his mind and memory like leaves quitting a tree. Even the hair, which tumbled with increasing urgency from his scalp, he felt represented the departure of his shaping spirit. The last letter printed in the Clarendon edition consists merely of these three lines:

> *An amethyst weeps in its crystal glitter*
> *Mineral jewels, Judas tears.*
> *King David too had the darkness inside him.*

And shortly after writing this, Richard Pelham disappeared from history. Where he died and how were never recorded, and if his body was placed in a grave, no one since had ever found it.

Withdrawal

To Withdraw: To take back; to bereave.

Johnson's *Dictionary*

One day I was in so much pain that I couldn't face the walk to the DSS building, so I didn't collect. Then it struck me how much I hated standing in line, as though posing for a posthumous L.S. Lowry painting, amongst the bowed down, the listless, the crooked and the evidently and permanently defeated. The place had a smell to it and that smell was failure, massive, inconsequential, state-monitored failure, mixed with a little disinfectant. The five flights of steps I had to walk up and down to get to my flat had become such a deterrent that I only went out at all when in need of food. Then one day my mother arrived, unannounced, by taxi and looked with wonder about the place, littered with debris of all descriptions, some of it once edible, some of it once wearable. The spaces on the wall where Alice's pictures had hung made the place look even more desolate.

'But Chris, you were always so fastidious.' She was already opening a window. Something else I'd stopped doing.

'Sometimes it's hard for me to bend down,' I said. But I was ashamed. I was surrounded by emblems of my own dissolution. There was even a smell in the air I could never get rid of these days, and I wasn't sure it was so different from the one at the DSS building.

A week later on the telephone my mother suggested I should sell my flat and go to live with her. Even three months before I would have found the notion absurd. But now, after pondering the matter for a couple of days, I called the local estate agent and told them to come round for a valuation that Friday. I needed three days to clean the place up, often on my hands and knees, and often doubling the dosage of my drugs to numb the pain. One of London's intermittent housing booms was booming away at the time and six weeks later we had clinched a deal. In less than four months, I was back in Tooting. Even after paying off my mortgage, I still had some money to put on deposit in the building society, from which I could expect a return each year. It wasn't much, but then I no longer had any bills to attend to. I always paid for the shopping when I accompanied my mother to the supermarket, but that was it.

In the process of clearing out my flat, I discovered at the bottom of my wardrobe a pile of papers. They looked familiar but neglected: it was the notes on my thesis from all those years ago in Leeds. I put them on one side, together with my Pelham books, and as soon as I was settled back in Tooting I placed the books on the shelves in the little room on the ground floor which I made my study, and I placed the sheets on the table.

One day I heard my mother, on the telephone to her sister

Agnes, saying she'd decided to nurse me back to health. I
thought perhaps she was simply finding her widowhood a
little too solitary for her taste. I certainly hadn't been round
much, and I had never once taken Alice to meet her –
couldn't face that. But now we had one another's exclusive
company, and I soon turned to that pile of notes and started
reading them again after such a lengthy interruption. By the
end of that first week of reconnoitre and retrieval, my
attention had turned once more to the mystery of Richard
Pelham. But this time I had nothing else to distract me, and I
certainly needed something to occupy the chill vacuum left
behind inside me, with the departure of Alice, my job, my
car, my running – and most of my walking too. The chaos
and grief of Pelham's life still needed annotating, so it
seemed, since no one had come forward to do it in the
meantime. His work had been out of print for the better part
of a century. Most people had never even heard of him.

But six months after my mother started nursing me, we
had to switch roles. She'd been growing slightly odd for
some time before that, and would occasionally be returned to
the house by one of the bemused local traders, to whom she
had confided that she hadn't the faintest notion where she
presently lived. I came back one day from a tentative walk
outdoors to find her carefully scrubbing used food tins with a
toothbrush before putting them in perfect rows in a
cardboard box on the Formica table – 'We've always had
clean rubbish, Christopher, your father insisted on it right up
to the end' – and I sat and listened to her elegiac monologue
about what life had been like when they had lived in the
colonies. But they never had lived in the colonies. 'I was so

sensitive to the climate out there that your father would say, "You're all wrapped in fly-skin, Sylvia'" – but my father had been an accountant in Tooting all his life, and had inherited our house from his father before him. She had carried on scrubbing and talking and talking and scrubbing. The bean tin's blue label was torn and flapping, so she healed it gently with a dab from the Sellotape dispenser which she kept on the shelf above the sink. An asymmetric sardine can, with its ragged remnants of serrated lid, had the blackened toothbrush applied with vigour into its awkward corners. And on it went. On and on and on.

'Probably Alzheimer's, I'm afraid,' the doctor had confided professionally, as we stood out of earshot months later. He leaned close to me. His breath smelt of peppermint. 'Premature senility, as we used to call it.' And I watched her mooning about the place, her grave, beautiful face turned incredulously towards the window sometimes. What it was that caused her so much amazement out there, between the grass and the swaying trees of the common, I never did find out.

But she didn't appear greatly troubled and still cooked and cleaned, though with increasingly eccentric results. I spent most hours of the day in my little study, scraping away at the patina that had accrued about the age of Pelham. I began to think that the problem with the eighteenth century was that you could only see it through the funnel of the nineteenth; could only see Pope through Wordsworth or Byron; only see Smart through Blake; only see Richard Pelham through Coleridge and De Quincey, or Baudelaire and Rimbaud. Even the forms of his degeneracy were contaminated by the future that still lay ahead. I would take walks across the common, over to the Lido and back again, pondering this or that conundrum. By now, despite my back, I did all the shopping and tried, as far as possible, to keep my mother from going out.

My mother took to saying grace before and after meals. 'Your father always insisted on it,' she said, but I never remembered any such insistence. My father, even in his Roman Catholicism, always seemed to me to be accountant all the way through, one who kept the gestures of his faith to an economic minimum. He counted and he calculated, he added up and he subtracted, and he smiled with his own small glow of satisfaction when the figures balanced. But I reckoned that the only agency he had ever truly credited with transcendent power was the Inland Revenue. The mention of its inspectors could, uniquely, hush his voice to a tone of reverence. For him, the atonement had balanced the books, and the ledger had thus been completed.

That Christmas my mother insisted we should go to midnight mass at Westminster Cathedral. I tried desperately to talk her out of it, but she would not be budged. She always had been strong-willed, and the onset of her mild senility had in no way modified that characteristic. On Christmas Eve I opened up the garage to look at my father's car. This last was at my mother's bidding, since I had no doubt it would be non-functional: flat-tyred, flat-batteried, untaxed, undrivable. To my astonishment, his old Rover started at the second turn of the ignition. The tyres were at the right pressure, and when I checked the tax disc it had been renewed three months before. Inside the glove compartment I found my father's motoring file and service history, and discovered that the insurance was up to date too, for any driver over thirty. I couldn't believe my mother had had anything to do with this, for she didn't even drive, so I asked her who had been tending the car.

'Harry does it.'

'Who's Harry?' I said.

'Harry who?'

'Never mind, mother.'

I had to some extent come to terms with my disability. Whether the pain had actually declined, or my accommodation of it had increased, I can't say. That's one of the curious things about any pain that comes to stay: after a while you can't remember what life felt like without it. I had simply learnt not to move whole sectors of my body whose fluency and strength I had once taken for granted. But it was the first time I had driven since my accident, and I had forgotten entirely what a great cumbersome beast my father's car was. It had been designed for a more genteel age, when petrol had been cheaper and the roads emptier. The smell of old leather and the dashboard's gleaming mahogany triggered memories of years before, but it hurt my back every time I had to turn the wheel full circle. The distance between the gears using that old metal stick seemed to require an acrobatic contortion. Whenever I leaned forward to find the indicator switch, the slack safety belt would tighten suddenly across my shoulder and jerk me backwards. There were frequent bleatings from the horns of other drivers. When we arrived at Victoria I was so nervous about parking, and having to twist my head around to do it, that I drove in and out of the

surrounding streets for twenty minutes before I found a gap
large enough to pull into without reversing. My mother sat
tranquilly at my side, gazing out with contented wonder at
the world beyond her window, flashing and flickering away
out there like another galaxy.

In the car on the way back that night, my mother was
silent for a few minutes, until she said finally, with a great
sigh of satisfaction, 'Well, amen to all *that.*' The next day I
couldn't even get out of bed. She brought me my TENS
machine and switched me on. The crowds of electrons
whirled and cavorted inside me, bearing their infinitesimal
burdens of negativity.

My mother's smile was much in evidence that spring.
Once I came back to find her chewing contentedly on a
piece of soap. It was a pink bar of Lux she had always been
choosy regarding the bathroom accoutrements. Then something entirely unexpected happened: my mother started to
speak to me as she had never done before, and using words I
never knew lurked in her vocabulary.

I was sitting at the table one morning, eating a boiled egg
and reading this line of Pelham's from the letters: '*I am the
age's gull, and every year that passes cozens me.*' My mother was
staring through the window with a copy of the New
Testament open on her lap.

'Do you remember what God said to Paul?' she asked. I
carried on reading Pelham, as I normally did these days when
my mother started on one of her monologues. 'He said: "*My
grace is sufficient for thee; for power is made perfect in infirmity.*" I
was thinking how true that is. In your case for example,
Chris.'

'How's that mother?' I said without looking up.

'Well, when you were successful, and a director, and had that lovely little car, I couldn't help noticing something about you.'

'What was that?'

'You were such a twat, dear.' I swallowed hard on the piece of egg I was chewing and turned to look at her. She was serene as usual, her face pointed towards the window. I thought I must have mis-heard.

'I was a what, mother?'

'What?' she said.

'What did you say I was a moment ago?'

'Oh,' she said. 'A twat. Such a fucking twat and you were so pleased with yourself about it, too. I found myself wondering if you'd ever given a bugger about anyone but yourself in the whole of your life. Your father was a bit like that, to be perfectly honest with you. Reliable, of course, like those cars of his. I think the people who built them might have done him as well, when they had a day off. But what a bloody bore he could be with his trial balances and all of that palaver. I don't think anything ever excited your father as much as double-entry book-keeping. Certainly not sex. He'd come home at night and sit in that armchair by the fire and talk to me about . . . cases of insolvency. Not surprising we only had the one child, is it, Christopher? Though probably just as well. Did you get those sausages, by the way? And I could see so much of your father in you that I thought it would be better if you became a priest, that's why I encouraged you in that direction, if you want to know. Then if you were going to be a selfish little shit you could be a selfish little shit amongst men, who wouldn't get damaged by it, since most of them were probably selfish little shits as well. How many women did you have, over the brush, as your father would have said?'

'I can't remember, mother,' I said slowly.

'Too many then. I only hope you gave them money.'

And when I thought about it, the only thing I could be absolutely sure I had given Alice *was* money. My mother sat in silence for a few moments, then she said brightly, 'I sometimes think that if they made a twat that didn't have a woman round it, there'd be quite a lot of takers amongst you chaps.' Then a slab of pain so hard it almost lifted me off the chair suddenly met my neck and brought tears to my eyes.

'Bayliss men don't weep,' my mother said evenly. 'Your father always said that. He always said bollocks to men who blub.'

We both coped in our different ways until the incontinence began. I've heard tell that the faeces of an infant can seem like fragrance in the nostrils of a doting mother, but I've never heard anyone claim the smell of a parent's shit can be sweet to the child, however loving. I came back from my walk around the common to find her smeared from the waist down with streaks of the fetid sludge. One of her fingers was brown from poking at herself in bovine incredulity.

It wasn't long after that I put her in the home. Unfortunately, I couldn't find an affordable one nearby. I can still see the silent reproach in her face as I left her there that day, but what else could I have done? I tried to visit every four or five days, when the state of my back allowed me to drive, but I think mother must have decided that she'd had enough for one lifetime. Her dignity had been mortally offended, I could see that, even as her wits came indisputably astray. But she still swayed in and out of focus and only when she was out of focus entirely did the distress appear to cease. Then she was nobody and nowhere. She was out of focus more and more often. Within a year she was dead.

'Save you a lot of money in bills anyway,' her sister Agnes said to me at the funeral, from under her freshly purchased, wide-brimmed black hat. 'Sylvia was always so considerate that way. Though if you'd only got her a home nurse in, I don't doubt she'd still be alive today. And after all that time she spent nursing you, Christopher.'

Right up to the end my mother had kept her silver hair swept back immaculately into a little knot of royal blue silk.

There was no ghost of her left after that in any mirror, for I'd not inherited her features, neither the high cheekbones nor the blue eyes, nor the tall, thin frame. I was once trim and taut enough in my climbing days up in Yorkshire. In fact, I always stayed fit, I had prided myself on it right up to the accident. But as I loped around, it seemed more and more that my body was merely an encumbrance to my mind. I no longer asked much of the flesh, except that it should leave my thoughts free from distraction and discomfort for as long as possible.

But now I had a whole house to myself – a big one, too. I transferred my thoughts completely into the eighteenth century, having nothing further to keep me in the twentieth. I would occasionally catch sight of myself in shop windows, or in the mirrored wall inside the chemist's. A dishevelled and dubious figure. Since I'd retired from public life, I shaved once a week, and that was with my father's old electric razor, so the results could often be sketchy. My clothes had grown rumpled and baggy and seemed suddenly too big for me, for I only ate these days when I occasionally remembered to do so. I had withdrawn, you see, into the world of study and reflection. Even my flesh had withdrawn.

In that ramshackle Edwardian house at the edge of Tooting Common, I lived by myself. I took no lodgers, and I received no visitors. I pursued my true work at last, with no Alice or anyone else to distract me from it. Now that I was seemingly free from both the pleasures and the burdens that the world afforded, I felt I had been left alone at last to elucidate the life and poetry of Richard Pelham, as I had set out to do so many years before.

Melancholy

Black sun of melancholy. They say the sun never sees a shadow, but the black sun never sees anything else.

RICHARD PELHAM, *Letters*

By the time Lord Chilford returned to Chilford Villa, many of its contents had been draped and shrouded in muslin dust sheets, even the virginals at which his wife had played so prettily. He had bought them for her as a wedding present from an instrument maker in Deal by the name of Atterbury, a man renowned for the tonal precision of his harpsichords. He would now arrange for Jacob to cut the strings. He found the idea of any other fingers dancing along its keys repugnant.

He walked up and down his geometric stairs and in and out of his perfectly proportioned rooms, halting momentarily to stare at the plasterwork on the grand ceiling. Mermen frolicked in the frozen white as their womenfolk taunted and teased them. In the middle of it all was Chilford in his most luxurious wig, as Lady Chilford's smile beckoned him, both her eyes and her breasts focused relentlessly upon the man who represented the centre of her world. Was it Francesco

Vassalli who had done that for him, or had he only been employed on the busts? He could no longer remember, but whichever Italian he had congratulated so enthusiastically on his work, he had hardly thought then that its contemplation could so soon become nothing but a source of nameless grief to him.

He made his way through sad, silent rooms. The multitude of long-case and carriage clocks had all ceased the measured clunks and hammerings which had once sunk so relentlessly through Richard Pelham's soul, for he had instructed Jacob to stop winding them the day after Lady Chilford's death.

At last he came to his study. Pompeo Batoni's portrait of him in oils still hung opposite the door, painted years back in Rome while Chilford was doing the tour. Batoni had given his sitter the airs and graces of an emperor, in contradiction to all Chilford's true beliefs, but still it had amused him and had become a part of the lore of his lovemaking with his wife, as she would whisper coquettishly into his ear about his pagan Roman customs, and he would oblige her with one or two to which his stay in the Holy City had in fact introduced him. One hot afternoon he had crushed grapes across her shifting thighs and then begun to lick . . . Ah leave it, he thought, as he turned the canvas to the wall. She's down in the earth with the worms now, so have done with it.

What confronted him next had always struck him before as of merely anatomic significance. One of the écorché studies so popular at that time portrayed a heavily pregnant woman, the flesh of her belly ripped back to reveal a hugely swollen womb, all the other organs neatly arranged like side dishes, as though to garnish the heavily veined and bloated egg they surrounded. Now for the first time it likened itself in his mind to an explosion, or the rising of a bloody planet over devastated, war-torn ground. Now it meant death, not anatomy. Or perhaps anatomy itself had come to mean nothing but death for him. That image, too, he turned quickly to the wall.

Around him were so many of the objects that had filled the mind of Richard Pelham with panic and confusion. The wax models, the flayed man, the skulls, the Byzantine array of medical implements, to hack into this piece of bone or saw through that one. Even a delicate point so finessed it could drill a tiny hole in a man's skull. 'Is that how you plan to let his spirit escape?' Pelham had asked him. He walked across to the small engraving which hung behind his desk, acquired while journeying through Nuremburg: Albrecht Dürer's *Melencolia*. He looked at it intently now, as he had never looked before.

It pictured a winged woman, the emblematic figure of the melancholy state, gazing off into impossibility, as around her were strewn all the tools of possibility, left immobile by her mystic stare. An hourglass trapped her wing. A magic square was incised in the wall above her head, its arcane promise of hidden knowledge and unworldly power somehow as muted and despairing as all the worldly implements of building and geometry scattered about her feet. Though her face was dark, the eyes were of a startling brilliancy. Watercress and ranunculus wreathed her head – watery flowers to offset the dry and earthy humour. Medieval superstitions creeping into the new learning. But he had been intrigued once by

Marsilio Ficino's distinction between *melancolia candida bilis*, or the white bile melancholy, and *melancolia atra bilis*, or black bile melancholy. The one was said to produce genius and the other mania. Indeed, he had once thought he might well need to apply the distinction to Richard Pelham himself, to show how a single personality could contain both states, or at least how one type might in time degenerate into the other. The compasses in Melancholy's hand could no more measure out a new state house or a basilica than they could fathom the bottomless dimensions of saturnine gloom.

On the table stood the pile of letters in Pelham's wild hand, which Jacob had told him had been arriving over the previous months. Chilford pulled the tug-rope and a bell rang elsewhere in the house. Jacob arrived with Josephine a foot or two behind him. She began to sob as she entered the room and her employer walked across and took her in his arms.

'I'm so sorry, my Lord. I'm so sorry for your trouble.'

'Thank you, Josephine. But we cannot stand about and grieve all day. Jacob, despite my previous instructions, I intend to move back here to the villa for a while, after all, and I'm arranging for my son and his nurse to join me shortly. Would you start making the necessary arrangements?'

Jacob's face brightened, despite the heavy fact of the death of her ladyship in childbirth, as he realised that the villa was not to be shut up after all. He had grown attached to it, he and his wife.

'You'll be able to help, no doubt, with the raising of the boy, Josephine.'

'I'd be honoured, my Lord.' It was one of the sadnesses of their marriage that they had not been blessed with children.

'Good. Then that's settled.' Chilford pointed briskly to the pile of letters on his desk, and Jacob nodded.

'Those are the ones I told you of.'

'How long have they been coming?'

'Over six months now.'

'And never any return address?' Jacob shook his head. 'Right, let's all make a start then, shall we?' Jacob and Josephine stepped out of the room and about their business, and Lord Chilford gazed out of the window at the river. The recent storms had converted the field in front of his house into a whin. He suddenly turned, as it seemed to him momentarily that he caught a breath of his wife's perfume. An absurdity, of course: no more than a trick of undischarged memory intruding on the mind's present calculations. No scent's particles could sustain themselves even in such static air for such a duration. Then he sat down at his desk and started on the unwelcome task of reading Richard Pelham's letters.

Catalogues and Litanies

A fine stock of poetry, biography, letters . . .

REDMOND & THRING, Advertisement

Medical treatises. Memoirs. Obscure works of theology. Volumes of letters so long forgotten that only antiquarian booksellers and lizard-grey librarians knew they still existed. Diaries printed privately in limited editions. All those distant, rolling mists of recollection. Faded obituaries in long-defunct journals. Holograph texts inserted into warped vellum bindings. Marginalia whose sepia inks were dying slowly in the intermittent light.

The only thing that ever took me out of the house these days, apart from simple provisions, was my forays in pursuit of my manuscripts and books among the dealers. I had tried but quickly given up on the London and the British Libraries. I found even the breathing of other people deafened me to the words of the text I was studying. A cough at the next table could end my concentration for the day. I had begun to realise that if I was ever to say anything of substance about this poet who had sunk into such universal oblivion, I was going to have to own some serious material, share my living space with it night and day, stare at it slowly as it stared slowly back, exchange intimate details, date of birth and year of publication, home town and place of printing. For borrowed texts, I had begun to understand, can be very coy in yielding up their secrets. Intercourse with books requires that you should marry them, and the sacrament is money (or theft, whichever one costs you the most), the estate possession. Books need to be owned and treasured, or even abused, not scanned swiftly and coldly in public places as though they were government statistics or pornography. It's no good wrapping them in dirty polythene coats and passing them from one subscriber's hand to another. Books offer illumination only to those they choose, and where and when they choose. A paperback wrapper is a mere illusion of availability, but then so is a luxurious leather binding, like the fur coat a whore wears in winter. Many who read, and often the richest among them, are given nothing whatsoever. The spirit of the text might be retained, however grand and stately the transaction, even while the letter is given. Books must always cost you a little more than you can afford, otherwise they'll keep themselves to themselves, hunch frigid and impenetrable inside their covers, shroud their secrets with a chilling baffle of propriety. And who wouldn't, after all? Whoever taught us to assume that the hearts of books should be easier to come by than our own? Or that their souls should be for sale at a lower price than anyone else's passport to eternity? What is a book, when all's said and done, but someone's heart, someone's soul?

Pelham himself was acutely aware of this. He wrote to his

fellow poet James Thomson that whenever he looked at one of Lord Chilford's books, he sensed the presence of the man, the severe crouch of his precision, beside him in the room. The one possession Pelham was never separated from, even in his last days in Grub Street, was his sextodecimo *Psalms* in the authorised version. A binding of red goatskin over birchwood boards. Tooled into the leather was an image of David playing the lyre, while Saul looked on from his throne, hoping the notes of the music could calm the unfathomed terror and torment that churned inside him.

I'd come to see that books are bound in time as surely as they are inside their covers, which was why my prize possession up to now was a first edition of the *Psalms of Solace*, with handwritten corrections, quibbles and second thoughts. In the margins were written fractions of comments, all inscribed in a tiny, cryptic, eighteenth-century hand. Whose? I needed each day to touch this book, for it was a physical link. The original years, Pelham's years, had rubbed off, they clung to its pages – they were still turning there. It hadn't yet been reset in modernity's font. When I held that book I took the poet's hand across the centuries.

But such items, it has to be said, did not come cheaply. And my appetite for them grew. My mother had left a small amount of money when she died, but not much. That had soon gone. And I was afraid of breaking into my building society account, since the interest on it was, after all, my only income. So one day I took a good look around the house.

The paintings were the first things I sold. I'd never liked them much in any case, since most of them portrayed Victorian sentiment up on its stilts, and I found a most sympathetic man, a Mr Surtees, who had an antique shop a mile or so down the road. He would turn up and I would point to the items I'd decided I could happily live without, then he'd scribble a few notes on a pad, and quickly arrive at a figure. He seemed reliable enough, so rather than waste his time and mine bargaining with him, or hunting about town finding alternative valuations, Simon and I (for we were soon on first-name terms) would sort it out between us. With a smile and a minimum of fuss. No paperwork required. Then he could go back to his business and I back to my books.

There were patches on the walls where the pictures and the mirrors disappeared, and gaps were opening up inside the rooms now as I cut down on the furniture, but the cash enabled me to buy books and batches of unpublished letters and papers; this was the only thing that was important. As for the mirrors, to be honest I was glad to see the silvered backs of them. They always seemed to turn my features round to face me like a silent accusation, though I never knew of what exactly I was being accused. Sometimes when I caught sight of myself as a ghostly blur in a window, I would ask momentarily who that man could be, since I had surely seen him before. My clothes were becoming too large for me. My greying hair was down to my shoulders.

Surtees had expressed an interest more than once in the sofa on the landing. He had even gone from offering me fifty to offering me a hundred pounds, and then a hundred and fifty, but still I demurred. It had memories, that sofa. In fact, it was stained with memories.

During my final exams at school, my mother and father had gone away for a few days to the seaside, and I had stayed on alone in the house to study. It was hot and sunny outside, so when I'd had enough of Robert Walpole's administration, I went out and took a walk over the common. I didn't go to the Lido any more. I think I might even have grown afraid of the place. It was a rendezvous where sex and violence were rehearsed, a hunting ground of physical display and wary counsel, where the smells of flesh and fear intermingled. I never heard tell of any fights actually happening inside – they all occurred later, but they had been negotiated in there, like the rumoured couplings they were so often about.

I had wandered over, drawn most likely by the noise, as the girls' cries threaded in amongst the boys' loud boasts and splashes. I didn't buy a ticket or go inside, but there is a corner near to the railway line where it is possible to climb through the bushes and see past the bars to the bodies within. I knew many of them – I knew them but was no longer friends with them, for I was the one who'd gone to the different school. As we had grown older this had become more important with every year. Then I'd made that big decision regarding my vocation, and had become entirely separate, no longer desirable as a companion. Among the boys, anyway.

Pauline Healey had a legendary status. Her father had deserted his family years before, bestowing on them in the process an indefinably anarchic and socially unanchored status. Her mother was known to take lovers, relationships which sometimes ended noisily and badly. I had even heard my parents talking in low voices about it. Pauline's two elder sisters were said to be notoriously free with their favours. But Pauline herself was famous primarily among the boys for her breasts, which had burgeoned and flourished earlier than any of those of her classmates. Everyone had found them impossible to ignore, whatever clothes she had on, whatever the time of year.

She was there inside in a bikini, and even more impossible to ignore than usual. The boys laughed uneasily as they strutted about her. One wrestled with her for a moment at the water's edge, and the consequence of his arousal was visible in the tightening fabric of his trunks. I had thought to remain invisible, but she saw me, saw me crouching and peering when the others had momentarily drifted away from her, and she made her way over to the rusting bars, where I stood outside looking in.

'Hello, Christopher. Haven't seen you for a long time. Working hard at your books, I suppose. They say you'll be going to Rome this year.'

'If I pass my exams, I will.'

'I thought you never failed any.' She bent down to scratch her knee and her breasts swung free from her ribcage. 'Aren't you coming in?'

'No,' I said. 'Just came out for a walk. I'm studying at home. By myself. Mum and dad have gone away for a few days.' She looked at me closely and smiled. There was an insolent bravado about Pauline's manner that made me nervy and unsure of myself. 'Drop by for a coffee,' I said, without considering my words.

'All right then, I will. After tea tonight.'

As I walked back over the common I felt a cold surge of fear going through me. What had I done? What was I expected to do? But along with the fear was an equally icy thrill.

She came as promised. In her white T-shirt and black leather jacket, and her tight blue jeans. And I made her the coffee. After, she asked to look around the house. She even bounced up and down a few times on my bed and laughed, but it was later, on that sturdily built Victorian sofa, that Pauline Healey finally said, 'Can't keep your eyes off them, can you?' and pulled the T-shirt over her head, leaving me to fumble with the fastening of her bra, while she unzipped me swiftly and took hold. She'd done all this before. Just like the boys had said, she knew what she was about. In one of Pelham's notebook scrawls he speculated whether the first joy of the flesh that an infant ever knows, when its toothless gums are pressed deliriously against the nipple, remains a marker in the hidden memory for all subsequent delights. That might explain why the snowy dazzle of Pauline's ample breasts had so overcome me that the stain was still there after all these years. A week later my mother had noticed it and given it a scrupulous examination, even dubiously sniffing it.

'Looks like milk,' she had said, though without conviction. I had said nothing, not wishing to inform her that it was in fact the spilt seed of Onan, her son. A week later I saw Pauline on a street corner with some of the local boys, and heard her laughter as I walked by. She called something out to me, and the boys laughed again as I hurried away. And in the amused tone of her voice I once more heard the question she had asked as she had left the house that night: 'Are you absolutely sure you want to be a priest, Chris?' Now I found myself asking a question I was often to ask again as the years went by: had Pauline been interested in me, or only in the priest I was destined to become? To tempt a priest with that which he has renounced is a ritual curiosity for some women, and I don't know whether it's meant to abolish all sacraments in bodily delight, or simply to consecrate the flesh itself; to see if it's true that a woman's body might become the altar on which we perform our little miracle.

So I never did sell that sofa. I seemed to be well on the way to selling everything else, though. I would put Simon Surtees's cash in my pocket, then I would strap on my TENS. Little flitters of electricity started flying, tiny stars flashing through my veins, a dance of dainty currents that caused a small hot commotion in the blood. And then, renewed and freshly charged like a milk float, I'd be off, with money burning holes in my pockets, to do the rounds of the London dealers.

London booksellers, I soon discovered, constitute an entire world unto themselves, where unpredictable alliances and bitter rivalries flourish. Some of the people who could supply the things I wanted were not in the centre any more, because they couldn't afford the rents. Charles Redmond and Josianne Thring in Hammersmith were among them.

Charles would open the door of the little house off King Street as though he had just woken up. He would yawn and stretch, whatever the time of day, then he'd push his long ginger hair back from his bony face and reveal his nicotine-discoloured teeth in an enormous grin. Usually he would have no shoes on, and his shirt would be unbuttoned, whatever the weather. He would never acknowledge that he was expecting me, even if I had phoned an hour before.

'Christopher, how nice. Come in. Come in. Good timing – Josianne's not gone out yet.'

Through we would go down the corridor and up the stairs, all lined with shelf upon shelf of neatly stacked books. And there, sitting at the table, would be Josianne. Apart from a few finely nibbed lines around her eyes, she always looked entirely ageless to me, small with brown hair cut short in precisely the manner that the hair of all twelve-year-old boys used to be when I was at school, combed straight in every direction, a shingle of fringe at the front. Blue eyes, wider than the dimensions of her face would have predicted, above a tiny, sweetly arced nose. Her lips seemed permanently sculptured into a good-natured pout, and fastidiously lipsticked. There was always a hint of white powder about her neck, and a meek blush of rouge on her cheekbones. She wore a double-breasted trouser suit, and appeared to be perfectly made, like the inside of a Swiss watch. And I could never see her body without thinking of Alice. They both had the same spare, boyish shape, as though neither of them could be bothered even trying to look womanish; as though they had both made the decision to be female at the very last minute.

'I'll make you some coffee, Christopher,' Charles said as he stepped nimbly over to the kettle. He'd already lit another cigarette. 'I was just telling Josianne about my trip to the East End this morning. Do you know Shadwell at all? Shadwell, the poet?'

'No relation?' I asked.

'No relation,' he echoed vaguely.

'To the Poet Laureate in the seventeenth century. You remember Dryden's lines:

The rest to some faint meaning make pretence,
But Shadwell never deviates into sense.

He was the first person ever recorded in England to die from opium addiction.'

'No, this one's alive and well. Alive anyway. He wasn't actually called Shadwell when I met him at university. He was called Dennis then, but I can see why he might prefer Shadwell. It seems to be a new thing, this single-name business.'

'What about Donovan?' Josianne asked vaguely, while staring through the window, smiling compassionately at the sky, whose thickening grey suggested that it would start to weep at any moment.

'True,' Charles said. 'Kitaj won't let anyone call him Ronnie any more, you know. He's just Kitaj from now on, apparently, even to his nearest and dearest. And there's a man in Brighton called Leon, who lies in a box for a week at a time.'

'Why?' asked Josianne.

'It's some sort of art.'

'Ah.'

'Anyway, I've known Shadwell, or Dennis as he was then, ever since we were at college together,' Charles continued, amidst the clinking of cups, 'before he packed it in, that is, after the first year, as a task unfitted to his genius. So whenever Shadwell's short of a bob or two, which is often, he calls me over to the Isle of Dogs to have a dekko at his first editions. It turns out that last night he gave a reading at a Whitechapel pub, and when he got back, worn out I suppose from the excitement of it all, he passed out in an armchair. After twenty minutes, wanting to catch up on the news, he started his usual search for the black-and-white TV set that he keeps in the corner, along with his other debris and bric-à-brac. Some time later, when this search had proved even more difficult than usual, he realised with sudden clarity that he'd been burgled.' Josianne had started to laugh very softly, and Charles continued, smiling. 'He then called the police. A constable arrives hours later and looking round the place, which was in exactly the same state it's been in for the last ten years, he says, "Like animals aren't they, sir? Just like animals."'

Josianne continued laughing, more loudly now. 'Ah Shadwell,' she said. 'We'll have to have him over again.'

'No good trying to phone,' Charles said as he brought the coffees over on a tray.

'Why not?'

'There's about two hundred empty milk bottles between him and the telephone. He says by the time he makes it into the hall, it's always stopped ringing. He reckons that's why none of his work gets published any more – the publishers have all rung off by the time he picks up the receiver. I raised the possibility of him getting rid of the bottles, and he just shook his head and smiled. A dark smile. A *poète maudit* sort of smile, Paris *circa* 1870. He found it amusing, I think, that I should have such a limited grasp of how complicated the situation regarding his milk bottles really is. Picked up some interesting stuff though. Lots of signed first editions. He's so vague he can never even remember where he got them all from.' I was looking at one of these. A copy of Philip Larkin's *Whitsun Weddings*. Larkin's neatly inscribed name was there, the ink apparently unfaded.

'Anyway, come through and have a look at what we've got,' Charles said. 'One or two things might interest you.' Josianne had stood up and was putting on her coat.

'Goodbye chaps,' she said as she started down the staircase. 'How's the neck, by the way, Christopher?'

'You don't really want to know.'

I bought the three-volume diary of a long-forgotten surgeon and a few books of minor Augustan verse. We finally arrived at a price of three hundred and fifty pounds, though I had the feeling he might have taken slightly less, had I been inclined to haggle, which I wasn't. As I left, Charles said, 'It's Pelham you're after, isn't it? Isn't that your subject?'

'Yes.'

'Now, didn't he have a patron?'

'Lord Chilford,' I said.

'That's him. Chilford. There was some dark mischief about him, wasn't there? Bodies in his basement, or something. Anyway, I could swear there was a rumour, oh years ago now, about a private purchase of Chilford papers. Just on the grapevine, you know. That's how this business operates mostly. The word was that Tewk had bought some material. All very hush-hush. Stamford Tewk. Do you know him? Down in Richmond, just at the side of the bridge. You should probably visit him, he'd have all sorts of stuff you'd be interested in, I should think. Only trouble is, of course, he won't let you in.'

Heart's Hornbook, Memory's Bible

*It pleased God that I should be born in a country where melancholy
is the national characteristic.*

WILLIAM COWPER, *Letters*

Lord Chilford stared at the page before him, with its wild
writing.

My Lord,
You will perhaps remember how in Swift's Voyage to Laputa *the
men of the Academy of Lagado carried on their back every conceivable
object to which they might need to refer, thus absolving them of the
need for vocabulary.*

*It seems in these dark days that it is so with me: for now I carry
every species of grief and sorrow, and cannot translate a single one of
them into a lighter word. I am indeed cropsick and addled, and
wonder whether the treatment you gave me, to which I so meekly
submitted, hasn't helped to turn the sun black.*

*Of course, even David the Psalm-maker had his wife Michal
taken away from him and given to another man, she who had cost
him a hundred Philistine foreskins. But David at least one day won
his wife back.*

What have I been given back for my gold coin but a scorched black disc? So that I could play Gobemouche to your lordly Jack-Know-It-All. And all the time I was privy to things your science couldn't discover in ten thousand years. I have actually been there, my Lord, to the land you told me never existed.

This text that Chilford had before him was not one of those included in the Clarendon edition. If it had been, I might have found it easier to diagnose what Pelham meant by the black sun, the image that kept recurring throughout *The Instruments of the Passion*. How often I seemed to be orbiting about this curious device, or was I merely going round in circles?

One thing I had at least become clear about: it was in the eighteenth century that the modern form of our confusion between fiction and biography began. We say there was a real man called Alexander Selkirk who was shipwrecked and prompted Daniel Defoe to write *Robinson Crusoe*, and yet we now read Selkirk's life through Defoe's novel. The biographical has become a footnote to the fictional. This was the time too when the biographical became, all too often, the servant of the sensational.

Edmund Curll, bookseller and publisher, and amongst the most hated of all the figures in Pope's *Dunciad*, was quick to see the potential of both these trends. He had already had both his ears cut off in a previous brush with the law, but his senses were still in fine working order and they told him to avoid all scrupulosity in regard to the facts. He kept in his rotting garret three particularly disreputable hacks who could be prodded into ill-paid service at a moment's notice. With their aid he produced 'biographies' of many of the famous figures of his day, including some writers. Besmirched on every page with libels and scurrilities, these were a great success. Because Pelham had gained a certain notoriety for his excesses, both alcoholic and religious, Curll brought out a little pamphlet entitled *Richard Pelham Esquire and the Quaint Muse of Dementia*. By the time this work appeared, Pelham was already incarcerated in the Chelsea Asylum, which was perhaps just as well.

We have grown accustomed now to the counter-hagiography of modern enquiry. We expect to be told not about miraculous gifts and healings, but about the full chamber pot stinking under Beethoven's piano while he composes work of sublimity, his own ears deaf to whatever sounds his fingers evoke. The novelty should have worn off by now, but the books do keep coming, and at the time of Curll's pamphlet people were still relatively fresh to the phenomenon. Alexander Pelham, in the Clarendon edition of his great-grandfather's work, could only bring himself to mention Curll's pamphlet once, in an acid footnote. I had finally managed to buy one of these pamphlets, at considerable expense. It was undoubtedly libellous and almost certainly profoundly unfair. It was also very funny. I had the distinct impression that Curll had been in some of the taverns where Pelham had done his drinking. He had seen him at it, probably even joined him in his cups, playing witling to the monarch of laughter.

But he couldn't tell me anything about the black sun, nor about another subject that was beginning to obsess me. After that day with Charles Redmond, I had come back home and pulled down my copy of Stamford Tewk's *Eighteenth-Century Bibliography*, the very place my interest in Pelham had started all those years before. And I read again that line I had first read up in Leeds, but thought nothing much about at the time:

> *Pelham the man, uniquely, underwent the terrors of both star-machine and lightning cage. Pelham the poet at least managed to tell us something of the experience.*

The only thing was, no lightning cage appeared in Pelham's collected works, nor in Curll, nor in Alfred Burnett's nineteenth-century essay. It wasn't in the *OED* either. There was no mention of it in Thomas Parker's *Chelsea Asylum*, even though the star-machine was there, varnished by then into a precocious mechanism of redemption. So where had Stamford Tewk found it? Chilford Papers, Charlie Redmond had said, hadn't he, acquired many years before? All very hush-hush. Whatever the difficulties, it seemed that I had somehow to get to see Stamford Tewk. His address appeared to be still the same as on that bibliography from thirty years before: Richmond, just up from the bridge. But with all the stories I had heard about him over the years, I did wonder if I could summon the strength to face it.

Stamford Tewk had developed a rancid reputation among antiquarian booksellers. In a trade famous for its league of cantankerous, malodorous, misanthropic ne'er-do-wells and bankrupts, Fordie – as he was universally known, even by those who'd never spoken to him – held a special position of honour. He was so indefatigably impolite, so sharply offensive to the most innocent intruder in search of a book, whether it be on Shelley or the Napoleonic Wars or Nietzsche's breakdown, that the stories accrued about him, glowing with venom, until they formed in effect a repolarised halo. Even old Jimmy Baskerville, with his poetry bookshop in Camden Town and his fondness for creeping up behind young female customers and grabbing their breasts, usually with the better part of a bottle of vodka sluicing around inside him, even that seventy-five-year-old bibliographer was as nothing in his legendary status compared with Stamford Tewk.

He had been one of the famous crowd of Soho poets, his first book published by Faber & Faber back in 1948. There had been two slim volumes, all written in strict forms, and all strenuously avoiding any of the whirling rhetoric and sonorous lamentation which so filled the air at the time. The new expressionism of Dylan Thomas and George Barker obviously had no appeal whatsoever for Stamford Tewk, since his bleak and weary eye would have none of it. After the second book he had fallen silent, cleared off and married a painter, who had been well thought of at the time and was now almost entirely forgotten.

But Tewk had become a part of the folklore of Soho and Fitzrovia in the 1940s and 1950s. You could pick up a book by Daniel Farson and read how Fordie had been one of the few characters capable of matching John Deakin rudeness for rudeness, or how he had been a true habitué of the Wheatsheaf, never at a loss for a spiked remark. There were anecdotes about his meetings and collisions: with Francis Bacon, Lucian Freud, or Dylan Thomas himself. How, in his expansive moods and conciliatory days he had picked up the tab at Kettner's, and on another occasion had actually dragged an abrasive companion by his leg along Old Compton Street, until a policeman enquired as to the precise nature of their business. Yet they said he had been kind to Paul Potts, putting up with his indigence and petty thieving, even enduring his company when the smell he emitted had grown feculent enough to drive away many others. He had always bought Sylvia Gough a drink in the Fitzroy, and had sat next to Nina Hamnet as she announced for the fiftieth time that Modigliani had assured her she had the finest tits in Europe, enduring the subtle reek of her urine as it slowly percolated though her underclothes. The drinks passed through her quickly by that stage.

And then one day he had left, and had never been known to return. He was one of the few people to turn his back entirely on Soho, having once inhabited it. And he had at some point opened his bookshop and published his own bibliography of eighteenth-century poetry, which could still be found in the libraries. Then slowly and imperceptibly he had settled down into the dusty eccentricity of his own myth. As far as I could see, no one had anything much to do with him any more. They made do with telling the old stories over again.

The bookshop, in a little road above Richmond Bridge, was permanently closed. Even when the sign said open, and the door was on the latch, it was closed. Tewk would look up with undisguised irritation from his desk if some unsuspecting punter should venture inside, and shout, 'But what do you WANT?'

'I was wondering if you might have a book on . . .'

'But we're closed, for goodness sake, can you not see that?'

'It doesn't say closed on the door.'

'I am here on urgent private business, sir. Now will you please leave the shop, or must I call the police?'

When it rained, he simply locked the door and imperiously waved his umbrella at any sodden individuals who banged upon it, shouting at them from behind the glass to kindly repeat their journey in drier weather, if they really had to repeat it at all. An occasional tyro bookdealer would arrive, looking about him knowingly with a professional frown, fingering the pockets of his leather jacket for his notebook.

'Do you have any modern first editions?' Fordie's response was always the same, and he would deliver it without even looking up from his desk.

'Clear off out of it, will you, sonny? I don't need your sort round here.'

The stock that filled up the front of his shop appeared to be largely a matter of indifference to him. Large rows of volumes that were often distinguished by their contents, if not their prices: mostly literature, history and a miscellany of theology and philosophy, often of an unexpected nature. This constituted the remainder of the auction lots, and country-house sales, after he had extracted the few volumes that truly interested him. But he seemed to regard it as no more than necessary lumber. He showed no interest whatsoever in its sale. His finances constituted an impenetrable mystery to everyone, though he was hardly unique in that respect, in a trade which thrives on Chinese whispers, systematic innuendo and downright falsehood. The only thing of importance to Stamford Tewk, so it was said, was the back room in which he kept his bibliographic gold. In locked shelves and cabinets, and in a large safe. There were a few, a very few, who had been permitted to enter that room and discuss its contents with him, or even handle the precious titles and manuscripts. But they were the chosen, who had fought their way through to the inside of his sanctuary. And God help any of the hoi polloi who disturbed him then, intent on one of his secret sessions. Those who had been in there would never let on to anyone outside what they had been shown, partly to enhance their own prestige as bookmen (for never, so far as anyone knew, had a woman entered), and partly for fear that someone else might have been handed an item of even greater value, of which they themselves still knew nothing. Thus had the mystique of Fordie's stock intensified with every passing year, its value wrapped in ever-thicker shrouds of speculation. That was why, dealers would tell you with a wink, the old boy never left the shop any more. That was why he was going to die in there, keel over in a shroud of manuscripts, rather than step out blinking into the light; why they'd have to chip out his fossil finally with a geologist's hammer, after his remains had begun to settle into a sediment of crumbling pages.

Tewk's age was as much a matter of dispute as his biographic details. One school held that he was seventy, another that he was at least ten or twelve years older; some claimed that his father had left him an estate in Bedfordshire, which he had sold off quickly and thus financed his life in the book trade. There was even a paranoid sect, so foxed by the total lack of sales or purchases which appeared to be Fordie's hallmark for much of the time, who claimed his shop was a front for either MI5 or MI6, an esoteric fascia behind which the murky doings of the intelligence services were being conducted. Given the sort of organisations capable of employing the likes of Burgess or Philby, who could ever be sure? And then there was the mystery of the marriage. People would narrow their eyes in concentration and say, 'Yes, Serena Tallis. Interesting painter, actually. Highly thought of, once upon a time anyway. Went completely nuts.'

So I plugged myself into my TENS for half the morning, until my nerves were honeyed with the flow of the electricity, then went down the road to wait for the red bus that would take me to Richmond. At some point beyond Wandsworth, a group of schoolchildren mounted. Two of them, one black and one white, sat in front of me, and as the bus started moving again the black boy opened the window, and spat randomly out of it. Then he did it again. The white boy next to him started laughing. Then a few seconds later the black boy took aim and spat hard, managing to hit a woman pushing a pram on the pavement.

'Don't do that,' I said and leaned forward to shut the window.

'Who the fuck do you think you are?' the black boy said, his face turned to me, his bright, round eyes absolutely fearless – he couldn't have been more than thirteen years old, but he was already my height. I looked up to see if the driver realised what was going on, for there was no conductor.

'Just leave the window shut,' I said, with I suppose some of the schoolmaster from many years before rising up inside me. I never had been able to put up with insolence. The boy pushed it open again and spat out of it once more.

'Right,' I said rising, 'off the bus.' And I grabbed him by the sleeve of his jacket and pulled him along into the aisle, but he struggled and before I could pull him any further a pain struck with such force down my neck and my back that I let go of him as I froze, then almost fell over. The boy shrieked with sudden delight, 'The poof's a cripple. The poof's a fucking cripple,' he shouted, turning to everyone around him so that they could share his joy. The bus stopped and I managed somehow to get out. I had to stand for ten minutes leaning against a wall, in too much pain even to register the humiliation I had suffered. Mercifully a taxi came by and I talked him into taking me back to Tooting. When I arrived home, I shut the door behind me and locked it, and after that I didn't go out any more even to see the bookdealers. I had them post me their catalogues. Thus was I confined to the little acre of my bare necessities.

Now Pelham took up the whole of my days and most of my nights too. Since I had improvised my own study downstairs, I seldom ventured into my father's on the first floor. I think its atmosphere must have retained something of the calculating precision of his spirit. Perhaps I felt the value of what I was doing was put too severely into question there and I already doubted how much questioning it could stand. But I meandered in one day and that's when I found the stash of postcards, all neatly stacked into filing drawers.

It had been a family tradition ever since I could remember: from each holiday location my father would post a card home, with a brief account of our vacation penned on the back. I picked one out and read it:

Dear House,

The weather has been mixed, but has not deterred us from the coastal paths. Christopher fell on the rocks and cut both his knees. Hope you are free from burglars and leaks. See you Saturday.

Bayliss, Bayliss and Bayliss

His clear copperplate script was festooned with unexpected flourishes, as though indulging an otherwise well-concealed decorative vitality. On the obverse was a photograph, heavy-handedly enhanced, of Fowey in Cornwall. The garish colours seemed somehow entirely of their period: that was precisely how I remembered the world of my childhood, as though the unsophisticated repro work corresponded in some mystical way to the reality around it. I kept flicking through the cards.

Manorbier in towering black and white, the castle a rearing cloud above the shoreline. Oast houses in Kent, herring stores in Hastings, the white cliffs of Dover, the Isle of Wight chines, the flatlands of East Anglia stretching away to meet an even flatter sky. Eastbourne, Worthing, Hove, Bridlington (how that Rover had purred contentedly at fifty miles per hour all the way there and back). Rocks from glacial valleys, limestone coves and blue-watered harbours, Marine Parade, Lyme Regis, the pier and pavilion at Weymouth, detailed line engravings of distant waterfalls and tarns. Each stamp bore the young queen's head in profile and a neat postmark clearly recording the date; each card seemed to have absconded into the future bearing a tiny shred of the past. How like my father to have filed it all away, these random thievings from chronology. And now of the three Baylisses there was only one of us left to count the years, while the locations themselves had shrunk to this house in Tooting. But then the past was my study, after all, since I had already put the future behind me as something too nostalgic even to think about. Simply remembering the word Alice was enough to bring on the pains in my neck.

Dust. The house had been filling up with dust. I'd started to notice it rising round my stockinged feet as I padded downstairs in the morning. I didn't care much about the curtains or the carpets or the wooden surfaces, but now it was settling over the books too. I didn't know how best to handle this. I could hardly clean each volume every week, for there were far too many of them, and I certainly didn't intend to open any windows. The very thought of it. And the notion of plugging in my mother's Hoover and introducing its querulous, wheezing clamour to the library that this place had become, struck me as sacrilegious. It would have been like weighing in with an organ during the more reflective passages of a string quartet. The whole house was gaining on itself in silent increments, but I didn't know where it was coming from, whether blown upwards somehow from below, or silting down gently from above. Perhaps it had always been there, except that mother had once chased it from room to room, keeping it furtive and fleet-footed.

But since I'd stopped pursuing it, now that I'd introduced this lax regime of silent laissez-faire, the dust was growing confident, claiming more and more territory for itself, covering my little world with its minutiae.

One day I noticed a bowl of dead oranges. How long had they been there? My mother must once have bought them, but how far back was that? Each looked like a little shrivelled skull, blood-blackened with rigor mortis; a pile of them, a headhunter's collection after a good season hacking the necks of pygmies. I picked one up and fingered its dry, dimpled dunes, the hide of some spherical foetus that had never made it through. Little dead stars, I thought, too far gone now for even the sun to touch them.

I had taken to thinking a great deal about the past. Not merely the past that had once held Richard Pelham, but the past that had once held me. I had spent nearly three years at the English College in Rome, but in the few months before I set out to embark on my vocation, I did start to consider very carefully whether this should really be the pattern of my life. Pauline Healey's body did not come to the house to confuse me any more, but her spirit visited my dreams most nights. I had begun to wonder if I were not simply too worldly to be a priest, and then a number of things happened. First, I started to have my dream, the dream in which a leprous disease would slowly cover the flesh all over my body, as I looked on in horrified paralysis. My skin would slowly erupt in small volcanoes of disfigurement. I itched all over with some nameless filth. And then right at the end, as the tears started coming, invisible arms would hold me and heal me, and I woke then sobbing with gratitude. I had looked up Matthew 8:3, where Jesus puts forth his hand to the leper and touches him, and tells him he is made clean, and the leprosy instantly vanishes. A new man walks away. First sign.

The second sign had been this: I had read an article about Merrim, the multi-millionaire businessman, in which one of his disgruntled ex-employees described the scene each morning when the mogul shouted to his advisers to join him in his personal lavatory, the one with the solid gold taps, and there bawled instructions at them, as they tried to avert their eyes from the fat, hairy thighs protruding out of his shirt-tails, and breathe as little as possible so as to avoid the stench of his abundant faeces. This image of earthly power had been sufficient to make me wonder once again whether I shouldn't in conscience try, in however small a way, to be a part of the world's leaven. The salt, its savour.

But the last sign had been the blackest and by far the most potent. There had been a boy called Midgely, who had lived in the neighbourhood ever since I could remember. In fact we were the same age. He had been arrested on a murder charge a month before, and was now awaiting trial without bail. Murky stories were circulating about what had happened, but one night I went down to the local pub and stood nursing my drink while I listened to the chatter all around me. Midgely, it seemed, had had a few pints and then set off unsteadily to a place in Streatham half a mile away, where a housing estate and a piece of wasteland between them provided the possibility of sex for sale. There was little doubt in the minds of the regulars that Midgely had been a virgin before that evening. It had not taken him long to be approached by one of the local rent-girls. The two of them had engaged in whatever grim and mechanical manoeuvres were on offer, then Midgely had informed his partner that he had no money. He had told her not to worry, he would return the following night with the five pounds that had been requested. The fact that she had not demanded the money first meant that she was no professional. After she had screamed at him, and even cut a part of his cheek with one of her nails, she had then started laughing, and had suggested they should call it quits after all, since he now had VD, though it would take a week or so before he started squirming with the pain.

Whether through terror or anger or shame, or a mix of all three, Midgely had dragged her back into the derelict building and, holding her down by the hair with one hand, had smashed in her head with a brick that he held in the other. They said that there had been nothing left of her face by the time he was finished. She had been nineteen years old.

This little trinity of signs, I had come to feel, was angled directly at me. You see, I've never believed anything to be accidental. There are no coincidences, only a veined complexity sometimes too deep to fathom. Only the wounds of time and what's hidden inside them. And so it was that I began to make preparations for my life in Rome. Whatever doubts I had, I knew that I still had to go. I had told all this to Alice once. 'What a God,' she had said, 'who only speaks through other people's misery.'

Once in Rome I was a most devoted student, and was highly thought of by my superiors. The minor orders presented no problem: porter, lector, exorcist and acolyte.

These ancient ruins of courtly degrees I received without demur. I even wore my tonsure with a kind of pride. But I started to falter as the subdiaconate approached, for it contained that fateful commitment to lifelong celibacy. In the *magnum silentium* after ten at night I would lie in bed and try to work out whether the women striding through my mind were shapes sent to distract me, like St Anthony's desert seducers, or merely a warning that I would surely fail, should I ever make an irrevocable commitment to forsake the intimate presence of women and the comfort that their flesh and their spirits afforded. How often the ghost of Pauline Healey ministered to me. How often she pulled that white T-shirt over her head and reached down again to take me.

So that's when I had started to slip into the streets outside, uncassocked, to find out before it was too late what it was I might be missing, and it was then I first discovered in that great city of pagan monuments that what I would be missing was too much, far too much.

Soon after I had left for England and that degree course up in Leeds, and had put celibacy behind me as one of those childish things, not fit for adults in an adult world. Or at least only possible for those for whom the passions burned with a dimmer flame than they did in me. The Christ of redemption shrank back into the Jesus of history, and the resurrection became whatever filled the chasm between hope and mortality. My mother found it difficult to speak to me for a while after that, and I had the dreadful suspicion she was praying for my lost vocation. Every night.

I had gone out to buy some vegetables and rice. I was walking along distractedly on my way back, carrying my meagre bag of groceries, when I suddenly stopped and stared down at the pavement. How many years before had there been brown paving stones? York stones my father had called them, though it seemed like a long way to bring them to me. Billy Haggarty and I had crouched opposite one another. We had both stolen chisels from our separate houses. He hammered first at the flagstone and made a white circle out of its ochre. Then I raised my own blunted blade and drove it down into the centre. Tiny flakes of stone had risen into our faces like sharp-sided hail.

'The rat is dead for another year,' Billy had shouted. 'Can't eat my toes, can't eat yours. He'll have to find a baby if he's hungry.'

Furtive and priestly, we had buried both chisels in his garden. I never did know what the ceremony meant. There were no rats that I knew of, not in his house, and not in mine either. Two months later I caught my father hunting through his tools and muttering, 'Where on earth has that chisel gone?'

That night I spent twice as long as usual with my TENS wrapped blinking round my neck. It would probably surprise you if I were to tell you that electricity can flirt inside your body. It can, though. It hovers in obscure muscles, and dawdles along the corridors of veins. It snuffles out little hidey-holes in membranous corners, and quivers foxily in there and won't be ferreted out. And so you end up walking around with all this electricity quirking and scrolling inside you. If they stuck a bulb between your lips, believe me, you'd light up a field.

My bedside reading was the little book of Count

Zabrenus's sermons I had managed to buy that week, the words faithfully transcribed by the faithful in the conventicle off Tottenham Court Road which Pelham had once attended:

> *Would you eat anything, my brothers and sisters? Would you swallow a nightingale live for the sake of its warm, liquid song, just to catch the pulse of it swelling? And if not, then why not? Do you imagine a cow is any less kind than a songbird? Jesus told us he was the lamb, and yet we continue to shed the blood of lambs as men once shed His.*

I had been brooding on this passage before I fell asleep, and in my dream I was in an abattoir, dressed absurdly in eighteenth-century costume and a periwig, but with a priest's stiff collar, shouting at the men, who in their blood-stained T-shirts ignored me and went about their business: 'Celery, carrots, potatoes and bread don't bleed, my friends, don't get dragged from their cribs before dawn, or stacked into lorries, knee-deep in blood-spattered straw and their own faeces . . .' My words were chewed up by the sound of machinery. Then the dream turned inside out and I was travelling through my own intestines, the internalised homunculus of myself, animula, little soul, and I saw how the walls inside my own body were stained badly by the dreadful yield and cull of slaughter. Then there was nothing but smoke in an oven, just black smoke stains and scratches inside a huge, municipal, over-used oven.

In the weeks that followed, and without ever consciously making a decision about it, meat disappeared once more from my diet, as though I were back with Alice in Battersea. I felt I couldn't face the smell of it cooking, or the sight of dried blood gathering inside its wet shrink-wrapping. I could almost hear the pitiful moans and demented whinnies in the butcher's shop window, and I thought I could hear Pelham at Smithfield on his knees, calling aloud for mercy for all the creatures of God's bounty, just before his second arrest.

The Zabrenus sermons made intelligible much of the fury in those late letters of Pelham. I lifted my eyes from the book in the early afternoon and saw with extraordinary vividness an image from my childhood. Billy Haggarty and I had found some old battered tins, still full of whatever it was they contained, but with all the printed wrapping long gone and with enormous rusted dents in each one.

'They explode,' said Billy, 'if you throw them on a fire. Let's start a fire.' So we pulled together pieces of old wood on the stretch of wasteland near where Billy lived. He had matches and after a while he managed to get a flame alive. Then we watched and coughed as the blistered paint of the timber belched out its black, stinking smoke. We started to throw on the cans, one by one, laughing at the danger we knew we were courting. There must have been ten or eleven of them, and each time we threw one into the flames our yelps of laughter grew louder. When the last one had been thrown, we stood in silence staring at our own private bonfire, our faces blackening from the sooty fumes. Then there was an explosion, so loud it seemed the world had stopped all about us, and Billy stood staring at me in solemn disbelief, his face and clothes spattered with red gobbets where the tinned tomatoes had hit him. I waited for him to fall over from his wounds, but he never did.

The next day I went down into the cellar for the first time since I had come back to live in Tooting. A spider had made its web across one corner, and it was littered with the eviscerated carcasses of insects. A few months before I had bought an eighteenth-century edition of Swift's *The Battle of the Books*, in which he meditates on how the spider, the representative of all that is modern, spins its new world out of its entrails. And then I saw the jar of money. It sat on the trestle table in the middle of the floor, an enormous glass jar, almost the size of an amphora, filled with coins; of copper, brass, silver and others unspecified, made of alloys unassayed. I had in my teens collected them from all over the world, but mostly England. Put there originally as a gesture towards possible redemption one day, but left finally to gather in their own gloom and for their own dull sake, rotting gently like outdated ordnance in a military dump. Even burglars wouldn't bother to touch that pile, should they ever come on a visit.

What had I done to earn them and, more to the point, why had I failed to spend them? Why had I not simply thrown them away? And what were they, anyway, these coins? Congealed labour, the symbolic issue of the sweat of someone's brow? Not mine anyway, so maybe only the random tokens scattered by the Goddess of Fortune spinning on her wheel, Lady Luck's hard-nosed gifts. Pennies and dimes, drachmas and centimes, Deutschmarks, pesetas, lire. And a few antique ones I picked up one day at a jumble sale and tossed into the pot. Most likely issued by a Roman quartermaster to some bored and randy legionnaires centuries before. Hundreds of sundry fingers had pressed most of them into my palm. In bars in Tuscany, French cafés, Greek doss houses, on the top decks of dirty buses in south London.

I remembered how I had once sat in the evening staring at that glassy vault, asking myself what happened to such money if you declined to use it. Did it become merely a ghost of itself in metallic retirement, forgetting at last the corrosive sweat of the flesh? It had been freed from any burden of its usefulness, that was for sure. The paper money, having no weight or gravity to begin with, had all long since floated into other people's hands.

It was odd to think that every head portrayed in relief in that jar had once been the centre of the circle of its world. This was my little protest at the hellish infinity of money, its ceaseless, monstrous, reproducible fecundity. I had only one use for it these days: to buy other men's words, written centuries before.

Simon Surtees would drop in most weeks to arrange my next asset-stripping session, though most of the rooms were now so void of furniture or ornament that there wasn't too much left over to strip. And two or three mornings a week I had to answer the door for the postman, as he delivered a holograph manuscript or a set of eighteenth-century first editions. That particular morning it was the postman. I opened the door and took his parcel, signing his little form.

'You all right, Mr Bayliss?' he said, peering at me solicitously. He was in his early twenties, with closely cropped hair, a single earring on one ear, and an open smiling face, always cheerful whether the weather was wet or dry.

'I think so. Why do you ask?'

'Just wondered,' he said, and walked off whistling. I took the package through to the kitchen and carefully cut it open. *A Doctor's Meditation on the Melancholic State* in two volumes, by Frederick Threlwall. I had been waiting for that. I laid the books out on the table and stared at them lovingly. Only then did I look down and realise I had no trousers on. Worse than that, my underpants had a big yellow patch across them. How long had I been wearing those? How long had it been since I had washed? That explained the postman's quizzical look. I went upstairs and found some trousers. They were stained too, and crumpled, but I put them on all the same and looked into the mirror on the inside of the wardrobe, the only mirror left in the house. It was weeks since I had shaved. What surprised me most was that my straggly new beard was entirely grey. And so was my hair, which had not been cut for months and months and now reached below my shoulders. Then the knocking on the door started up again. Probably the postman, come back to make sure I wasn't ill.

It wasn't though. It was my Aunt Agnes, my mother's sister, the newly hatted comforter at the funeral.

'I've come for lunch,' she announced as she stepped through the door and past me. 'Good God, Christopher, you look like Ben Gunn.'

'Lunch isn't possible,' I said quickly, following her. 'I have an appointment in an hour with some bookdealers. But have some coffee.'

She walked about the place, emitting sounds of ill-tempered incredulity. 'Where has all the furniture gone?'

'I decided to refurbish the house.' Had I picked up that phrase from Simon? It can't have been one of mine.

'It's yourself you should be refurbishing, by the look of you. All Sylvia's lovely wooden chairs gone, even the little coffee table. What have you done, sold them?' I didn't answer. She ran a hand along one of the remaining surfaces, a 1930s sideboard even Simon had balked at buying, and held out her finger towards me, smudged in black. 'There's more dust in here than where your mother is. Are you seriously telling me you're not going to make me some lunch, after I've come here especially all the way from Surrey?' She had ringed her mouth with a dangerous streak of red lipstick.

'You should have phoned.'

'I did phone. About ten times. Nobody ever answered.' It was true I seldom picked up the receiver any more, either to call or to be called, except to place my orders with the dealers. 'And just look at you. You look like death warmed over. You're fading away, you are. You'll be with Sylvia soon, if you carry on like this. Anyway, at my age going from one county to another is not something to be taken on lightly. You'll have to drive me back, then. I told Ernest not to bother coming till four.'

'I can't drive the car today,' I said. 'My injury.' I gestured at my shoulder. 'It's playing up.'

'Injuries. At your age. Your uncle's been waiting for an operation on his rupture for three years, but it's never stopped him driving me around.'

I made her coffee, but the milk was rancid – I couldn't

remember the last time I'd needed to use it. I found a biscuit for her. She looked about in unremitting pique at the state of the house.

'You've started to look like somebody in one of those films,' she said, shaking her head. Her hair had been frozen into place with aerosol. 'Fresh out of the desert. And you used to be quite presentable.' People simply didn't come here any more, I wasn't used to it, and I soon grew so exasperated with the ceaseless scissoring movement of her jaws that I excused myself. I grabbed a book from my study then made for the bathroom on the top floor, where I read a whole page slowly in an unsuccessful attempt to cleanse my mind of the clutter of my jabbering aunt. When I came back down the stairs I stopped on the landing. There was a humming sound coming from mother's bedroom. 'Greensleeves' – a tune of which she was never fond, so it seemed unlikely to be her ghost. I peered round the door. Aunt Agnes was trying on my mother's shoes, flipping her toes in and arching her instep for size. She'd already pulled three pairs out of the wardrobe.

'I'll take these, Christopher,' she said matter-of-factly, 'it's not as though you'll be doing much with them, is it? Even you wouldn't have the heart to sell her personal effects, though you're obviously hell-bent on selling everything else. She'd have wanted me to have them, I can promise you that.'

Finally, in speechless relief, I steered her to the bus stop clutching her bag of shoes, and loaded her on to the first bus that came, claiming I myself would have to wait for the second to go and meet my dealers. Then I slouched back to the house, even more crook-backed than usual, climbed to the bedroom and connected myself up to my TENS. AC/DC. Take the AC out of Alice and you were left with the one word *lie*. Even the bedroom was now denuded of all furniture except the mattress, and besprinkled all over with an inch of dust. This was a domicile of ghosts, even if my mother's wasn't one of them. Desire hadn't died with Alice's departure – those ghosts moved from room to room as well. And I suddenly realised lying there, with the great clarity of the totally isolated, that if I didn't try to pull myself out of the eighteenth century, I would shortly disappear entirely from the twentieth.

And so that weekend, with the hesitancy of one doing it for the first time, I bathed and shaved. I went to the barber's in Tooting Bec, who stared at me with wonder, and told him to cut it all off. I called into a shop and bought myself some clothes. And finally, all dressed up and with nowhere to go but home, I looked around the house and realised that my Aunt Agnes, selfish, hard-nosed bitch that she was, had been right: I *had* turned the place into the inside of a tomb. There was enough dust in there to start a cemetery. So I took the vacuum cleaner out of its retirement under the stairs and set it loose to wheeze brutally about the place. Now without dust the house looked unnervingly empty (what a lot of things I'd sold). And, for the first time, I didn't want to be locked inside it: I wanted to be out instead. So I tried to think of some place I needed to visit. And then I remembered Grub Street. Except that it wasn't called that any more. Nowadays they called it Milton Street, but I'd never actually been on a visit.

I had to breathe in hard before descending the steps at Tooting underground station, but I persevered. Half an hour later I was there, and I wondered why I had bothered. The street has been truncated and surrounded by a fearful symmetry of modern offices. Could this really be the place where for ten years Pelham learned to drink deep and taste corruption? So many windows glittering with City prosperity, but no sign of any life at all, just stonewall anonymity. At the top now stood a tower of darkly tinted glass that I tried to peer through, but I couldn't make out very much. I had to walk right round it before I found a tiny sign, informing me that this was a British Telecom building. Odd to think such an eye-deflecting, enquiry-refracting pile should be one of the centres of the country's communications. So uncommunicative. I'd always thought the idea was that the century decided to dispense with Victorian façades and make buildings out of glass, so that the machinery of life could be transparent with modernist hygiene, no need any more to hide away the golden facts in inner sanctums. Now they had darkened the glass so much that no one could look inside, and the glass had become its own façade instead. Could this place really have been such a thriving nest of vagrant brilliance and journeyman cynicism, learning and hypocrisy, all seasoned and poxed with lust? Johnson's Dictionary was pert and personal: 'Grub Street: A street near Moorfields, much inhabited by writers of small histories, dictionaries, and temporary poems.' And from the *Walks Through London*: 'The residence of sorry authors . . . From this street has proceeded an infinity of wit and humour: perhaps authors were poorer in former days than at present, and therefore chose this cheap part of the town for their residences.' That was a mere two centuries before. Now it was a counting machine, curtained by steel and glass from the inquisitive air outside. An occasional besuited figure, carrying a sandwich and a slimline drink strode efficiently up the pavement. I was out of place. Even freshly bathed and shorn, I was still ragged with distraction compared to these functionaries of the financial machine. They looked at me with faint suspicion, as though I might be about to ask for money. There'd have been no use in telling them I was in pursuit of Richard Pelham, for they wouldn't have known who I was talking about. There are no blue plaques to him in the City, or anywhere else for that matter. Even most academics have barely heard of him, so why should some fresh young accountant be expected to know? Anyway, Pelham and money are incompatible, we've established that much surely, if no more.

So I made my way over to Museum Street, to collect the book I had ordered on the eighteenth-century houses of Twickenham, and that night, exhausted but pleased with myself at my re-entry into the world, I opened the old folio volume carefully and started to read the section on Chilford Villa.

Dilapidation

To Dilapidate: To go to ruin; to fall by decay.

Johnson's *Dictionary*

In *Twickenham's Georgian Houses* there were three pages on the building of Chilford Villa and another ten on the lengthy saga of its ruin. This was material I knew nothing about.

It seems that after the death of his wife, Lord Chilford raised his son at the villa, with the faithful Jacob and Josephine in attendance, as he devoted himself more and more to his scientific studies. Many members of the Royal Society visited him there, including Benjamin Franklin, who became a great friend and who was reputed to have collaborated in Chilford's experiments in the laboratory which he had constructed inside the villa.

On achieving his majority, Chilford's son promptly embarked on the life of a libertine, to the lifelong regret of his father, who became more and more reclusive and was reputed in his final years (here I stopped reading for a moment, startled) to take his solace in ever-deeper draughts of laudanum. On his death, his son began to use the place as a weekend retreat for whoring and other, more spectacular variants of Georgian debauchery. The villa's precipitous decline had now begun. By the time of the early death of the third earl of Chilford, the building was already in poor repair. It was acquired by a number of figures in the nineteenth century, two wealthy industrialists, and a local dowager of considerable means. But although renovation began on at least two separate occasions, it was never completed satisfactorily. By the turn of this century, the place was half-decayed, its gutters fallen, the lead from the roofs stripped out, the copper plumbing gutted, its interior a damp and windy haunt of bats, birds and the occasional tramp. Then during the First World War it was requisitioned by the army for storage purposes, and by the time they'd finished with it, anything of any remaining interest in the interior had either been vandalised or entirely destroyed.

In 1908 the Royal Commission on Historical Monuments had been set up, but the buildings it was required to list needed to have been erected before 1714, and Chilford Villa was not completed until 1745, so its sad dissolution carried on unhindered until finally in 1935 its condition was deemed so unsafe as to call for demolition, which is why no stone of it remains standing today. During the demolition, human remains were discovered in the foundations. This was the 'black mischief' which Charles Redmond had mentioned. Their presence had never been satisfactorily explained, but the corpses had evidently been experimented upon.

I lay in bed that night with images of the ruin of Chilford's Palladian dream going through my mind. I tried to listen to a story on the radio. I fell asleep with the radio on and I woke early on the Sunday morning to its grim announcements. Princess Diana had died after a car crash in Paris. Later I bought some papers for the first time in months and in reading them found myself more affected than I would have expected. In the week that followed, I forced myself out each day, to practise my freshly found worldly expertise, and I became intrigued to see London transformed into an open-air mausoleum and shrine. The newspapers started to report that the driver had been out of his head with drink and drugs. It seemed that as she lay mangled in the dark concrete underpass, the photographers' flashlights had still been exploding in her face. As in life then, so in death. One day I left all the bookshops behind so that I could walk back through the parks. Great masses of bouquets, still glistening in their cellophane wrappers, had burgeoned around St James's, Buckingham Palace and, most spectacularly, at Kensington. I read some of the messages: 'Hope you are happy at last among the angels.' Children's toys had been dropped in among the forest of flowers, little funerary gifts for her journey beyond. One evening I stayed up in town and walked, as the dark was settling, to Kensington and there I looked with wonder at the thousands of silhouetted figures queueing almost silently, shuffling along like the shades in Dante, to add their condolences to the great black book, as the rings of candles flickered prayerfully around every tree. I had never seen anything like it in my life. Even Rome's exuberant processions had never matched this.

That night I left the station at Tooting and stopped a moment later outside a pub. An old man, diminutive, bewhiskered, with an aluminium walking stick, whirled, danced and juddered, as though under compulsion from whatever force had taken hold within him. His jacket was a putrid grey above his black and baggy trousers, and his bare, blistered feet were inserted into massive overshoes. He could only move forward by splaying his feet sideways, and as he twisted, jerked and convulsed along, his shiny walking stick described chaos manoeuvres about him. His unruly other hand drew surrealist maps of fork lightning in the air, and it was impossible not to think of Chaplin, his sad little clown now terminally plagued by St Vitus's Dance. I resolved never to allow myself to disappear into that interior at Tooting again.

Back inside the house I stared at those pages about the ruin of Chilford Villa, and I knew that the next day I had to start out once more to see Stamford Tewk.

Part Two

Stamford Tewk

Where each man reads the book of himself.

RICHARD PELHAM, *The Instruments of the Passion*

This time my journey to the shop was uneventful. I walked up and down a few times outside before I finally managed to step through the door.

'Closed,' he shouted from the desk, without looking up. I didn't move. Finally he raised his face from the desk. He was wearing a black double-breasted suit, which looked as though it had put in at least one decade of service too many, and some species of college tie, darkened from many years of use. But what I hadn't expected was his face. His face was ascetically thin, thinner even than his short, trim body would have led you to expect. His nose was both delicate and prominent, his eyebrows arched and coal black, even though the hair above was entirely grey, parted immaculately in the manner of film stars of the 1940s. Could that really be Brylcreem he was using? When he took off his glasses to stare at me, his eyes were vivid green, and seemed not to blink at all. Stamford Tewk was that rare thing: a beautiful old man.

His voice when he spoke had a depth of resonance and a precise inflection, which in more conscripted times would probably have been referred to as commanding.

'I said we were closed, or do you suffer from an auditory disability?'

'Not much point asking me, if I do, is there?' I think I might have detected the rictus of a smile about his features then, the merest twitch of the possibility of amusement.

'Is there anything specific you require?'

'Lord Chilford,' I said. 'Edward Allingham, the second earl of Chilford. Royal Society publications. Letters. Diaries. Related material from other sources. Holograph texts. I was told you might have something.'

'Why?' The eyes unwavering in their focus on mine.

'I'm writing a book on Richard Pelham.'

'Is it likely to make any money, this book of yours? Or is it a requirement of your career? Might you perhaps be a member of a university department?' These final words were uttered with a quiet, but maximum, disdain.

'I'm not a member of anything at all any more. And I'd say there's a fair chance the book will never even get published, let alone make any money.'

'So why write it, then?'

It's an odd thing, one I came to note more and more as the months rolled on, but when Fordie asked a question, it tended to get answered.

'I can't help myself, if you must know,' I said. 'I don't think there's anything left for me to do but write it. Otherwise I'd just be a waste of space.' And with those words I suspect I smuggled myself into the environs of

Fordie's heart. I might just possibly have fallen outside the innumerable categories of people whom he detested. Or could it be that he'd simply grown tired of telling the whole world he was closed?

That first day he suggested I return the following week, after he'd had a chance to check on what he had stored away. And so it began, my lengthy dialogue with Stamford Tewk. We spoke of almost everything, and my visiting days increased until I would be there for several hours four or five times a week. The only thing he wouldn't discuss were the Chilford papers, which were the only reason I'd come in the first place. I had to make do with other topics and study Tewk's curious way with customer relations.

I was sitting there one day reading a first edition of Pope which Fordie had placed in my hands. The man who entered was small and more boyish in appearance than his age should have allowed. His hair was golden but with a lacing of grey here and there, and studiedly unkempt. He wore jeans that were faded to the precise fashionable requirement and a suede jacket. He had slipped through the door, and managed to evade the proprietor's scowl and the little intermittent barks requesting his departure.

'Do you have any pomes?' he asked Fordie, after a few minutes of idling about the place. A Liverpudlian accent. Fordie looked him over from head to toe with evident distaste.

'Pomes?' he said finally, and the man nodded. 'Do you mind if I ask your nationality?'

'I'm English actually,' the man said, looking confused.

'That's your country of origin,' Fordie said. 'Your

nationality, I think you'll probably find, is British. Your occupation?' The man looked even more confused, but he responded, as I mentioned people often did when Fordie interrogated them. Did they hear some tone in his voice that demanded a reply? Was there an atavistic requirement to answer the pressure of his rudeness?

'I'm a university lecturer.'

'Subject?'

'What?'

'What is your subject, man? What is it we're paying you to teach?'

'English literature.'

'Then, given the silver threads among the gold in your hairpiece, I'd have though you might have realised by this stage in life that the word is poem. PO-EM. Not *pome.*'

'I was raised in Liverpool,' the lecturer said with sudden indignation.

'I daresay you were, but you must surely have grasped the principle of the English diphthong by now, whatever the peculiarities of your rearing in the north-west. I seem to recall you lot are more than capable of chanting EE-AYE-ADDIO. Over and over again, if memory serves. A diphthong. A rather *melodramatic* diphthong at that.'

The small man left then, without another word, and banged the door fiercely behind him. The dusty little bell tinkled sadly, gently turning into an echo of its former self.

'An educationalist,' Fordie said evenly, pronouncing each syllable of the word fastidiously, before turning back to the book on the table before him.

We would spend hours like this, as I watched in silent

amazement at his treatment of all those impertinent enough to try to get into his shop. If anyone managed to enter and then find a book of interest, it would only take a few seconds before he would call out, 'You really must take care not to crease the spine, you know.' The bemused figure would look up from the book being inspected, nonplussed.

'But I'm only opening it enough to read it.'

'READ IT?' Fordie pronounced both words slowly, to emphasise how exotic he found the idea. 'I see. Well, if you're finding yourself at a loose end today, there is, I believe, one of those Christian Science Reading Rooms a mere five minutes' walk from here, and I'm sure they'd be more than delighted to accommodate you. Alternatively, in the other direction there is a public library. I believe the spines of books there are specially strengthened with binding tape and apparently shrink-wrapped in some species of plastic, so no matter how much you bend, bump or scuff them about, no one's likely even to notice. You could probably even tear the pages out, while sitting in the reference section, without attracting a moment's attention. Sing an ethnic folk song while you're about it. Claim it's all part of your people's inviolable traditions.'

This last was usually uttered to white members of the middle class whose inviolable traditions stretched back no further than Ealing or Slough.

One morning as we sat together in silence, Fordie gazed with a melancholy eye at his newspaper. He was staring at a photograph of the island of Montserrat lying under a carpet of grey volcanic ash, a huge dead cake floating disconsolately in the middle of the Caribbean. Another picture of the volcano itself, coughing out its dragon's spew, showed the earth under her aspect of malignancy, an apocalypse of fury scorching only inches beneath her leprous hide. Vulcanologists were still in dispute, so the paper reported. Would *la Soufrière* return at last to its mighty slumber, or continue to lavish its lethal fumes and dust upon the acres of earth that now lay gagging beneath it?

'*Soufrière*,' Fordie said thoughtfully, looking up. 'Sulphurous. Yes, it must be. From *le soufre*. Odd they should have made it feminine though, isn't it? Or maybe not, come to think of it. The mons. So much bloody turmoil inside, once everything gets started. It seems that hell's for real, after all: here we are walking round its rim.'

'Another coffee, Fordie?' I said. His silence was the nearest he ever came to an affirmative.

'Do you really believe in hell?'

Fordie pushed his delicate, well-manicured fingers across his neatly swept hair, a gesture he often made prior to speaking.

'My wife, you know, believed in nothing but the imagination. The trouble was she thought the imagination was a temple of light, a great big tower of illumination. No real darkness there at all. Then she went mad and started dying, rather horribly in fact, and after that her paintings . . . you have *seen* her paintings?' He gestured at the wall behind me.

I'd wondered whose they were. A tiny monogram, ST, thinly inscribed in white paint with a very delicate brush in the bottom right-hand corner of each one, had had me speculating whether they might not be Fordie's own work. I turned and took them in again at a single glance. They were all small landscapes in oils. A copse in Surrey: silver birch, bracken, heather, pine and sand. A window showing on to the grand arc of the bay at Tenby (every time I looked at that I thought of Alice, and the last time I had ever seen her) with the Victorian buildings rain-scumbled in their pastels above it, and the boats heaving and bobbing at anchor in the little harbour below. A prospect of the Isle of Wight: sherbet-coloured sands sifting the headlands and chines. Another showed the battle between harshness and gentility in the great swathes of open colour, spliced by lattices of drystone walling, up in the Yorkshire Dales. And then there was a tiny pair, my favourites, picturing granite promontories thrashed by angry, roaring seas, with the winking lights of a fishing port, somewhere or other on the Cornish coast at night.

'My wife was called Serena Tallis,' Fordie went on, 'very well thought of for a time, among an admittedly small and discerning group. She exhibited with the 7 and 5 Society a few times, before they all lost their heads about abstraction. Her studio in the 1930s was in Hampstead. Just round the corner from the Mall Studios. Five minutes' walk, and you could meet Ben Nicholson, Barbara Hepworth, or Henry Moore. Even, for a little while, Piet Mondrian, before he moved on to New York, to the great city of grids, which I should think must have fitted his Puritan soul as though it had been made to measure.

'Now, you have a good look at those things behind you. They're not at all bad, you know, not at all bad.' They weren't either. There was a luminous quality to the brushwork and colouring that often held me for minutes at a time as I walked past, on my way to find a book. They all seemed to delight so much in their fluency and uninhibited palette. 'But they lack something. Impress me, Christopher, and tell me what it is that my wife's paintings lack.' I couldn't. 'They lack black, that's what. The colour of no colour at all, the colour of no belief and no comfort, let's call it the pigment of extinction. Oh, they display a great delight in the rainbow, I grant you, but she never did find a space, either in her mind or on her canvases, for the shadows, my poor old Serena. And then, when her mind set off on its own strange journey to the grave, shadows were all that she could see around her, but she simply had no way of exorcising them by that stage. She'd never had any practice, to be fair. So, after a while, she put down her brush and just got on with being mad, there being nothing else to get on with.

'I've always wondered what might have happened if she could have started to confront that dark before it overwhelmed her . . .'

The bell on the door had once more clunked its dread dull summons. A long-haired young woman in a voluminous, floral-printed dress meandered over to the poetry section, pulled down a volume with what seemed an insouciant rapidity, and dropped down on to the floor cross-legged, laying the book open on the tented fabric now pulled tight between her knees. Fordie watched her for a moment in silence, then, with the stoical air of General Gordon stepping down into the sea of spears, he stood up and walked across to the window, where he picked up the pole and started to pull down the blinds. The young woman looked up at him, confused, as the light by which she was reading was curtained off, section by section. Fordie turned to her finally, a kindly expression on his face in the sudden morning gloom.

'Oh, I'm so sorry,' he said, 'I hadn't seen you down there, catching up on your homework. If you'd like to have a word with my young colleague over there the next time you come in, he might be able to arrange the provision of a torch, but now I really must get some sleep. Migraine, you know.'

He led her to the door and I couldn't help noticing how caressingly his hands upon her back gently ejected her from his little Eden. (I wondered if Fordie's mysterious afternoon off once a fortnight could be connected with women? He simply wouldn't say where he went.) He put the lock on then, and we sat in the semi-darkness for a few minutes. But he didn't continue his monologue. Finally, after about ten minutes, he spoke again, 'Fancy a drink, Christopher?'

I nodded, and he went into his back room where, among all the other treasures, he kept the white wine chilling in his fridge. A few minutes later we were sipping contentedly at Fordie's Chablis.

'And you,' he said as we sat there, 'do you believe in hell?'

'I'm a Roman Catholic,' I said. 'All Roman Catholics believe in hell, even when we no longer believe in heaven.' He looked at me with a renewed interest.

'How Roman Catholic are you?'

'Enough to have nearly become a priest. Enough to be a lapsed Catholic but never a non-Catholic. Do you really have the Chilford papers, Fordie?'

'I think I probably do, yes.'

'Can I read them?'

'Would that be with an eye to a purchase?'

'You must have had them a long time,' I said warily.

'You still have much to learn about this business, Christopher.' He reached for the bottle and refilled our glasses. 'Look at Christopher Smart, for example. No edition of his work for a century and a half, and no edition of *Jubilate Agno* ever, but when Cape brought out Stead's edition in 1939, the book didn't make a penny. Now admittedly, publishing an eighteenth-century English madman's poetical ravings just as a twentieth-century German madman was about to drag us all through another world war was less than ideal timing.

'Do you know how they found Thomas Traherne's *Commentaries of Heaven*? An autograph copy was pulled from a smouldering tip in south Lancashire in 1967, three hundred years after the things were written. Isn't that extraordinary? One of the occasional delights of this sort of work is that now and then one finds a treasure.'

'What sort of price would you be asking for them, if you were to sell?'

'Do you know that you're the first person I've ever heard express the slightest interest in Pelham in all my years in the book trade? I thought everyone had agreed to forget him, though I suppose people might start to look at him again these days simply because of his madness. Is that possible? That seems to be very much on the curriculum. I've never really understood it, this new vogue for insanity. The last critical piece I looked at seemed to give the impression that the whole of the eighteenth century was a great formal deceit, waiting to explode into Blake's eccentric authenticity. What do you think he might have meant, by the way, your man, when he spoke of the *ancient haunting ground of English mercies*?'

'Are you sure that's Pelham?' I asked.

'Assuming the authenticity of the text, then it's Pelham. Don't often mix up my quotations. *Poetic licence* is the most foolish phrase ever used about literature, since poets, even very minor ones like myself, traditionally make such a large effort to be precise.'

'That phrase is not in any of the published work that I know. And I know all of it.'

'There was a correspondence . . . but we're getting ahead of ourselves here. Whenever two men are alone together there's always the spirit of a woman present, at least one, and I'm trying to work out which one it is with you. Your mother perhaps? A wife maybe? I use that term loosely.'

'There was someone called Alice.'

'I note your use of the past tense, so what was the problem?'

'She'd never really been born.'

'That could be disadvantageous, I can see. It is, however, your mother's house where you now live, isn't it? I wonder if it might perhaps be time you moved.'

'What?'

'I am prepared to sell you the Chilford papers, Christopher, along with half of the stock of my shop. And you can have the whole lot when I'm dead, which won't be too long now. I always knew someone would come through that door one day to fit the bill. Besides, you seem better qualified than anyone else to sort out the Chilford and Pelham business.'

'Why?'

'Well, you still believe in hell, for a start.'

'But how much are you asking?'

'How much would that big house of your mother's be worth on the open market these days?'

'I don't know,' I said honestly. 'I suppose about a quarter of a million.'

'I'll settle for two hundred thousand,' Fordie said and I started laughing. Then I stopped laughing. 'You're serious aren't you?'

'I'd be giving it to you cheap, very cheap, I'd say. You have no idea what I have back there. In any case, I'd also teach you the business. Or did you have something else planned for the rest of your life?'

I lay awake that night and thought about the sheer absurdity of Fordie's scheme. The next morning I rose early and padded barefoot as usual round the empty house. I stared down at my feet and saw the busy clouds of dust motes jumping up in little spasms where I padded. They were coming back. They seemed inescapable. So I dressed myself and set off down to the local estate agent to have a chat about the value of my mother's house.

Resentment #1

Where does this man make his peace
In Athens, Jerusalem or Rome?
So I replied, In none of these:
It's in resentment he has made his home.

STAMFORD TEWK, *Soho Ledger*

Now I went over to Richmond every day, unless prospective purchasers were coming to view the house. We'd had one offer, but it was too low. I tried to pump Fordie about those famous Soho years, and he would occasionally reminisce glancingly as we took a glass of white wine in the afternoon.

'You know, Christopher, half the people I knew back then have stopped writing, stopped whoring, one or two of the poor sods have even stopped drinking, and some they tell me have long since stopped breathing, but the one thing none of them ever desists from, as far as I can see, not even posthumously, is the never-ending anecdote about what a sappy, spunky crew we were, unable to tell day from night, as we ripped the buttons off Soho's blouse. Jazz clubs and Colony Clubs and big-hearted tarts in doorways, and all those brilliant queers. I think I might have declared war on the anecdote, Christopher. All I know is that if an old man's reduced to anecdotage and self-congratulation for his earlier sins, he should have the good manners to get on and die – which I'm doing, by the way, if you're interested, though I do seem to be taking an unconscionable time about it. The last occasion I went near the Coach and Horses, I peered round the door and there enthroned in the middle of the floor was Jeff Bernard, in a wheelchair, with one leg and a stump, and on her knees beside him, on her *knees*, mind you, was a young black lady tending to his every need. I couldn't face it, honestly couldn't, so I didn't go in.' He looked out through the window. 'They say he made a good end on't, all the same.'

Positioned here and there in the shop were photographs of writers Fordie had known, fading in their battered little frames. One was a picture of T.S. Eliot, his Chinese smile aslant under a well-brushed bowler. I pointed to it one day.

'Ah,' he said, smiling, 'old Tom. Now there was a grave, gracious and tormented man. Used to come here, by the way, though not often. I read some of these things about him recently. It seems there's a growing crew now who want him remembered only for one or two early abstract hatreds – ugly hatreds, I grant you, but abstract nonetheless – now do you know what I call that, Christopher?' I shook my head. 'I call that resentment.

'I've seen these people with their television smiles, but underneath the smile is a little reservoir of resentment. They flatter their vanity and usually seem to be doing very nicely for themselves, thank you very much, and every single one of them is a devoted disciple of resentment. Resentment says that what is mighty shall be brought down to my size or preferably even a little lower. Resentment says that all achievement is rigged, all greatness a sham, and that tradition is always and everywhere a lie. Resentment says one early sin obliterates all later virtue.

'What was that phrase of Nietzsche's? The soul squints, that's it. And what it squints through is resentment.

'It's my personal conviction, for what it's worth, that Shakespeare underwent just about every emotion including at some point the annihilation of faith in anything at all. And yet it never did issue in resentment, did it? Poison goes into the system and comes out as growth – that's the opposite of resentment.

'Look at this book.' Fordie picked up a recent novel he had received through the post. 'Now listen to the opening paragraph:

Albert was at first a little bitter when he realised that, after the girls had anaesthetised him, they had then gone on to cut off his penis. But, on reflection, it struck him that now at least he didn't need to fret any more about that infection of his.

'And that's it, it carries on with that idea for three hundred pages. What would have passed for a half-way decent joke at the bar in my Soho years is now proclaimed a classic of modern fiction. One of the theologians you, in your wisdom, have abandoned said the only spiritual advice he could give was to receive everything that happens as though directly from the hand of God. I suppose the gospel of resentment receives everything as coming directly from the hand of the Devil. Or could they possibly be the same thing? Anyway, beware resentment, Christopher.' By now he was filling up my glass again. 'It causeth the bookman to make a great hoard of his books and look with unkindness on those at his window.'

'Fordie.'

'Mmm.'

'I went to see the solicitor today. There's always been a family connection, so you must understand he's not being difficult.'

'And?'

'Would there be any chance of an inventory?' Fordie looked at me with some disappointment.

'What do you think, Christopher?'

'We are talking about a large sum of money here. Everything I own in the world, to be precise about it.'

'I was under the impression that it involved everything I own in the world too.'

'I know that.'

'Did you show him the proposed new draft of my will?'

'Yes. He was very impressed, but he did keep saying that we had somehow to establish the worth of some of the stock and archive here, at least up to the value of the house. He said it was only prudent.'

Fordie sat back and eyed me dispassionately.

'Prudent? You do remember what Blake had to say about that? *Prudence is a rich old maid courted by incapacity*. There are things here no one has seen but me, and no one will until you do. What do you think an independent assessor is, Christopher? Do you imagine they don't live on this planet, or have tongues in their mouths; do you think that people employed to assess the value of books have nothing to do with the book trade? It's up to you, entirely up to you. But you must either take my word, or we'll forget the whole thing.'

So it seemed that I had to choose between what my solicitor wanted and what Stamford Tewk wanted, and I soon realised that there could be no choice, whatever the risks. I asked, 'Can I at least see my quarters, then?' Fordie smiled and led me up the stairs to the small bedroom overlooking the road, across the corridor from his. Every wall was covered with books, most of them eighteenth century. Even the sides of the staircase were solid with obscure titles. On the way back down I stopped before the safe set into the wall.

'Yes,' Fordie said brushing past me, 'that's where I keep the stuff. Fordie's gold, they call it. Now let's go and talk theology, to make sure you're qualified for this job.'

So it was that, after listening three times to my solicitor's exasperated warnings about the reckless folly of the course of action on which I was embarking (he had evidently begun to wonder if I was truly my father's son) I sold the house, and gave the better part of the proceeds to Fordie, who then made himself scarce for a day or two. When he returned he gave me a chequebook for an account called Tewk Bookshop, which had two printed signatories, namely myself and him. The solicitor had looked carefully over the new will Fordie had made out, which stipulated that in the event of his death all the assets and liabilities of his business passed to me in their entirety, but without specifying them. So there we were.

I used the car to carry my own books over to Richmond, then I sold it. My whiplash injury had stopped bothering me so much over the previous six months, though it's true that I'd learnt to avoid any sudden movement or exertion. But the whole palaver of moving brought it on again, and when I was finally settled at the shop the first thing I did was to go to my room, rig myself up and lie down. Fordie came to take a whimsical look at me, supine on my new bed. He offered me a glass of wine, which I refused. I had learnt in any case not to try to match him glass for glass. He asked what I was doing and I explained about the TENS, then he went downstairs again. A few minutes later he came back up, brandishing a book. He read the passage out to me, a little gleefully I thought, given my discomfort:

'*I advised one who had been troubled many years with a stubborn paralytic disorder, to try a new remedy. Accordingly she was electrified, and found immediate help.* John Wesley's journal, Sat 20th, 1753. Here's the machine he had made for himself,' he said, as he sat down on the bed and showed me an old sepia frontispiece with a picture of Wesley's electrical device. 'Yours is a lot neater, but you are shamming aren't you, Bayliss? All this is nothing but eighteenth-century research disguised as pathology.' He left the book with me and I started reading it as I lay there. It seemed that Wesley was in the habit of prescribing the use of electricity for stomach pains and angina. The current flowed like the Holy Spirit, according to him, and often removed all diseased obstacles in its path. It was an aspect of the healing portion of creation.

He even used it on some of the troubled young women who made the pilgrimage to see him. Wesley had his own recharging box then, just as I did.

Fordie's arrangements with regard to food were curious: he seemed to eat nothing but eggs. I asked him about this, and it transpired that he had shopped for some years at the supermarket a quarter of a mile down the road, but then one day he noticed that everything had been rearranged. Though irritated, he made the effort to reorient himself and once more memorised the positioning of all the items he needed. Then, a week later, everything was moved again. He took the matter up with the management, who were finally driven by Fordie's relentless questioning into admitting that the company's retail psychologist advised on these moves, which were due to continue, and which were said to increase overall sales.

'Retail psychologist,' Fordie said with wonder, shaking his head at the very fact of it. Anyway, that had been enough as far as he was concerned, and he had decided to trim his requirements, so he made arrangements with a local store to supply his newly simplified needs. Now a delivery arrived once a week: fourteen bottles of dry white wine, five boxes of eggs, a few loaves and some salad. And that was his diet. He boiled four eggs close to hardness every morning, until the yolk had the texture of friable yellow soil. One he ate warm with toast for breakfast. Two he ate with a tomato and a few sprigs of lettuce for lunch, and one he would have for his dinner. He had a whole repertoire of exotic things he might do with that one. White wine accompanied all these meals except breakfast. Once a week he might venture out, and then he would eat anything, as long as it had no egg in it. So, vegetarian that I was, I simply joined in. Fordie merely doubled his previous order.

Letters arrived all the time inviting him to take part in interviews regarding his Soho past. One arrived from a graduate student asking for the opportunity to talk to him about English surrealism.

'English surrealism,' he growled, throwing the letter on to the table. 'He might as well write a thesis on English bull-fighting.'

'Wasn't there any, then?' I asked.

'Oh, it was in the air when I was a young man, of course. There were even those of my circle who wrote what I believe was called surrealist verse. It was tedious enough then, and I'd have thought it entirely unreadable now, though I suppose people will go to the most extraordinary lengths to get themselves called doctor. I can't help thinking that anything based on relentless novelty is tedious. The random and disconnected is only shocking for about two minutes, then it becomes completely predictable. It's the battle between intellectual control and disorder that makes for interesting writing – or interesting anything else, if it comes to that. It seemed terribly exotic, of course, Rimbaud's systematic derangement of the senses. I suppose drugs seemed terribly exotic too, though we had to make do with booze on the whole. Not quite so exotic, though I don't doubt we managed to be every bit as tiresome as most highly intoxicated people are.

'Outside Fortnum & Mason, on a little wooden box on the Piccadilly pavement, an old fellow sits playing the harmonica. He's been there day in and day out for the last thirty years, blowing and sucking and sucking and blowing. And he's never been known to master a single tune. Every so often you might catch a glimmer or a fragment of something recognisable – "When Johnny Comes Marching Home", or "Once in Royal David's City", but never for more than three or four notes, then he's off again, howling away at his discords. He actually has a number of different mouth organs, so that he can shift the key of these tuneless drones, for variety's sake I suppose. Witty slogans are chalked on a board: *All Music Half-Price Today* and *Quiet Please, Concert in Progress*. He keeps a hat in front of him which always appears to have three coins in it. Never two and never four.

'He strikes me as a living disproof of those devotees of the random who used to proclaim that an infinite number of monkeys left to themselves with typewriters would one day produce the collected works of William Shakespeare. What they would produce of course would be an infinite amount of gibberish. Issue them all with a harmonica apiece and you would probably bring about the collapse of the universe. The deafness of the gods. Oblivion.

'Now, give me again that definition of final impenitence.' I was as reluctant to talk Catholic theology with Fordie as he was to memorialise Soho with me, but he simply wouldn't let me escape.

Thus did I settle down to life with Stamford Tewk: the endless conversations, the boiled eggs, the Chablis seven days a week. I even started to put on weight. Fordie's diet might have been eccentric, but it was considerably more regular than what I'd grown used to in Tooting. So, at his insistence, I started to walk up to Richmond Park each morning when the weather permitted. I had to bring back with me a clutch of fallen leaves and we would match them up against the hand-coloured illustrations in his copy of *The Botanist*.

I even took to walking there sometimes in the early evening. My back had stopped giving me so much trouble. I might not have to use my TENS for a week at a time. This particular day it took me about twenty minutes to reach Pembroke Lodge. It was the beginning of autumn and I stood facing west. The air between me and the horizon was soaked through by what was left of the sun's rays. The space about my head felt suddenly saturated with light. Down from where I sat I could still see antlered roots torn up by the Great Storm, and one or two charred corpses of trees, fingered by lightning. An occasional wood pigeon crashed out of the leaves; grey squirrels sprinted and posed; crow's claws skirred over the flora's debris. I picked up a leaf from the ones scattered about my feet. A fig like an outstretched hand beseeching from the anorexic stem of its wrist. Another one: the dead leaf of a smoke tree mottled into a small apocalypse of colour, like the carapace of a sinister tropical beetle. There was also a grape vine, parching into the shape of a drying estuary, its veins dehydrating swiftly into sand and sere. Pelham's contemporary Christopher Smart made out the markings of the Hebrew alphabet in the barks of trees. *Aleph* and *zayin* and *lamed* and *taw*, etched there as a sacred lectionary. But then for him the blown spikes of the cornfield spelt out the Tetragrammaton every time the weather grew salty.

Then the children arrived, shouting, followed by a woman with a mobile phone pressed into her cheek. She laughed into it loudly and continuously. I stood up and started walking back home to Richmond. Home. I started to smile to myself. For over two months I'd hardly even thought about the Chilford papers, since it had become evident that Fordie would show them to me when he chose and not a moment sooner, presumably at the same time that he would begin to teach me the business. I had the curious feeling I was very nearly happy, except for the memories of Alice that still lamed my soul. She had taken precisely what she wanted and then gone. She had used one brief unkindness by me to walk away for ever. If I ever found my mind moving in the direction of acknowledging that she had only done to me exactly what I had done to every other woman I'd ever been with, namely stayed around until it no longer suited her, I then had to remind myself that I had paid for everything, cooked everything, driven everywhere, cleaned everything up. Alice had had an easy time of it with me, for all the thanks I'd received. Resentment. Was that resentment? Beware resentment, Fordie always said. Still, apart from Alice's white snake still coiled inside me, I was almost at peace. When I arrived back, I let myself into the shop, and laid the leaves carefully on the table, and it was not until a few moments later that I found Fordie lying at the bottom of the stairs.

The Combination

Combination: The action of combining or joining two or more separate things into a whole.

Oxford English Dictionary

I bent over him and gently brushed his face with my hand.

'I'll get an ambulance,' I said, but with what strength he still had, he held my arm and pulled me down towards him. My face was against his as he whispered his urgent words. I caught the mild reek of his wine breath.

'No, Fordie, I can't do that. Listen . . .' But the pull on my arm represented an effort too supreme to ignore, I knew that. So I bent down as requested and heard his confession, and when he had finished I made the sign of the cross over him and said softly, '*Ego te absolvo in nomine patris et filii et spiritus sancti. Amen.*' And even then, as I tried to pull away to call that ambulance, he held me and with another effort that cost him too much, he said, 'Six six, four three, one two.' I stared at him, not understanding, and I could see the life already ebbing out of his features. He said it again, each word separated by a void of his breath. 'Six . . . six . . . four . . . three . . . one . . . two.' And still not understanding, in my confusion I went to the table and wrote the numbers down on a piece of paper. I brought it back to where he lay on the floor and held it above his face. He managed to nod and close his eyes then. Finally I called the ambulance. Fordie died that night in the hospital. He had suffered a massive heart attack.

Back in the shop in the early hours of the morning, I realised as I stared blankly at that number amidst the scattered leaves I had dumped on the table that it was the combination to his safe.

More people turned up at the crematorium than I had expected. Even Charles Redmond and Josianne Thring.

'We hear the bookshop's yours now,' Charles said, trying to keep the disbelief out of his voice.

'Yes, that's true.'

'We must come over some time. We could probably do a bit of business.' And after drinks in the nearby pub, the usual chatter started up about editions and prices, and which poor sod's stock was about to be sold off for a song to save him from liquidation, and whether they should all agree between them not to buy at the requested prices anyway, thereby forcing them down even lower. And then it was all over, and I was back in Richmond sitting in a bookshop which was now mine in its entirety. I wished that it weren't.

That night I dreamt that the amice was wrapped about my shoulders, and the alb flapping at my calves. I dreamt that I had prostrated myself as prescribed, and that the sacred laying on of hands had passed on to me the holy orders of priesthood. I was shaken awake by fear, though fear of what I couldn't have told you, but what I woke to was the realisation that my first mass was still postponed for ever, despite the curiosity of my unorthodox absolving of Fordie for his sins. For some reason the smell in my nose was Alice's hair, its tart mixture of peach blossom and turpentine, and it simply wouldn't go away. I lay there and thought of Rome, that parish of ritual slaughter and consecration, where the smell of incense, however pungent, can never quite overcome the smell of the flesh.

One or two people started coming into the shop. I didn't stop them. I was glad for the moment to have people around, even those I'd never seen before. A few of them asked where the grumpy old man was and I told them. Then they fell silent. One Friday afternoon the will was read and produced no surprises. Everything was as agreed, though the two hundred thousand I had paid him to become part of the business appeared to have vanished entirely. I couldn't help wondering where it had gone so quickly, though the fact was, I suppose, it was none of my business. We had made a deal. It took me a few weeks before I opened the desk drawer and took out that piece of paper on which I'd written the combination to Fordie's safe. By then the fridge was stacked with eggs and Chablis because I kept forgetting to change the weekly order.

Another week passed before I could face the safe's contents. My first reaction when that heavy metal door creaked open was a profound shock of disappointment. I had been led to expect a stack of eighteenth-century papers crammed in there, of incalculable rarity and value. The legendary hoard. What I had sold my parents' house to own.

And instead there was one folder, a substantial one admittedly, but that was all. On the folder was written in Fordie's hand: Chilford/Pelham. This had cost me a year of my life and one Tooting house. I remembered the last words of Fordie's confession, but then I dismissed the words as scrupulosity. An excess of conscience at the moment of death.

I uncorked a chilled bottle of the Chablis and sat down at the desk where Fordie had always sat. Then I started to read.

A good bibliographer is a historian in miniature, chronicling the journeyings of certain texts through time and space, and Fordie was nothing if not a good bibliographer. And yet this wasn't in fact bibliography, for what was being tracked had never become a book, or never yet anyway, though it soon became apparent to me that Fordie had meant it to, all the same, for what I held in my hands was evidently the book he had once started out to write. Why had he never mentioned it to me? And why, I wondered, had he never finished it? What had made him falter? In the meantime, I was now where he had once been, in that borderland between bibliography and philology, between textual criticism and biography, between religious belief and diagnosable mania.

Fordie's writing was crabbed and difficult, and it took me a while before I managed to start reading it fluently. There was this uneasy preface:

It is certainly arguable that the eighteenth century gave us the terms of modernity with which we've had to live ever since. Somewhere between the bent and crippled Pope, wielding the weight of classical learning to crush his opponents with ridicule, and William Blake and his wife, naked in their garden as they attempted to recapture Eden, we still seem to be rediscovering our dilemma. Pope ridiculed the mad, but for Blake madness was simply the condition of the visionary — no more and no less. He has Cowper come to him in his vision and ask for lessons in insanity: 'O that I were insane always. I will never rest. Can you not make me truly insane?' It is doubtful that the unfortunate Cowper would have wished to express the matter that way. There is one curiosity worthy of remark, though: how much more hate there is in the orthodox Roman Catholic Pope than in the outrageous antinomian heretic Blake.

Behind the perfect façades of the Augustan manner we can always hear the inmates' cries at Bedlam. This is not a metaphor, it is actual fact. Many of the eighteenth century's poetic voices speak to us from inside one species of asylum or another. Cowper raving, Collins in distress, Smart incarcerated, as Clare was to be later. Even Johnson, that massive arbiter of Augustan measure, in constant fear of madness, constantly praying to be saved the ultimate indignity of insanity. The great sloth that would descend upon him amounted to an autism of the spirit, whose sole antidote was the clatter and clamour of London. It was Johnson's 'vile melancholy', which 'made him mad all his life, at least not sober', what he himself called 'this dismal inertness of disposition'.

We have the dreadful prospect of Swift contemplating his end, knowing that he would die like a tree: from the head down.

If the study of the relatively unknown work of Richard Pelham might teach us anything, it might be to be wary of imagining that we explain much when we use words like melancholy, any more than we can approach the pathos of Nietzsche with his arms around that beleaguered horse in Turin by using the word syphilis. It is interesting to note how many of the Palladian houses built in England at that time had grottoes beneath them, as though

*acknowledging the Gothic terrors that accompany always the classical
lines of perfect proportion.*

*The eighteenth century is not a distant time, not in this regard
anyway. Remember how many of our own poets have been afflicted
with the same conditions: madness, alcoholism, suicide. Hart Crane
re-joining his sailors, Sylvia Plath, back in Pelham's London, with
her head in the gas oven, Lowell's mind divided between the bottle
and the psychotic ward, Berryman crashing through the ice on the
Mississippi, Paul Celan diving into the Seine – poets do seem very
fond of water when the time comes for them to leave us.*

Then the first section began, a history of the manuscripts. It
seemed that in his seclusion at Twickenham after his wife's
death, Lord Chilford had completed his study of Pelham's
melancholy condition and his madness. And then he had sent
his essay to the Royal Society.

The President of the Royal Society at that time was
Martin Folkes. His portrait had been painted by Hogarth.
Folkes had gained a certain notoriety from marrying Lucretia
Bradshaw, an actress much applauded at the Haymarket and
Drury Lane. *The History of the English Stage* of 1741 called her
'one of the greatest and most promising genii of her time'.
Folkes took her off the stage though, the better to facilitate
what he called her 'exemplary and prudent conduct'. By the
time Folkes died, she had been confined in Chelsea for many
years, her mind having long since sunk into derangement. In
the margin Fordie had written, 'Seems as though Pelham was
in good company then. Half of England was barking.'
According to Fordie, Folkes did not appear to have been one

of the Society's more inspiring presidents. The wits of the time had put it thus:

> *If ere he chance to wake in Newton's chair*
> *He wonders how the devil he got there.*

There was a grand sale of the Folkes collection in 1756. The library, gems, drawings, coins and prints fetched between them the considerable sum for those days of £3,090 in a sale that went on for fifty-six days, and in amongst those items was Chilford's study of Pelham.

It appeared that, as Lord Chilford's noble family had begun its decline, so the line of Pelham began to prosper. Thomas Pelham, the poet's son, returned from Ireland to London a wealthy man, having established for himself a lucrative practice as an architect in Georgian Dublin. Jealous of his family's reputation, and probably at least partly at the bidding of his adored mother, he set about retrieving any biographical data concerning his father which might one day find itself set in print. Curll's pamphlet was by that stage already a rarity, and the Pelhams wished Richard to be remembered as a poet of some distinction, not as an intermittently violent lunatic. It was Thomas Pelham who acquired the Chilford lot at the sale of the Folkes collection. And there he doubtless read of the 'correspondence in my possession' with his father, which Chilford off-handedly mentions in a footnote.

Lord Chilford would not grant Pelham an audience, despite repeated requests, but he did make him a curious promise: namely, that he would bequeath all the material relating to his father to him, so that it should all become his or his family's shortly after Chilford's own death, as long as no further attempt was made to contact him during his lifetime. This agreement was kept on both sides. In the intervening years Thomas Pelham continued busily about his appointed task, even tracking down the relevant portions of the Chelsea Asylum log for the period of his father's incarceration.

As has been said, a great deal of the motivation for all this activity was undoubtedly propriety. The material was being gathered in by the family so that it might never again become available for public scrutiny or ridicule. A rumour of insanity in a family's lineage was already becoming a grave social handicap. By the end of the nineteenth century the Pelhams were wealthy and established, and once more based in England. In the best Victorian tradition, business was used to finance scholarship, and Alexander Pelham became one of the most promising young scholars of Anglo-Saxon at Oxford University. He also took it upon himself to edit the collected works of his forebear. His summers throughout the Edwardian years were spent at what was now the family seat, Guisely Manor in Oxfordshire, working his way through all the material Thomas had so carefully retrieved. After the edition finally emerged in 1912, the manuscripts were donated to the British Museum. Or at least some of them were. There were occasional references in the Clarendon introduction and notes which suggested other material had been consulted, material that seemed to have been made available to the editor alone. There was one particularly cryptic note which said merely, 'If that scientific age treated

him badly in life, it treated him no less disgracefully in death.'
This could be read simply as a protest against the oblivion
into which Pelham's reputation swiftly sank, but there might
have been another way of reading it.

Perhaps Alexander Pelham had been considering a further
volume of Pelham's work, or even a definitive life. It is
possible he had retained some material for this purpose,
without ever clarifying the matter. But by 1914 he had
acquired the status of Captain Alexander Pelham, and his life
was soon to be lost leading his men into battle at the Somme.
Now whatever was left of the archive was lodged with his
wife and, after she died in 1940, with his only child Amelia,
who had been a mere three years old when her father the
captain was killed. Fordie's notes made it seem likely that she
had left the materials in her father's study exactly where they
were, as her mother had before her, to gather dust and
provide a domicile for spiders. But Amelia too grew old and
frail in her turn and her inherited rentier income became
more and more flimsy. Her one foray into romance had
failed long before the prospect of an engagement could
flower, and Guisely Manor could now no longer be
adequately sustained for its sole occupant. And so she had put
the entire building, with most of its contents intact, up for
auction, on the assumption that with the money gained by
the sale, she could take herself off to a retirement home in
Hove and live comfortably there for her remaining years.

But this had been during Stamford Tewk's glory days, the
time when his formidable reputation had been established,
and little escaped his attention then. He had seen the
announcement of the auction, and he had registered the

name Pelham. The next day he was there and managed t
talk the old lady round to giving him access to her father
papers. He only needed to read a few pages to know that l
wished to buy them. He gave her a reasonable sum too, f
more than she could have expected or would have agreed tu,
and this peripheral sale made no difference whatsoever to the
price finally agreed at auction. But all this had been years
back. Many years back. I found it extraordinary, as I turned
the pages, that he had not published any of the material. I
flicked forward to the manuscripts at the back of the folder.
Pelham's writing. He was obviously crazed by then, but it
was his writing. But I would work through what was before
me in the order in which Fordie had left it to me – I felt
firmly obliged to do this, though I'm not sure I could have
told you why.

The doorbell rang. I hesitated for a moment, then decided
that I needed a break. The figure that confronted me might
have stepped out of the mirrored wardrobe at Tooting. The
grey hair that fell to his shoulders and the shabby clothes.
Also an unfocused look I had occasionally noticed in myself
back then, as though there were nothing in the field of vision
that the eye could rest on. Except for words on a page. I
stood there silently and after a moment he spoke.

'Hello,' he said hesitantly, though the voice was deep and
almost seductive. 'My name's Shadwell. We have some
mutual friends in Charles and Josianne.'

We sat down together and I soon saw why Josianne's face
shifted into a smile whenever his name was mentioned.
There was beneath the vagueness an indisputable charm,
though charm is a quality that normally makes me dubious.

(It was a quality that Fordie had come to detest. He spoke of it with the same contempt that he used when talking of those who made nothing but money.) There was enough charm, in any case, for him to help me through a bottle of the Chablis and to sell me two signed editions of Lawrence Durrell, a writer I have never had any interest in whatsoever, and even a signed first edition of his own book of verse, *Megalith*, which seemed to be much preoccupied with the question of prehistoric Wales. Then he went, leaving me to consider the fact that I had just parted with the better part of fifty pounds and a bottle of wine. I felt suddenly exhausted. Not merely exhausted, but irritated at the time it had taken up. So it was not a good time for Shadwell to return, which was what he did ten minutes later. He stood in the doorway, neither coming in nor going out.

'Do you think there might be any chance that Stamford Tewk would be interested in having poetry readings here?' he asked, looking around speculatively. 'It's a long way for me to come, of course, but I do have a feeling this could become a very good venue.'

'I honestly couldn't answer for him,' I said, 'he's resting at the moment.' Then I gave Shadwell directions as to how he could get to the crematorium, though carefully avoiding the use of that word for his destination. 'Only take about twenty minutes, walking. Ask around when you get there, you're bound to find him.' Fordie would have been proud of me. Then I did something I had seldom known Fordie do: I actually locked the door and pulled down the blinds. I took out my TENS, for my back had tightened over the last few days into its rigour of rotting muscles. In mourning probably.

I switched on and sat there blinking in the gloom, hidden away inside the twilit murk of Fordie's bookshop.

Dark-Backward

What seest thou else
In the dark backward and Abisme of time?

WILLIAM SHAKESPEARE, *The Tempest*

Alexander Pelham had had to work from the few abbreviated references in the Chelsea Asylum log and from the poet's occasional remarks to Lord Chilford. Fordie had merely glossed these sources with further references and definitions, but the story in regard to the lightning cage had finally emerged plainly enough. Fordie had snipped this cutting from somewhere and pasted it in:

For the Entertainment of the Curious
There is to be seen at the House of Capt. John Williams, near the
Golden Fleece in King-street, Boston, A Great Variety of curious
Experiments of the most surprizing Effects of Electricity, wherein will
be shewn the wonderful Force; particularly the new Method of
electerising several Persons at the same Time, so that Fire shall dart
from all Parts of their Bodies, as the same as has lately been
exhibited to the Astonishment of the Curious in all Parts of Europe.

This had been an advertisement in the *Boston Evening Post* of 1747. Then he began with the English equivalent of that same material.

It seemed that Stephen Gray, a pensioner of Charterhouse, and a man of legendary irascibility, whose papers appeared intermittently in the *Philosophical Transactions* of the Royal Society, was conducting his experiments in the electrification of objects throughout Richard Pelham's lifetime. The objects were various: a guinea, a fire shovel, a poker, a copper tea kettle – on one occasion filled with hot, and on another with cold water – flint, chalk, a map of the world stretching to twenty-seven square feet, an umbrella, a dead cock and, on 8 April 1730, at long last, a young boy. This diminutive fellow was attached to a multitude of silken threads, chosen for their non-conductivity, and suspended from the ceiling of the Charterhouse. Then he was electrified, and Gray noted that his hair stood on end and large sparks could be coaxed with little effort from his nose. Word got around about this spectacular display and it was soon repeated across Europe, becoming a particular favourite at the court of Louis XV.

Thomas Parker wondered if electricity, particularly the natural variety that God himself supplies from heaven, might not have therapeutic as well as spectacular possibilities. Committed as he was to the idea of forces of nature invading the body and ridding the mind of all blockage and distortion, he then set about devising the structure known as the lightning cage. It was made of metal rods, and riddled with a lattice of vacancies, not unlike the type of construction in which circuses would once keep animals for show, and devised in such a manner that the cork floor was meant to ensure survival. The asylum inmate was inserted into the cage, often with substantial potions of brandy to render him at least partly insensible, and then frame and madman were suspended in midair from a makeshift gantry, from which they proceeded to dangle and turn in the shudder of storm and rain, until the lightning arrived. Depending on the temperament of the internee, or the efficacy of the brandy, the figure might crouch on the wooden base, or kneel to pray, or stand clamouring and weeping at the bars. When what Parker called the great electric veining of the sky finally occurred, the darkness about the the Chelsea Asylum's grounds would blanch into momentary illumination, and then, after the thunder, an odd silence would often quench the rattle of the storm. They would quickly take down the cage and Parker would examine its occupant. According to Ebenezer Hague's notes, only one caged member was actually eloctrocuted (this being before the perfection of the cage's construction), but he, as Hague put it drily, was also the only one whose turmoil ever terminated with the experiment. Two others died subsequently, one of a fever brought on by his drenching, the other apparently of unassuageable fright. And then there was Richard Pelham. The word on him was that the lightning which flashed around the bars touched but didn't kill him. It sealed his tongue for three whole months, and lit his eyes so brightly that one of the attendants could no longer bear to look at him. But the memory of much, including the chronicle of his recent torments, was temporarily deleted. According to Pelham's own lines in *The Instruments of the Passion*, it stretched him out between hell and heaven and, in the scorching brilliance of that moment, permitted angels and demons to travel through him, as they passed incorporeally from one realm to the other. And one stayed, he said. One settled in and made a temporary home of him, and from then on it knew his address when it needed a sojourn from the middle kingdom. This was Agarith.

Now Lord Chilford valued his friends from the Royal Society more highly than any of his other acquaintances. He was particularly close to Peter Collinson, the confidant of Benjamin Franklin, and soon became close to Franklin himself. Collinson was the man who disproved the common belief that swallows hibernate underwater during the winter, a belief shared at the time even by Linnaeus, and mentioned frequently by Chilford, who must undoubtedly have been aware of the considerable interest in electricity, in its experimental and its atmospheric incarnations. Yet one day he pointed to the crescent-shaped cicatrix, which stretched from Pelham's left ear right across his forehead, and asked where he had received it, but he merely laughed when Pelham replied quietly, 'From lightning. Heaven and hell branded me both at once.' His lordship's laughter was both sceptical and mildly bored. Pelham had noted before that his patron laughed often, but seldom with any passion.

'I ask for data regarding my philosophical investigation, Pelham, and you give me metaphors. Sadly, we don't live in a world made of verse, or I might be able to use what you have told me to some effect.' Fordie remarked acidly in his notes, 'Thus did his lordship miss Thomas Parker's one genuine scientific discovery: his anticipation of the radical effects of electro-convulsive therapy, later to become such a popular tool in the hands of our psychiatrists. Serena.'

I was growing less inclined to unlock the door. I was also growing less inclined to open the mail. However else Fordie had spent the money I'd given him, he didn't appear to have used any of it to clear his bills. I suppose if I thought about it we had lived well during the time we'd spent together, what with our daily Chablis and our weekly trips out in search of food without a hint of egg each week. Fordie had always signed for these dinners using a bookshop cheque. Now and then I had spotted some item in the auctions which might conceivably be relevant to Pelham or Chilford or both, and he had always insisted that we should purchase it immediately on the company account. I had felt grateful to him at the time. Soon after his death, however, the bank informed me that our overdraft was now nearly twenty thousand pounds, and given the changed circumstances of ownership, it might perhaps be better to clear it and start again. After that, the amount I had left in my building society account began to look increasingly unimpressive. And the bills kept arriving, many of them printed in red. But they were my bills now. I kept signing cheques. I wasn't sure I wanted to open up the bank statements any more. I had to make an effort sometimes not to entertain some black feelings about Fordie. *Beware resentment, Christopher* . . .

I woke from a dream in which water was cascading down on to my face to discover water cascading down on to my face. It took me twenty minutes to fathom how to get up into the roof. I found where the water had been pouring through, but by the look of all the surrounding insulation, or what was left of it, water had been pouring through for a long time. It had only just found its way into my bedroom, but it had long before been going somewhere. Down the walls, into the timbers, along the joists. I could see the sky flickering through various small holes in the slating. There was some tarpaulin up there and I managed to get enough of it into place to hold off the weather for the present. That morning I stepped outside the shop and walked to the other side of the road. It didn't require much architectural expertise to see that Tewk's Books was considerably more dilapidated than the buildings to the left or right of it. Some of the concrete façade on the first floor was actually coming away. Much of the outside timbering had rotted. I went back inside and hunted through the various papers that had passed over to me at the time of Fordie's death until I found the details of the landlords who were head lessors. I then wrote a brief and tetchy note asking them if they might perhaps like to call in and have a look at the property for which they had ultimate responsibility, since it appeared to be in a state of remarkably poor repair. With that done, I went back inside and locked the door again. After downing some Chablis and a boiled egg, I settled myself once more in front of Fordie's folder.

He had spent a considerable amount of time elucidating the rudiments of *The Instruments of the Passion*. The single note at the top of a page stated: *The title explains everything.* It seemed that Pelham had simply described more instruments than anyone before him, or anyone since, for that matter. In addition to the scourge and the column, the nails and hammers, the crown of thorns and the spear, he had thought up many others. Fordie had scrupulously noted that many variants could already be derived from the *Speculum Humanae Salvationis* of the fourteenth century. He listed them: Judas's kiss, the thirty pieces of silver, the torches and staves of Christ's captors, Malchus's ear, the open hand that struck the saviour, the blindfold, the cloak, the spitting mouth of one of his tormentors, the stick that struck the crown, the column, the ropes, the whips of the flagellation, Pilate washing his hands, the cock which crowed, the nails, hammer and ladder, the casting of lots, the sponge, the lance. To which Pelham added Mary's tears (more acid than the gall they had given him on a stick apparently) and Magdalena's body, twisted in grief, the body that might have twisted in ecstasy beneath him instead; the water into which Pilate's fingers sank; the sighs of the sleeping apostles in Gethsemane; the stars in the sky above Jerusalem; the tune that Joseph hummed as he planed wood; the wine at the last supper; the lost dreams of bliss that are hidden inside the poppy, and every species of sharp point that can cut a man's skin, whether a Roman's or a woman's nails.

Pelham had simply started to write his own book of truth, effectively doing two things in the process: rewriting the history of his own life and times in terms of the passion of Christ, and rewriting the passion of Christ as though he were Pelham's contemporary. And with this dialectical manoeuvre in action he had escaped the conventions of Augustan verse and accepted freely the condition of fragmentation. As Fordie stated simply in his marginalia to one of Pelham's lines, *Modernity is here getting ahead of itself.*

In fact, I began to suspect more and more with each page I read that Fordie had decided Pelham was not mad at all, that he had, as he put it, entirely eschewed the romance of insanity. Why else should he have quoted with such emphasis these words from Alexander Cruden's attempted self-vindication, after his own incarceration for imputed insanity only a few years before Pelham: *That the way to be mad, was to be sent to a Madhouse?* I couldn't think of another reason why he had written out so carefully this quotation from Hester Thrale: 'Mean observers suppose all *Madness* to be *Phrenzy*, and think a person *Insane* in proportion as he is wild, and disposed to throw things about – whereas experience shows that such temporary suspensions of the mental faculties are oftener connected with delirium than with *mania*, and, if not encouraged and stimulated by drunkenness, are seldom of long duration.'

I was now ignoring all knocks on the door, but this was not knocking, it was banging, and finally in fury I went and opened up.

'What?' I almost shouted at the diminutive, bearded character in the leather jacket outside.

'Christopher Bayliss?' he asked merrily.

'Yes.'

'Christ, mate, it's taken me long enough to find you.' And with that he pushed past me into the shop.

'But who are you?' I said, as he fiddled with his hearing aid.

'You what, mate?'

'Who are you?'

'Ah. Got it adjusted now. I'm Harry.'

'Harry.'

'Used to do jobs for your mother. Sorted out the car and everything.'

'Oh, Harry,' I said, trying to quench the expression of unremitting hostility in my features by an act of will, but still incapable of smiling all the same. 'Harry, of course, what can I do for you?'

'You could pay these bills for a start,' he said smiling. 'I've been holding on to them long enough. Comes to nearly six hundred pounds all told. I wasn't expecting you to just bugger off like that, to be honest.'

Harry, it became apparent, was from Manchester and had recently spent a lot of time back up north, which was why he'd missed my departure. But now, however affable his manner, he obviously wanted his money, and sooner rather than later. I wrote him a cheque, the fifth I'd signed that week.

'You wouldn't have cash, would you?'

'You're right, Harry,' I said. 'I wouldn't.'

He had heard about my mother's death from a neighbour and expressed his condolences at some length.

'They say she went a bit doolally at the end.' This was a subject I didn't wish to be drawn on, not just at that moment. So without thinking much about it I asked Harry what it was he did.

'I'm a builder, mate. Got my own business up in Stockport.'

'Ah. Spare me five minutes of your time, would you, Harry? I'd just like you to have a look at my roof.'

Ten minutes later Harry came back down, shaking his head and muttering.

'That should have been seen to years ago,' he said, 'years and years ago. Those slating nails have been rotting away ever since the war, I should think. Surprised any of the roof's still up there.'

'How much would you say it might cost to sort it out? The minimum decent job is what I'm talking about.' Harry mused, twitching sometimes his eyebrows and at others his lips, and always fiddling with his hearing aid as he considered this.

'I could probably do it for about three grand,' he said. 'But let's understand one another. We're talking cash. Forget VAT and forget the taxman. Otherwise we'd have to be talking more. I'd see you right though, mate, the way I always did with your old mum. What's the point in you paying all that money to the taxman anyway, and then me having to do the same?' I could see his point. I also wanted the simplest solution to my roof problem, and I did not want to be distracted from my studies.

'If I agreed to it,' I said, 'would it be something I could just leave you to get on with? What I mean is I've a lot of work to do, and I don't want to be taken away from it.'

'Your father and your mother always trusted me,' he said with a slightly wounded tone. 'Trusted me to do anything, they did. There'd be one thing. There's a mate of mine, well a relative actually, could do the job with me for a lot cheaper than anyone you'd get down here. But he lives up in Manchester, and I don't have any digs at the moment. Could we stay here, while we did it? It wouldn't take us long anyway.'

A week later Harry and his nephew Neil moved in. I gave them my bedroom and Fordie's and I made myself a temporary sleeping place down in the shop.

Descensus ad Inferos

These drear delightless London days.

RICHARD PELHAM, *Letters*

I tried as best I could to ignore the hammering and crashing, and the blare of the transistor radio in the roof, and concentrate instead on what was before me. I was fascinated by the way Fordie had tracked the image of the black sun in Pelham. At first he had thought it merely a parahelion, a falsity of illumination, the mirage of a god, but little by little he had come to feel that it was more significant than this. Its later manifestations, as in de Nerval's *Les Chimères*, he felt added nothing to Pelham's original usage. He looked instead at the following possibilities. Could it be, he asked, if wired up as he had been by the age's new obsession with electricity, he had in some uncanny manner come to sense that the earth had an iron core and that the currents hunting around it which generated the globe's magnetic field were also part of that same field of force that created electricity? Fordie made plain from his readings that the oddest thing about Pelham's black sun was not that it was black, but that it was at the centre of the earth, buried cryptically beneath his feet. Could some unaccountable shaft of insight have taught him about the currents around him and the force they generated? Pelham was obsessed with force fields, and there were these lines from *The Instruments* to prove it:

> *The earth, the world, this spinning globe*
> *Charmed still with lines of force invisible.*

By now I was beginning to wonder if I was anything more than a field of negative forces myself. I switched on for a while, but I wanted to be cleansed. I went up to the bathroom and stared down at the porcelain of Fordie's Victorian bath begrimed with black. Anthracite black. As though a bevy of pitmen had just doused themselves there, and no one had bothered to scrub it out later. Obviously Harry and his young relative had been making use of my facilities without feeling any need to leave them as they found them. I thought briefly of marching up into the roof to order one of them to come down and clean up, but the hammering and the shouting and the disintegrating blare of the transistor dissuaded me. I cleaned it up myself, and then I lay in the hot water for a while and tried not to consider my financial situation. In the halcyon days of the work's commencement I had also told Harry and his young relative to help themselves to whatever was in the fridge. That evening, they went through three bottles of the Chablis and eight eggs.

'Haven't got anything else apart from eggs, have you?' Harry shouted happily from the kitchen.

'No,' I said. 'No, I haven't.'

'Must be very binding, this diet.'

I had given them two thousand on account already. Now Harry returned on the Monday to confront me.

'I'm sorry, mate, but it's going to take us a bit more work than we thought. And we're having to replace more stuff up there than I'd realised. It's not cheap, you know, that sort of material. You're going to have to have it done, though, or you'll be in real trouble next time.'

'How much?' I said.

'Another two thousand.'

'When do you need it?'

'Well, now really.'

'In cash obviously.'

'The only way we'll get the job done on time, to be honest.'

So off I went to the building society and took out another substantial chunk of my rapidly diminishing resources. I realised as I handed it over to Harry, and he fiddled with his hearing aid, that I didn't like to look at his face any more. The permanent bonhomie of his grin had begun to grate. He had a gold filling between his two front teeth that seemed always to glint at precisely the wrong time. I just wanted the job done and both of them out. I soon had the latter anyway, for they didn't come back the next day. I crept up into the roof. A part of it was still tarpaulined over, but there were no gaps now that I could see. The following day, when they still didn't come back, I read in silence and with relief Fordie's notes about the black sun.

At its worst, it seemed, the black sun of melancholy cast its chill rays on the black river of bile in which a man sank, as the gummy lava bore him slowly towards hell. Not forgetfulness, though, not Lethe. Hell, where nothing was ever forgotten except for the possibility of forgiveness. And this image had become associated irrevocably in Pelham's mind with the dark king, David. David the Psalmist and the murderer, he who could summon from the night inside him either evil or good. This blended, by a process hard for the rational mind to track, with Pelham's conception of the parables, in which all must re-enter the dark womb of meaning, and thus learn how to be born in intention as well as flesh. This for him was the true burden of the words Christ speaks to Nicodemus, and of all the other parables too. The world assures us that we have been born, but the spirit informs us otherwise. And so the language of the parable refuses the language of the world as merely a jargon of the unborn. Why else would Jesus insist that a man must be born again? Why else would he constantly speak in such a dark and riddling manner? And the ultimate king was God himself. He darkened too at the time of the death of Jesus when, according to the disciple Luke, the sun went black. And if you found yourself inside the darkness of the Almighty, whose light could you call upon then?

Harry did not come back the next day either, nor the one after that, and I found myself wondering if he might not be coming back at all. This had never even occurred to me before, and I shrugged off the idea as the paranoia of a once-more solitary man, but after a week I had to accept that I'd been right the first time. Being paranoid and being right are not incompatible conditions. I also realised then that I had no address for Harry, not even a phone number, not even a mobile phone number. And what a lot of cash I'd given him. For another week I did nothing, then one night I climbed up there during a storm and thought I heard the whole structure gently creaking and moaning. In a panic the next morning I telephoned the district surveyor and explained my dilemma. He had someone round an hour later, a thin, besuited young man in his twenties who had a quick look at what had gone on up there and whistled quietly.

'Just as well you called us, sir. Did you realise these cowboys have taken the purlins out from both sides and not put anything in by way of replacement? Another month or so and the whole of your roof would have started sagging. It's already moving now, in fact. Do you mind if I ask who did it?'

'Harry,' I said quietly.

'Who's Harry?'

'Harry who?' I said and started laughing, though a little bleakly.

'I'm not sure I'm following this.'

'Sorry,' I said, 'one of my mother's jokes. Do you know anyone we can get in straight away to sort all this out?'

'Not technically supposed to answer that question,' he said, 'but here's someone you'll be all right with.' He took a card from his wallet and handed it to me.

'You know him?'

'I know him.' I called ten minutes later and arranged for Mr Birkett to come and sort out my roof. He spent half a day shoring it up, then said he'd be back on Monday to start the reslating.

'You do realise they've gone off with half your slates?'

'No,' I said, 'I didn't.'

'Worth a few bob these days. Now you're going to have to pay to replace them, I'm afraid.'

So I made more visits to the building society and took out more money. I noticed that my balance had some time before moved from five figures to four. I decided not to get distracted and sat down to the next section of Fordie's notes with my eggs on my plate and a bottle of Chablis open on the table before me.

This was the stage in his study where Fordie had obviously started to falter. An unsureness of tone began to affect his formulations, and as I read on I understood why. In the final part of his paper on Pelham, Lord Chilford gave his own account of that night when he had been summoned from Piccadilly by the frantic Jacob.

I entered the room to see for myself at long last the effects of one of these apparent fits of insanity of which I had heard so much from other, unreliable sources. Pelham was seemingly comatose. The temperature in the room was remarkably low and I was initially afraid that he might be suffering as a result. He was speechless, seemingly without consciousness. He appeared to be in a state such as that of one who has endured a violent accident. His pulse was weak. There were no reactions to my promptings.

I had intended to leave him for a while until some glimmer of consciousness returned, when my servant Josephine, who had attended him in our absence, directed me to his chest. On removing the sheets that covered him, I observed the following phenomenon.

Red welts had appeared upon the skin, which had formed themselves into the following intelligible sequence:

PEIIIAM

In other words, what appeared to be the subject's own name had been inscribed in his flesh, but with this curious anomaly: that the bridge between the two verticals of the letter H had not been formed.

Why hadn't the bridge of the H been formed? Perhaps that was the message: the message lay in the very distortion of the signature. That was what was being signalled, that a desire so strong, or an aversion so terrible, had separated itself from the main character, gained its own tortured autonomy, and so wished to sign itself differently.

A displacement of the agency of selfhood, pressed into a writing upon the flesh by an aetiology we cannot at present track, leaves its calling card. We might describe this as yet another, though an admittedly extreme, manifestation of the melancholy temperament. It might also surely begin to explain certain phenomena which have always previously been described in the terminology of superstition.

In its milder phases Pelham's condition was not dissimilar to hypochondriasis, and what would traditionally have been called a leucocholy. All his symptoms were compatible with religious monomania. It is doubtful if his residence at the Collegium Insanorum in Chelsea did anything other than provide the time required for remission.

In his hypomanic phases, Pelham believed that he was thronged with angels, some of whom confided in him visions of paradise. But in his black phases, his occlusions and eclipses, it was the landscape of hell that confronted and confounded him, peopled by the inferno's personnel.

And so to conclude, if we are to apply the characterisation **melancholia** to Richard Pelham, it must be with the clear understanding that the notion of bodily functions which once underlay the humoral system is now clearly defunct. However, just as remarkable nuances of planetary observation were possible within the Ptolemaic system, despite its fundamentally flawed conception, we may also remark the highly detailed, and frequently accurate, observation of melancholics over the years, made from the perspective of the humours.

While Pelham was in my care, the most alarming symptoms of his condition were never much in evidence, until this extraordinary occurrence. But the overall cast of his mind remained one of distraction, and I would continue to argue the following:

Pelham's immersion in often barbarous and fanciful modes of thought and literature, whether of a devotional, theological or poetical kind, exacerbated a form of disjunction between himself and observable reality which grew more acute during his periods of affliction. The Society has been only too aware of the pernicious function of fanciful language in the process of mis-perception, and the remarkable retentiveness of Pelham's mind meant that this grand language-hoard, standing so aslant to the actual world, created in effect a massive screen, which could at times protect him from unwanted stimuli, but at other times could isolate him inside his own dreadful confinement.

It is quite possible that this misalignment with general perception is precisely what enabled some of the unfortunate poet's more notable observations, but I have no doubt that the Members will be in agreement with me when I say that such mental deformations are surely not a price worth paying for these, increasingly exiguous, achievements.

Descensus ad Inferos

When writing moves from mind to flesh, it is perhaps because it has become unworthy of that higher realm.
Richard Pelham Concluded
Edward Allingham

In his notes, Fordie had written:

Any student of the mind's morbidity, the spirit's contagions and infections, must end up sooner or later with a simple question – does the mind in its bleakest and blackest descent reflect a reality or create one? Either way, it strikes me, the mystery is by no means diminished. Either way the consequences appear to be just as dreadful for humanity.

Then there was a further note, in Fordie's margin: *Might Chilford himself have been mad?* And he had answered his own question thus: *I don't think so. Not yet, anyway.*

Now my roof was finished. All that had been required of me was one more trip to the building society. I had resolved now not to think about money. Fordie had assured me that he never did, though he had been astute enough in acquiring mine. When money worries take command of the mind, he had said, the whole of life translates itself into that loveless language. I knew this, I'd been here once before, with sandwiches half-eaten turning back suddenly into the price you paid for them, or a mouthful of beer becoming metallic on your tongue as it solidifies into the coins you just handed over to have it poured. And I remembered again Fordie's utter contempt for those who make nothing but money: better to make none at all, he had said, and I tried harder than ever now to believe him. I didn't want to think about money and I didn't want to think about Pelham or Chilford for a few days either. I might have had the first hint as to why Fordie had put it all away in that safe of his and left it there for so long. I, too, was beginning to feel contaminated.

I locked the bookshop door and set out walking. Without even considering the matter I went off down the river in the direction of Twickenham. I'd never spent much time on or near the Thames. We lived too far away and didn't go to it often. It was simply a river I occasionally encountered in making my way across London. But for Pelham it was the mystic snake of life itself. I looked at it, but I couldn't see whatever it was that he saw. It was only as I came towards the town that I realised where I was heading, and I turned off into the centre. I didn't want to stand before the ghost site of Chilford Villa again at the moment, so I was simply meandering, no more, when I stopped in front of the little gallery window. Ten seconds later, the man at the desk looked up affably from the table where he sat.

'The painting over there,' I said, 'the *Chimera* painting, I wonder if it might be possible to get the artist's address. We were once great friends, you see, but we seem to have lost contact over the years.' He disguised his irritation that I wasn't about to buy something and riffled through a drawer until he found a piece of paper, which he then handed to me and turned back to his magazine. And I wrote down the following:

Alice Ashe
47 Bingham Road
Whitby

There were a number of restaurants in Richmond where Fordie had signed a bookshop cheque for our food. That evening I took my own Tewk chequebook and set off to the Italian one, hoping the time for the cheques to start bouncing had not yet arrived. The owner had heard about Fordie's death and was solicitous. I placed Fordie's order: 'Anything. Anything at all, so long as it's without eggs. And the usual wine.' He smiled sadly, and went off to provide for me a meal of the sort he had provided for Fordie over so many years. Then, between the drinks and the food, I wrote my letter to Alice. It ended like this:

So, discovering to my surprise that I don't seem to want to kill you any more, I now find I'd like to see you instead. I'm so pleased that you're still painting. I'm not the man you left behind in Tenby, believe me. Stopped running. These days I don't even drive. I now own the bookshop whose address is printed at the top of this page. But please don't imagine that means I'm wealthy. The opposite is increasingly the case. But I do have a fridge full of white wine and eggs. Should you ever be passing through London, I'll give you some of both.

The next day I posted it, and as I came back to the shop I saw a man in a white raincoat standing on the far side of the road, staring up at the building and then making notes in his little book. When he saw me unlocking the door, he came over and introduced himself.

'Mr Harrison,' he said, 'from Hamgate. You wrote to us.'

'Did I?' I said, opening the door and stepping inside.

'We are the head lessors.'

'Ah yes.'

'Any chance of a look around?'

'Feel free,' I said. 'I've just forked out for the roof, but I've kept the receipts, well some of them anyway, so if you've brought your chequebook with you, maybe we could settle up.' So off Mr Harrison went on his inspection. When he came back down half an hour later, he was putting his notebook into his pocket.

'It's worse than I thought,' he said.

'What do you intend to do about it?'

Mr Harrison sat down on the chair by the side of Fordie's table and placed his folded white raincoat across his knees. He was a short man with attractive regular features and a healthy mop of black hair. There probably wasn't much real difference between us in age, but with his hair so unimpeachably black and mine now so irreversibly white, we looked as though we came from different generations.

'Have you actually read your lease, Mr Bayliss?'

'No,' I said, 'I have a low boredom threshold.'

'Well then, let me explain something. It is what is known as a full-repairing lease. And its ten-year period is about to expire in six months.'

'Fordie said they were always renewed,' I said.

'Indeed, they always have been. But we did warn Mr Tewk last time around that the state of repair had become a major cause for concern. Of course, he did nothing about it, we didn't really expect him to. We suspected he'd become something of an institution around these parts, to be honest, so we decided to do nothing about it ourselves, until . . .' He stopped.

'Until he died?'

'Let's say until there was a substantial change in the situation.'

'And now there's been one.'

'What I think I'd better do, Mr Bayliss, is to have a schedule of necessary works properly prepared and sent to you.'

'And what do I do with it?'

'You effect it, sir, by the time of the expiry of the lease.'

'Or?'

'First, your lease will not be renewed. Second, you'll be held liable for all the works deemed to be necessary. I should warn you that a rent-review is imminent, in any case. Given this property's worth now, if realistically valued . . .' I had already walked into the back room and I was opening a bottle of Chablis. At least we still had plenty of that left.

'I'd offer you a glass, Mr Harrison,' I said, 'but I have the feeling that I can't afford it any more. Wouldn't you agree?'

'I don't actually drink,' he said, 'and I have to leave now, in any case. We'll be in touch shortly.'

That night in a dream I pulled hard at Harry's hearing aid and more and more of something came out, some long intestine of white flesh that kept winding out of his ear the more I pulled. Ectoplasm. I woke then, and remembered the last words Fordie had spoken to me, the last item in his confession. 'And I cheated you,' he had said. I hadn't wanted to think about it, but now it was impossible not to. But even if Fordie's gold had turned out to have all disappeared except for the Chilford papers, the stock of books must have considerable value, surely. And with that thought to comfort me I managed finally to sink back into a fitful sleep.

The sound of the motors outside whirring and thrumming up and down the road from the bridge abraded memories, eroded certainties, like a circle of fifths making a ghost of tonality.

Idle Fellowes

*How these curiosities would be quite forgott, did not such idle fellowes
as I am putt them downe.*

JOHN AUBREY, *Brief Lives*

The next day, I took the folder out of the safe once more.
Fordie had done what work he could on Prince Zabrenus
and the Children of Bethany, but the truth was that this
obscure sect had simply become more obscure as the years
had passed. No one knew much about them. They were part
of that antinomian tradition that threads its way through the
religious history of these islands. Zabrenus preached an
exhilarating freedom from the slavery of both sin and guilt.
He preached the redemption of the spirit and stated
emphatically that those on whom the spirit had alighted
could no longer sin. Their bodies might sin, in their
aboriginal attachment to darkness, but such sins could never
beslime the anointed soul. If this was bad theology, it appears
at least to have been good therapy, where Pelham was
concerned at least. Some of his more eirenic letters were
dated to this period, including this one, in which he was very
nearly friendly to the lord whom he otherwise appeared to

consider his tormentor:

> *My prayers can no more summon the presence or assistance of the Almighty than a hobby-horse can fetch in a fecund season or start to sprout the tiny hairs that grow between a virgin's legs. If my liturgy inclined all one way, my vices leaned always to the other side entirely. I wonder all the same if one might anticipate in Paradise the disreputable noise of gaiety? Perhaps you and I might still expect to be merry there together one day. Or at least to share the ancient haunting ground of English mercies.*

Fordie had written in his notes: *Richard Pelham: both mystic and occultist. He believed all darkness had light shrouded within it. Who can say whether or not he was right? Lightning from a black sky. What did Serena see when they put the charge through her?*

But Pelham's alcoholism and drug addiction could by this stage have been terminated only by incarceration or death. And the single-line letter he sent Chilford towards the end showed the true terror of his condition:

> *Self-slaughter in wanhope, without housel or shrift.*

I'd had enough for a while. I would have taken a walk, but the weather had turned bad. It was raining in Richmond. A dreary infinity of rain. A relentless drench from the heavens that hammered down in wet insistence upon Fordie's lean-to roof. The autumn was pressing on into winter.

Maybe I lacked Fordie's strength of character, but I couldn't leave whoever it was standing outside and tapping on the door. Not in that rain.

The man shook his umbrella fiercely as he stepped forward, and then smiled a broad, red-faced smile. He looked like a farmer come up to town for the weekend.

'I came to offer my condolences,' he said.

'That's kind,' I said. 'Who are you?'

'Fordie's vicar,' he said. 'And you must be the new proprietor.'

'Here, take your coat off. Can I offer you a drink?' I gave him a glass of wine and he sipped it and laughed.

'What's funny?'

'I'm sorry. I didn't mean to be impolite. It's just that it's nice to know some traditions are maintained. It is Chablis, isn't it?'

'It is.'

'Always what I was given on my infrequent visits.'

'How often did you come?'

'Maybe once a year. Fordie would occasionally come to me.' He paused then for a moment. 'Correction: Fordie came once to me. And I'm afraid I wasn't a lot of use to him. Though his quest at the time did strike me as a trifle cryptic.' I liked this vicar. He was one of those men who set you entirely at your ease merely by their presence. He'd probably found the right job, I thought.

'Do you mind if I ask what it was, this cryptic quest? Or would that come under the rubric of secrets of the confessional?'

'You must be a Roman Catholic,' he said, and I realised that his glass was already empty. I brought the bottle over and filled it. 'We don't share many secrets of the confessional in our church. No, I don't believe there was any

confidentiality in our discussion. Fordie was after information about . . .' He stopped.

'About what?'

'About a demon,' he said finally. 'Can't remember its
name.'

'Agarith,' I said quietly.

'Yes, that was it,' he said, mildly startled. 'How did you
know that?'

'I've picked up his studies where he left off. Let me fill
your glass again.'

'Sorry. Drinking all your nice wine.'

'There's plenty, believe me.'

'I've been stomping about out there for hours, but I'm
afraid that most of the addresses I visit aren't as hospitable as
Tewk's Bookshop. First glass I've been offered all day.

'I wasn't much use, I'm afraid. In fact, the truth is I was no
use at all. A shame really. The only time Stamford Tewk ever
went to consult his vicar, and I had to shrug my shoulders
and say I didn't have a clue. It's simply not a realm with
which we concern ourselves. Not these days, anyway.

'I heard about the ceremony, by the way. I would have
been happy to help of course, but . . .'

'I'm sorry,' I said, realising the extent of the slight, 'my
fault entirely. It honestly didn't occur to me. Fordie'd made
no mention. I'm sure he'd have wanted you there, probably
wanted you to conduct it. Sorry.'

'Not to worry. But we thought, perhaps, a memorial
service. Not immediately. But he was a local figure of some
importance, however eccentric.'

'Very good of you,' I said. 'Anything I can do, just let me know.' He had finished his drink now and stood up to go.

'So you're the new proprietor. Planning any changes?'

'Not planning anything at all until I've sorted out this Agarith business.' His smile vanished momentarily as he looked at me.

'No good asking me, I'm afraid. Just don't regard it as my job.'

'No,' I said as we reached the door. 'Maybe it isn't.'

'Are you actually planning to, I mean, unlike Fordie . . .'

'Sell any books?' I said, and he started laughing.

'Well, he never did seem very keen, did he? It always struck me as a bit of a shame really. By the way, I'd just like to say one thing, which I hope is not presumptuous. But Fordie did come to see me once more towards the end, to ask me if I would do something for him. Something I was more than happy to do. But perhaps you know all about this?' I shook my head. 'It was in regard to his daughter.'

'Fordie has a daughter?'

'Ah. You don't know about it. Well, a stepdaughter, in point of fact. His wife Serena's child. And now suffering her mother's illness, more's the shame. It's just I know what Fordie was like, not a great communicator in such matters, and I just thought you might want to know how much it meant to him, you investing in the bookshop in the way you did, so that he had the money to make sure she could be properly looked after. She's over fifty now, of course. Knowing she'd be properly cared for till the end was important to him. More important than I could tell you.' So now at least I knew where that money had gone. It should have made me feel better, I suppose, but I'm not sure it did.

'What was the favour he asked you?'

'Oh, just to visit her, that's all, once every couple of weeks, as he used to. It's not my parish, of course, and Fordie was not as I ever understood it a believer, but these things are given one sometimes, and perhaps it doesn't do too much to question them.'

'Will you come back?' I said.

'Sorry?'

'Will you come back and have another drink sometime?'

'I'd be delighted,' he said, looking slightly astonished, and then he set out into the rain again.

Something had confused me entirely in working my way through Fordie's notes. From time to time he would make a reference, only by initials, and then with a page number appended. For example: BLJ, p.623, or ITPC, p.147, or MD, p.223. They corresponded to no works I had seen referred to, and I simply couldn't imagine what they were or what purpose they served. I was sitting at Fordie's desk looking behind me distractedly at the two shelves of books he had assembled. I had assumed they were merely a miscellany, since they appeared to have no connecting thread that I'd ever noticed. Then I took out Boswell's *Life of Johnson* and saw the marked pages, and I thought: BLJ. I turned to the markers and found pencil lines and comments in the margins. Then I got down on my knees and started carefully scanning the titles. Could MD be *Moby Dick?* Again I pulled out the volume, and once more inside there were markers and pencilled marginalia. It took a while to locate ITPC, but I found it finally inside the single volume of Kafka: *In the Penal Colony*. I felt a strange sense of exhilaration. Then there was a knocking on the door. I had locked it. I could see far enough behind the closed sign to recognise Mr Harrison and a companion. I went and opened the door but I didn't invite either of them in.

'Hello, Mr Bayliss,' Harrison said, smiling his meaningless diplomatic smile, 'I've brought a colleague with me who's a little more expert than I in these matters. Could we come in for half an hour, and do another little survey of the works required?' He was already stepping forward. He hadn't been asking a question, he'd been making an announcement.

'No,' I said, 'you can't come in. I'm busy. Go away.' He looked nonplussed.

'We are entitled to get a court order, you know.'

'Then go and get one,' I said, 'and don't come back till you have it in your grubby little paw. Whatever the state of it, I've still got six months in this place, according to you.'

'Yes, but . . .'

'So bugger off,' I said, 'and take your little friend with you.' As I banged the door shut, and heard the bell's startled merriment, I sensed that the spirit of Stamford Tewk had never left his bookshop after all; it had simply taken a while for me to absorb it fully.

'I'm still fighting them off, Fordie,' I shouted into the depths of the bookshop. 'They haven't evicted us yet, even though you did set me up for it.'

So I started elaborating that little concordance of Fordie's. I didn't understand what he was up to at first. Then it began slowly to shift into focus. When Ishmael first meets Queequeg, the writing on the harpoonist's body, his tattoos, is like the mark of Cain, something that sets him apart to be shunned. But as Ishmael learns to read that writing on his body, horror turns into acceptance and finally love. In Kafka's story the dreadful punishment in the penal settlement is to have a machine write on your body the commandment you have ignored. This is script as capital punishment. Fordie was trying to understand the ways in which writing on the body had been understood. He had written at the end of this section: *All these questions resolve more and more into one question, one question it was surely impossible for Chilford, given his beliefs, to ask: Grappin.*

Back I went to the little bookshelf, and found the book he was referring to. It was a study of St John Vianney, the Curé d'Ars. And I began to wonder if I should have ever become involved in this business, because now it seemed I was going to have to read the life of a Catholic priest, and not just any Catholic priest either. Resentment. A real resentment was beginning. This time I went out and had a French meal on the bookshop account. And how much longer would I be able to get away with that?

For someone who had once never remembered his dreams, who had stepped into wakefulness the way he stepped into his well-pressed clothes, I was certainly turning into a serious dreamer now, and the dreams were all bad. I would roll over to take Alice in my arms and find Queequeg instead. I would wake to the chattering needles of the penal colony's machine, as they bit into my flesh. I always woke a moment too early to read whatever the commandment was that I had failed to obey. It wasn't much after dawn the next day that I rose and went downstairs. I thought I'd better get this Curé d'Ars business out of the way. I poured myself some coffee, picked up the copy of *Grappin,* subtitled *The Disciple Against Reason* and started. I knew well enough who Vianney was. I had even attended his feast-day mass in Rome and been exhorted from the pulpit to emulate the humble parish priest as far as possible in my own sacerdotal life. The problem was not who Vianney was, but what he was. He was either what his status in the Church proclaimed, a man of almost infinite obedience and humility who had stared down infernal powers for decades, or a credulous rural priest who, in reaction to enlightenment and revolution, had once more conjured all the Gothic palaver of medieval diabolism, so as to keep his flock well within the Church's grasp, to frighten the good citizens back into craven belief. And the interesting thing, it struck me now, was that I'd never been able to answer that question, even while I was in Rome. Hence my resentment now at being forced to confront the question once more.

As for the title of this book, *Grappin,* that was what everything hinged around. This word was the name the Curé had given to the Devil, the Devil who visited him, screamed abuse at him, called him a dirty little potato-eater, threw excrement at his holy pictures, and on many occasions even tried to kill him. The problem, simply put, was this: either the Curé was mad, or the Devil did indeed exist and had arrived in Ars each night to torment his humble little enemy. The surrounding testimony, of which a considerable amount still survives, corroborated Vianney's story. Even the severest scepticism had been overcome finally by the severity of the phenomena with which it had been confronted. If the Curé had been mad, then it seemed that he had made the better part of a French village mad with him.

I suppose it had been a curious time in the Church, when I was studying to enter the priesthood. There had been a strong sense that a great deal of outdated paraphernalia now needed to be dispensed with. At the time of the Second Vatican Council, Pope John XXIII had announced that he was opening the windows. It was time to let some fresh air in, and for the dark shapes of superstitious dread to fly away for ever. At some point between my childhood and my young manhood, the words in the creed that said of Christ after his crucifixion *He descended into hell* had disappeared, and they had never returned. The implication appeared to be that Christ had not made any such journey after all, in those hidden times between crucifixion and resurrection, and if he had never made that journey, could it perhaps be because there was no such journey to be made and no such place to disappear into? And if the dark kingdom had been quietly declared null and void, then perhaps its famous lord and master had also been dispensed with once and for all. There had been one or two ancient Jesuits about in Rome during my stay, who were whisperingly reputed to have conducted exorcisms many years before. But nobody ever spoke of anyone conducting such ceremonies any more. Except for half-smiling accounts of sinister goings on in Africa, or voodoo mumbo-jumbo in Haiti. Hell and its fallen angels had simply ceased to be a fit subject of concern for a modern Roman Catholic.

All of this had undoubtedly suited me in many ways, because I had felt uneasy for a long time about what I had come to think of as the Church's baggage of idolatry, its little black shapes that rose like mists out of Irish bogs, its weeping madonnas, its plaster saints with bleeding wounds, all those absurd hagiographies in which St Patrick in his chariot ran over his unchaste sister, or the fairy-tale daily miracles of *The Little Flowers of St Francis*. I was aware too that this heritage of superstition was not always blithe and innocent. The anti-Semitism that coiled itself around the legend of Hugh of Lincoln, the fear of the foreign, the hatred of the strange – these were a part of that heritage and they troubled me greatly. Even during my time there, Roman rumours had abounded about the Vatican's role in spiriting the Nazi Croatians of the Ustashe out of Europe after the war, with a series of monasteries used as safe houses, as a link in the rat-line. That's not what they're for, I remembered thinking angrily to myself as the details leaked out, that's not what they were built for at all.

And now here I was, trying to work out if Jean-Baptiste Vianney, the saintly Curé d'Ars, was a psychotic liar, or if the Devil might not, after all, have disappeared with the dim and unenlightened centuries that had been so fearfully fascinated with him.

Fordie had put a lot of work in here. I started studying his notes, and as I did I realised the significance of all those questions Fordie had put to me. I had thought it an intellectual game for him at the time, but now I could see that was the last thing it had been. He had been trying to get at the truth of the matter.

He had experimented with a variety of psychological stratagems, seeing if he could square St Jean-Baptiste Vianney's evident goodness and candour with his reported visitations. He noted that Jung had written how he himself had been menaced by a psychosis, one that had threatened both his sanity and his well-being. He had described the force as both real and dangerous, and yet emanating from inside him, but how could that be? Fordie had wondered how such an inner force could arise; where was *its* source? If one were to place the locus of the diabolic attacks within Vianney, rather than without, the potency and projection still remained inexplicable. Freud's account of the diabolic contract signed in his own blood by Christoph Haizmann in the seventeenth century was written largely in the manner of a scholarly amanuensis, simply writing down indisputable events. It was as though Freud expected such things. He even explained the logic and attraction of a deal with the Devil. But the last trustworthy account Fordie had been able to locate of an actual encounter was that of Huysmanns in Paris a hundred years before. The evidence suggested that the writer had indeed attended black masses and involved himself with a number of sinister figures in the world of the occult. The accounts were so specific that Fordie found it hard to doubt them. More to the point, Huysmanns became so terrified of the powers he believed had come to be directed at him, that he spent the last years of his life in a monastery, surrounded by alternative powers he believed to be redemptive, not infernal. That struck Fordie as a very large gesture to make, for any mere *poseur*.

But none of this resolved the problem he had with Vianney himself. The little priest had been brought up at a time when Reason, that pitiless French goddess, was enthroned. The cathedral in Paris was reconsecrated in her name, while the churches whose names did remain dedicated to the worship of Christ largely ran free with pigs and cattle. All the darkness of the past was to be left behind. Humanity would live henceforth in the glare of the light. Time had been revised to match the ticking of a different clock. The calendar had started all over again. It seemed ironic to Fordie though, that when humanity finally stepped on to the evolutionary platform of enlightenment, it should find itself metamorphosed into the Committee for Public Safety, ritual daily executions, a true terrorism of the spirit. Terror was, after all, what Robespierre had called the hygiene of the Revolution. And Vianney had seen priests come and go in secret amidst all this, risking their lives to administer the sacraments. The first definition of a priest he'd ever been given was this: a man who's prepared die to be one. So there he was, at the cusp, with on the one side a medieval battle between heaven and hell, and on the other a violent, evangelising Enlightenment. Enlightenment: where had the light come from, sitting so securely enthroned in the heart of that word? The supreme notion that the goddess Reason would now put everything to rights, and shine her brilliant eyes into everyone's darkness.

In the middle of this disquisition, Fordie had suddenly

stopped. He had written across the page: *We cannot answer this question. Or at least reason gives one answer, faith another. Is this why we have portraits of poets? Pelham's.*

I pulled out the first edition of *Psalms of Solace* and looked at the frontispiece portrait, then I turned back to Fordie's notes, trying to fathom where his mind was taking him. He pointed out that Pelham's period was the age of the portrait of the poet, though the tradition itself stretches back a long way, back to those busts of Homer in his blindness, the whole of his expression turned inwards from the world, reconnoitring now the landscapes and the battles he must find inside himself; or Euripides darkening, as humanity prances its rituals of destruction before him. But with the frontispiece to the folio edition of the works of Shakespeare in 1623, a new trend was begun, or rather an old trend of codex and scroll re-established: having an image of the poet attached to his works, so that one could study the shape of the head through which the flashes from above had been transmitted. Incompetent and inexpressive as this engraving is, it inaugurates our modern cult of inspiration.

Alexander Pope seemed set to fill the nation with his likeness, making it his business to have as many portraits painted and engraved, and as many miniatures of them distributed as possible. They often show him in a melancholy solitude, chin on hand, as though the present age had provided no one with whom he might truly speak; as though all his converse was with the line of artists threading him back in hermetic communion to antiquity.

One tradition had it that Hogarth's 'The Distressed Poet' of 1737 was a portrait of Pelham in penury, his wife

Susannah dutifully repairing his only pair of hose, his son Tom rubbing his eyes with incredulity at the bleakness of the world into which he has been born. The poet, booze-blotched and bleary, is scratching the hair under his wig as he dreams up fresh tropes and modern instances for the epic he labours away at, which carries the title 'Poverty'.

Godfrey Kneller had painted him as a young man and this image provided the early portrait of Pelham which was the original for the engraving on the frontispiece I was now looking at. A later portrait, by an otherwise obscure Dutch painter named Droet, shows Pelham already embarked on his dissolution, the startling clarity of his eyes beginning to be imprisoned by the encroaching flesh about them.

On an otherwise blank page, Fordie had written: *So we make the poet into hell's journeyman, and look into his eyes in portraits to see where he has been. Just when we have stopped believing in hell. Except we didn't stop believing in hell, did we? Only its externality. Serena again.*

The River's Last Drink

The river's last drink is the sea.

RICHARD PELHAM, *The Instruments of the Passion*

Fordie annotated as best he could the sad life of Lord Chilford following his wife's death. His stoical cheerfulness had perhaps always concealed a bleaker temperament. There was in him, too, a melancholy thread he had done his best to lose in scientific compassings and analytic precisions, a thread that perhaps tied him a little more closely to Richard Pelham than he ever cared to consider. But now with the sudden death of Lady Chilford, this unilluminated seam became the sable threading his psyche. Not that he communicated this to anyone. Even if he had felt any inclination to cry out, his quinsied distemper would probably have inclined him back to silence. But he too started to take lightning from the bottle.

It was only as I reached the last manuscript section, and the last of Fordie's notes that I came fully to understand why he might have put all this away in his safe, and left it there. I read through it all once and then I put it away myself. Time to go outside again.

I hadn't even noticed that it was snowing. But Richmond was white and I looked around, a little dazzled, at all the countless blank sheets of snow-sugared windscreens on the endless parked cars. On one or two a finger had already entered its script, but most were pristine, untouched, aboriginal. For an hour that morning the world was fresh, but the thaw had started by lunchtime. By then I was sitting in a café eating a sandwich and making my decision. I decided that one way or the other I had to get this business over with. Fordie had obviously shelved it for years. But I didn't have years. In a few months' time I would be out, and I had an odd feeling that I might soon have to be selling off anything of any value. Including possibly the Chilford papers.

When I arrived back I opened up the last bottle of Chablis – it had stopped coming, along with the eggs. I suspected that the non-payment of bills might have had something to do with this. Then I telephoned Westminster Cathedral. On the back cover of *Grappin*, there was a note that the author, Monsignor Templeton, had spent many years in various missions and now tended a parish in south London. There was one line in his book, one line about the confrontation with the face of evil, which made it evident to me that Templeton had either conducted or been present at an exorcism. Out of that had come the particular slant of his work on Vianney, its undeniable passionate engagement. There was no doubt in this monsignor's mind about the reality of Grappin. So when the lady at the other end asked me the nature of my enquiry, I said that it was a matter of some urgency that she give me the address of Monsignor Templeton. Thirty seconds later she did. He was now resident in a little church at the edge of Clapham Common.

I could have telephoned or written, but I had a feeling he'd have found a way of fobbing me off. Had he guessed the nature of my enquiry, he would probably have refused to collaborate at all. So I simply went there on the train. On the way I did something I seldom did any more: I bought a newspaper. Inside I saw a photograph I recognised and read the headline *Poet Shadwell Jailed in First Editions Scam*. Shadwell, it seemed, had been topping up his exiguous income by signing early editions of other writers' work, using their own style of signature (so much for my Lawrence Durrells). He had done so much of this that the judge felt obliged to have him put away for three months. In his first prison interview Shadwell pointed out that there was a long and intimate connection between poetry and criminality. I read the names Villon, Verlaine, Rimbaud and Ben Jonson before I threw the paper aside.

I have often thought about the shock that must be sustained by those in England who turn to the Church of Rome without knowing much about it, imagining that they are about to enter an earthly shadow of the heavenly city, particularly those who have spent any time studying the buildings of the Italian Renaissance. So often our buildings are no more than bleak machines for praying in. This one looked particularly bleak, and the presbytery seemed to be falling down. The stucco had gone almost entirely, revealing the uneven bricks beneath. I rang the doorbell twice and at

last a tall, anxious-looking woman appeared. She gave me a
sceptical look and asked, in a sharp Irish voice, what I
wanted. The housekeeper.

'I have come to see Monsignor Templeton.'

'You do not have an appointment, do you?'

'No,' I said. 'I don't.'

'Today is his day off. He has no appointments today.'
Housekeeper and protectress. 'If you would like to leave a
message for him, I'll see that he gets it.'

'I'm sorry,' I said, 'but it's a matter of some urgency.'

'There is another priest on duty . . .'

'No, I'm afraid it has to be Monsignor Templeton, for
reasons I can't go into.' This was a nasty trick, and I knew it.
No Irish housekeeper would ever take on the responsibility
of sending someone away in a state of mortal sin, and
therefore in peril of his immortal soul should he step under
the first oncoming bus. With a sniff of irritation she showed
me into the reception room and left. I looked around at the
slowly rotting furniture and sub-Murillo framed kitsch on the
walls, and wondered once more how any high Anglicans had
ever walked the path to Rome, without promptly turning
back. At last Monsignor Templeton came in and gestured
with his arthritic hands for me to sit down at the oilcloth-
covered table. I felt guilty. He had about him a look of utter
exhaustion. I would have said he was in his late sixties and
had probably already retired from the usual parish duties.
There was a little grey hair on his head, but his milky blue
eyes, though rheumy, were sharp and sceptical. The veins on
his forehead were visibly throbbing. He wore the shabby

dark clothes of almost all elderly priests when they are trying to pass for civilians.

'How can I help you, Mr . . .'

'Bayliss.'

'Forgive me, Mr Bayliss, but have we ever met? It's just that Moira, sorry, Mrs O'Connell, said you wanted to see me in particular. I don't believe we're acquainted.' My eyes had wandered up the wall to the ceiling as the monsignor spoke. Along the ceiling ran an enormous crack from corner to corner, a threatening, gaping crack that augured worse to come. The priest's eyes had followed mine.

'Not in very good repair, I'm afraid, this house.'

'Hope it's not a full-repairing lease,' I said.

'I'm sorry?'

'Never mind. Monsignor Templeton, I've called on you during your day off on false pretences. I'm sorry, but I didn't know what else to do. I read your book *Grappin* and you are the only person I think might be able to help me.' Suddenly he stiffened.

'Are you from the press?'

'No.'

'Not the television?'

'Nothing like that, believe me.'

'Ever since that film *The Exorcist* we have been plagued with enquiries of a dubious nature.' I had expected something like this and that's why I had brought the manuscripts along with me. I took them carefully out of my bag. No scholar can ever resist looking at unpublished manuscripts from centuries before.

'What are these?' he asked peering across at them and fumbling for his reading glasses.

'You are going to have to spare me a half-hour of your time for me to explain.'

He looked up from the papers, still a little wearily. 'Perhaps you would like a coffee?' He went to the kitchen, and a few minutes later he carried the mugs in one at a time, with enormous difficulty, in his arthritic fingers. I should have offered to help, but I had been staring out of the window at the snow, which had started falling again.

I told the story as briefly as I could. Occasionally he would ask for some clarification and I realised by the astuteness of his questions that whatever was going wrong with Templeton's body, there was nothing at all wrong with his mind.

'Do you know of a demon named Agarith?' I asked him.

'Minor Babylonian deity. Re-emerged infrequently as a demonic power. Enlisted at some point as one of our devils, like so many others.'

'What were his attributes?'

'He appears in certain grimoires and necromantic instructions for raising the dead. He was called upon to bestow special gifts in the sciences. A certain penchant for fanciful violence. But you haven't told me what finally happened to your Richard Pelham. You'll have to forgive me, but I'm afraid I know nothing about him. France was my area of specialisation.'

'What happened to him has been a mystery for over two hundred years.' He looked at me once more a little warily. He would be a good man in the confessional, I could see that, as hard to shock as he was to impress.

'And now your manuscripts here are about to bring light where previously there was darkness, is that it?'

'Can I read something to you?'

'What is it you are reading?'

'Lord Chilford's diary of events.' He nodded and I started to read.

'*The weather had already turned into snapping winds and howling showers. Unexpected blusters ruffled the water of the Thames into petulant swells. It was only an hour after dawn when Jacob noticed the rope tied to the willow's trunk. At the other end of this tether, dragging slowly in the outgoing tide, was the poet's mutilated body, attached by a well-executed bowline. (I couldn't help remembering Pelham's boyish pride in his knot-tying.)*

'*The wounds appear, for a suicide, inexplicable. All five fingers on each hand pierced, the lobes of both ears, an aperture passing right through the flesh of the nose, and the appalling stabbing through the right eye that sent him plunging down into the water. It was only some time later that I noticed the wound to the tongue. All of the wounds had been effected with the lancet Pelham had stolen from my laboratory.*' I looked up. Monsignor Templeton was staring through the window at the snow, which was now falling more heavily.

'Do the wounds mean anything to you?' I said.

'Oh yes. They are a parody of the mortification of the senses. Sight, hearing, taste, touch and smell. Most lengthy ascetical rites or penitential practices would work their way through them one by one. It does rather sound as though your fellow decided to get them all over at once.'

'That's assuming he was still deciding anything.'

Monsignor Templeton stood up and started to walk slowly

around the room. He held his hands before him, laid one over the other, palm upwards. That, presumably, eased the pain of the arthritis. He stopped at the other side of the table and stood looking through the window.

'So, you've decided he was possessed, have you?'

'The business that night in Twickenham. The writing on his flesh. The prediction of the future. The speaking in voices belonging to another person. The unaccountable fall in the room's temperature. What else can it all mean?'

'What else can it all mean?' he echoed, and I realised how very tired he was. 'Well now, let me see. Signs on bodies are a curious business, you know. Let's start with the saints, not the sinners. The stigmatic is in some ways rather like certain types of demoniac – both of them are said to have their bodies written on by preternatural powers, the one divine, the other demonic. The Church is extremely circumspect about stigmatics, did you know that? The reason? The phenomena could be produced by means other than the pressure of the divine. A sufficient degree of psychological identification with Christ in his passion might inscribe the wounds on hands and feet, sometimes on the breast. This in itself might well be a form of saintliness, but does not necessarily imply divine intervention. And the same is true the other way about, with the apparently possessed, or obsessed: the devil is too often no more than another word for repression. You could say that he is, in that sense, the primal force of the hidden, the unacknowledged, all that is unconfessed and unshriven. The force of your man's mind might have become so darkened and intensified by his trials and turmoils that it could write distorted messages upon his body. Such spectacular feats are not unknown in India, practised by the conscious mind in meditation. Why should it not be possible also for the unconscious mind under the constraint of hysteria? Anyway, with hundreds of years separating us from his life and death, how could we ever possibly know?'

'But what about the other manifestations?'

'The other manifestations can all be answered for quite straightforwardly, and if anything can be answered for without the need of preternatural intervention, then so it must be. That is the teaching of the Church. Your man predicted the death of Lady Chilford in childbirth. What were the statistics for death in childbirth in the mid-eighteenth century?'

'I don't know,' I said.

'Then might I suggest you go and find out? I think you'll find that this particular prediction has about it as much of the preternatural as my statement that it will probably rain for three days next week. From one of those letters you read me it is quite evident that Pelham was sexually besotted with Chilford's wife. When the conscious controls of his mind crumbled, that obsession was made manifest.

'So he spoke in Jacob's voice, spoke words Josephine thought were known only to herself and her husband. He had been almost alone in that place with the two of them. One presumes that unless there was some impediment, they would have consummated their vows with reasonable vigour when given the opportunity. So Pelham heard them. You've already remarked on his astuteness of observation in those reports you read, so the same astuteness led him to internalise not merely the vocabulary employed, but the inflections and intonations too. Mimicry is native to human beings. We don't have to introduce the inhabitants of hell to explain it.'

We stared at each other over the table for a moment in silence.

'You seem to be agreeing with Lord Chilford,' I said finally and with obvious disappointment.

'I probably am,' he said. 'The man was evidently a Deist on the way to atheism, but it sounds to me as though he behaved in a most exemplary fashion, despite all that. There is no problem at all with reason, you know, except that it sometimes oversteps its bounds. It is usually preferable to superstition. I wish *I* could look forward to ending my days with the kind of care that Lord Chilford provided for your poet. His asylum by the river sounds really very tempting. What is the purpose of your study, Mr Bayliss?' I thought about this for a moment before answering. But I didn't really know the answer.

'I'm not sure any more,' I said. 'I just wanted to work something out, that's all.'

'For your benefit or the benefit of Richard Pelham's memory?'

'Could it be both?'

'We can't very well exorcise his demon for him, can we, even assuming he had one? The fact that he himself could identify it suggests, by the way, that he was not possessed. His imagination might well have been in the grip of an entity he had come across in his studies, but that is far from being the same thing. What's left for either of us then, except speculation and remembrance?

'Whatever can be known with any certitude does not belong in the realm of demonology, that is the only certainty I can offer you in regard to it. Everything there has at least two meanings, which are always contradictory and self-cancelling. Like the business with waves and particles: it can't simultaneously be both, but nor can it be separated solely into either. Do you know that de Tonquedec, the official exorcist for the archdiocese of Paris for over forty years, said that not a single case had ever been placed before him, not one in all those years, which he could, with absolute certainty, diagnose as a genuine case of possession? And they were living cases, not ones from two centuries ago. The best human response to the world of the demonic is simply to leave it alone, avoid it entirely, and tread the path of love and faith instead. And now you really must forgive me, but I'm very tired. I've not been well lately, and I need my rest. Thank you for coming to see me. I hope it's been some help.'

When I arrived back at the shop I put the manuscripts into the safe, and wondered if I'd ever take them out again. What, after all, was the point? Maybe it was better to let the matter rest in peace. Was that what Fordie had decided? I set off walking to Richmond Park. But the weather was relentless, it thrashed and skewed the trees. And that night as I lay in bed I sensed the mist edging towards me like a cautious animal, blinding the windows one by one with its smear.

My dreams were riddled with these images of writing on bodies. Christ and his five wounds, and St Francis reproducing them on his flesh, so that it had itself become a ceaseless act of devotion, a prayer. Queequeg's tattoos, and blue numbers on ceaseless processions of white flesh; Kafka's story, where the master of the machine submits himself to be the page the needles need to write upon. And then Pelham himself: was he no more than writing paper, the age's submerged hysteria encrypted with its signs, or had the age's science placed him in a realm that science itself could neither understand nor even credit with existence? I woke at dawn in the freezing cold, since the heating had ceased a week before – I hadn't paid the gas bill. I went downstairs and opened up the safe. I took out the papers and read them over and over again.

Why had I simply taken Lord Chilford's word for it? It was true that the letters appeared to form Pelham's name on his chest, with one oddity, namely, as Chilford pointed out, the fact that the H was not properly formed and looked more like an I. I had read this now at least four times and had wondered before, Cannot those demons, with their preternatural powers, even spell? Or might it simply have been that Pelham in his dementia had lost the faculty of stringing letters together sufficiently even to form his own name? What I had never done was simply stare straight ahead at the information before me. I took out a piece of paper and wrote out what Chilford had set down, and what it said was: Pell I am. I took down the N–Poy volume of Fordie's *OED*. Pell: substantive. (1) A skin or hide. (2) A skin or parchment. Quickly, I hunted back through *The Instruments of the Passion* to the lines I remembered:

See how the flesh of Marsyas
Provides Apollo with foul papers

Nothing was misspelt then. Whether it was some force beyond him inscribing him with its own infernal torments, or whether it was merely the skin of his mind that was peeling off, and the mental disintegration had started to manifest outside his mind, the words on Pelham's body meant precisely what they had always said: his own skin had been turned into parchment. He was not writing now, but being written upon.

I went back to bed and slept soundly for the first time since I could remember. I was only woken by the knocking at the door. It was Charles Redmond. I made him coffee, for I had some of that, but without milk, for I had none.

'God, it's cold in here,' he said.

'Gas has been cut off.'

'Ah. Bill went astray?'

'No,' I said, 'the bill's over there. It's the money to pay it went astray.' He looked at me dubiously.

'Do you have any of Shadwell's signed copies?'

'I have two fake Durrells and one bona fide Shadwell, each one signed, for all the good it'll do me.'

'Would you like to sell them?'

'How much were you thinking of offering?'

'I'll give you what you paid for them.'

'Done,' I said and went to fetch them.

'Why?' I asked. 'Just out of interest.' I was handing over the books as he handed over the money.

'I think they're turning into collector's pieces already,' he said. 'There's a story attached. Shadwell's about to become a sort of icon. Prison was a good move. Warmer there than here as well, Christopher.'

'How do you know?'

'I went to visit him yesterday. He'd like to think he caused no one too much inconvenience.' I started to laugh.

'While you're here, give me a quick valuation on the stock, would you?'

'What all of it?'

'Yes. I might need to sell quickly.'

Charles wandered about for half an hour, pulling down books and putting them back. When he had finished, he came over to the table.

'On sight, maybe seven thousand pounds.'

'Is that all?'

'There are some very distinguished titles here, but not many distinguished volumes you know.'

'Not many distinguished prices, you mean?'

'Same thing. Some of the things I sold you are much more valuable than anything here.'

'That's all upstairs. My personal collection. Not for sale. I still need it.'

'And what about the secrets in the back room?'

'I don't think there are as many of them as you might have imagined. Certainly not as many as I imagined.'

'Ah, Fordie. How much did you pay him?'

'Mind your own business,' I said sharply, then relented. 'I'm sorry. Let's say that I didn't cut a very good deal here. Or anywhere else either.'

'I'm afraid I can't go higher than seven thousand from what I can see.'

'And you would take it away?'

'I would take it away.'

No eggs. No Chablis. No heating. It wouldn't be too long before the lighting went too. The days of Tewk's Bookshop were numbered. I had been down to the Citizens' Advice Bureau. They hadn't extended much hope in regard to the terms of the lease. A sufficiently draconian rent-review, on the other hand, might make a local campaign possible. Though the fact that I hadn't bothered opening up the place to the local residents except for a couple of hours a week might stand against me. Now if Fordie had still been alive . . . I could always claim the rights of a sitting tenant for the rooms above apparently. Or alternatively, I could do what I was thinking of doing, namely sell up and clear off with the bills unpaid, preferably to a place sufficiently remote for Hamgate to find it very difficult to locate me, and finally to give up trying.

There was a knock on the door. I was sitting at Fordie's table absorbing the electricity from my TENS, one of the very few pleasures I could still afford. I had no intention of answering. But Alice managed to crouch down far enough to be able to see me from under one of the blinds. Her face was unmistakable, even out there in the dark. I went to the door and opened it. I was still unfastening the blinking TENS attached to my neck.

'What's that?' she said.

'My electricity machine.'

'What does it do?'

'Eases the pain in my muscles. Helps me to move around again. It's nice to see you, Alice.'

'I wanted to have a look at your bookshop.'

'Take a good look now, then,' I said, 'because it won't be

mine for much longer.' She walked around for a moment looking at the rows of titles. I couldn't help noticing the briskness of her manner. Alice had changed. This was Alice #2.

'Like father like son,' she said at last.

'How's that?

'Both book-keepers. You promised white wine and eggs.' She was no longer dressed in construction boots and jeans, but in a battered brown tweed suit with a long skirt, and what looked like school sandals. Polished though, and her hair had been evenly cut.

'Ah,' I said, 'I seem to have run out of both of those. How about a coffee with no milk?' In the way people have when they can't think of what to say, I started to talk and talk. I explained quickly about the accident; the bizarre circumstances of my buying into the business; how I had only subsequently discovered the state of the building and the status of the repairing lease. How one by one the utilities were declining to provide their services, hence the cold. And the last thing I explained was that I didn't have any money left. I decided to spare her the value of the stock.

'I don't suppose you'd like to buy some books, would you?'

'No,' she said evenly, 'but I'm going to take you out and buy you dinner instead.' So it was that when we walked down the road to the Italian restaurant, it was Alice's treat. As we ate our pizzas and sipped our wine she told me about the house where she lived up in Whitby. There was one other painter apart from herself, a carpenter, a dressmaker and a car mechanic who doubled as a hairdresser. I felt immediately jealous of all of these unknown people, and wondered if any of them had made love to her.

'I saw a painting of yours in a shop in Twickenham,' I said, 'that's how I got your address.'

'I've had a few exhibitions up north,' she said offhandedly, trying not to sound boastful. 'I've come down to supervise the next one over in Whitechapel. That's why I'm here. What are you going to do, Chris? Where are you going to go?'

'I don't know,' I said. 'I can sell off the books to start with, that'll give me some money, but not too much, it seems. Fordie wasn't exactly straight with me about it all. I don't know how much he deliberately misled me, or how much he just didn't want to think about it – the lease, the actual value of the stock, how badly he needed the money so that he could provide for his stepdaughter. Anyway, it seems that all he really left me were the Chilford papers, which are probably not all that valuable on the open market anyway. But they're the only work I have. The only trouble is, I don't know now that I'll ever get to finish it. I keep stopping, anyway, because so much of it is tied up with things I thought I'd finally escaped from. And now I have another problem. I might not have anywhere to live where I can do it.' And then I realised, as I stared across at Alice's shadowed face, that I was begging.

'You once took me in,' she said, 'don't think I've forgotten.' I looked down at my wineglass and tried to remember. It all seemed like a different life, with different people in it.

'I took you in because I wanted you.'

'You still took me in.' I was staring over the glass at her hands now. I had forgotten how her veins twisted and knotted over the backs of those small, quick hands of hers. She had painted her fingernails the colour of wild blackberry. However much I had changed, she had changed to the same degree or more. I looked up at the lines across her forehead announcing, I suppose, that there was death inside her too, death and calculation, however white her body. And my white hair probably made me look twenty years older than I had the last time she'd seen me.

'Are you saying I could come to Whitby?' I asked as quietly as I could. 'Be careful what you offer. You're talking to a desperate man. I'll almost certainly take you up on anything.'

'It wouldn't just be up to me, you know.'

'I suppose I'd have to be interviewed,' I said and laughed.

'Yes,' she said, but without laughing. 'Everybody has to agree. I suppose they might take you, but you'd have to explain what you can do.' Alice had become brisk and efficient. She had obviously decided at some point that she couldn't do all her communicating with a brush.

'Well,' I said, 'I can cook eggs, clean paint off carpets . . .'

'I didn't say that,' she snapped, and then regretted the snapping and spoke more gently. 'I didn't say what you can do for *us*, did I, Chris? That's not what I said.'

'Then what?'

'What you can do. What you would be doing with your days. We only once had someone in with us who didn't have something to do, and it became too exhausting for everyone.' I thought for a moment.

'I can write a book,' I said uneasily, 'about an eighteenth-century poet, who was thought to be mad.'

'Was he mad?'

'Yes and no.'

'Never thought I'd hear you use that phrase. Well, I can ask them. You can write the book, can you?'

I watched how carefully she made out the cheque and filled in the details on her stub. Once I had done all of that, but with more of a flourish, as though it really didn't matter at all.

Back in the shop, I made her another coffee as she wandered about. Out in the back she found the stack of canvases. They were all Serena's. She pulled them out one by one and leaned them against the wall.

'You know what these are?'

'Fordie's wife's paintings,' I said. 'I think they're pretty good myself.'

'You always did have taste, Chris. That's how we met, I seem to recall. These are Serena Tallises.'

'That's right. That was her name.'

'They're not worth a fortune, but they are worth something. One was sold at auction a while back for a few thousand. There's more than ten of them here. Maybe your old friend Stamford Tewk left you a little more than you think.'

'You've just made an old man very happy.'

'Which one?' I wanted to touch her, but I knew that I mustn't. She didn't seem greatly inclined to touch me. There were new rules here and I didn't understand them yet. She couldn't take her eyes from one picture, the storm-whipped canvas of the coast at night.

'You really like that one, don't you?'

'I think it's beautiful.' I picked it up and put it in her arms.

'It's yours.' But she looked unsure.

'You know, Chris, I think you used to give things to people as a way of controlling them.'

'Yes,' I said, 'I think I probably did. Never worked though, did it?'

'And I used to do things just because somebody asked me to.' For the passing of a moment, a look of that old distraction covered her face 'I miss her sometimes, you know.'

'Who?' I said.

'The Alice who used to do things just because somebody asked. Now I seem to have ended up in charge of the house up in Whitby, and now people do things because I ask them to. Which means that I must be always reminding myself what I'm supposed to be asking them. There are some days when the whole of my head is so filled up with all those questions, there doesn't seem to be any space left in there for pictures at all.'

'Ah,' I said, 'then both our lives have changed.'

I offered her, very tentatively, Fordie's room for the night, but I sensed that she wouldn't be staying. She explained that she had to drive over to the East End. She was expected. Her exhibition.

'Drive?' I said.

'I have my little Morris outside.'

'When did you learn to drive?'

'Oh, I could always drive.'

'You never drove when you were with me.'

'You never asked me to.' Silence for a few moments.

'You won't forget, will you, to talk to your friends in Whitby?' She shook her head. 'Hermann Siegfried?'

'I don't do it any more. It served its purpose.'

'You got born then?'

'What?' she said, and the lines on her forehead deepened.

'In Tenby I asked you to marry me. Said we could have children. No embryos from embryos, is what you said. Remember?' Alice looked at me in silence and then started to laugh, very slowly at first and I realised that I had never heard her laugh in all the time we had been together. Once it gained its full momentum, there was a hint of wildness about the sound, as though something new had been born inside her, and was only now beginning to try out her senses for size. The laughter continued and increased and I realised that it was not an entirely comforting sound. There was menace in it as well as joy, but even so I had started to laugh along with her.

'What's so funny?'

'I was talking about you, Chris, not me. You should have read Siegfried, you know – I was always leaving the bloody book about for you to pick up. You might have learnt something, except I suppose you couldn't imagine how silent little Alice could teach you anything back then. One of Siegfried's rules was this: complete changes are no changes at all. They're disguises. Every time you were given the opportunity for a birthing you ran away. There was that girl you told me about, what was her name?'

'Pauline Healey,' I said uncomfortably.

'Then your priesthood. You could have taken something away from it all, but no, not you. You couldn't just become a non-priest, you had to become an anti-priest. Then you dropped your thesis, at least partly because you couldn't stand your supervisor. So instead of working occasionally with one dreadful man, you ended up working all the time with that other dreadful man, what was he called again?'

'Andrew Cavendish-Porter,' I said edgily. I wasn't enjoying this.

'And now you're here with the ghosts of the priest, and the Olympic runner, and the high-flying businessman, and the racing-car driver and I suppose you've added Stamford Tewk's ghost to the mix as well. All Siegfried's book said finally was that getting born is a long, slow change, not a sudden transformation. You're a mammal, Chris, not a butterfly. Could you get that machine of yours out again? I was intrigued by the way it squatted on your neck and gave off those little blips of light.'

So I took it out and explained how it worked. And that was how, before she left that night, Alice's final courtesy was to fit me up and switch me on and give me a good long look before she went out of the door and left me flickering away inside, as though, in amongst the thousands of books, I was trying to signal to someone out there in the dark.

Resentment #2

The melancholy of this day hung long upon me.

SAMUEL JOHNSON, *Diaries*

The next day the knock on the door kept on, until I went
and peered cautiously through the blind. It appeared to be
some sort of uniformed courier. I opened the door and he
handed me the package. It was a painting, the painting I had
given Alice the night before. And attached to it was this note:

Dear Chris,
I reckon you might need this picture more than I do.
Why don't you finish your book first, then maybe we can talk
about Whitby? There are some things we can only get done by
ourselves. I think I've learnt that much at least.
Take care of yourself.
Love,
Alice

I still had the money Charles Redmond had given me, so I
went out and bought a bottle of whisky.

Late in the afternoon, and half-way through the bottle, I

shouted out a single word, a single obscene word, at the top of my voice. I just wanted one of them in front of me, that was all, just one, whether it was Fordie or Harry or Andrew Cavendish-Porter or Alice. I wanted someone to yell some truths at, you see, I wanted to get a few things off my chest. I didn't want to hurt any of them. If I had taken hold of them, which I probably would have done, it would have been merely by way of restraint, to stop them leaving, to make them concentrate on what I was trying to say, upon the importance of it, for you must realise by now, as I did, that everything had gone, and even what hadn't gone yet was about to. It seemed to me that I'd paid a fortune, the whole fortune of my life, for the pleasure of these people's company. And now Andrew was in Bath in his grand Georgian house, and Harry was back in Stockport counting the money I'd given him, and Alice was in Whitechapel supervising her exhibition. Even Fordie was probably up in heaven, with my blessing on his head, redeemed through his beneficence to his crazy stepdaughter. Financed by me.

And the whisky poured down, without even a single egg to absorb it. It scorched my throat and made my memory blaze with anger, until I stumbled round the shop picking up the photographs of Fordie and all his literary friends and smashed them one by one against the walls. There were tiny shards of glass everywhere. Finally, sometime in the evening, I decided it was time to talk to Alice. A little unsteadily I held up that card she had sent me so that I could read the telephone number of the gallery. I picked up the phone, then I banged the receiver up and down on the cradle until my befuddled brain realised at last that the phone was dead. I had been cut off for not paying the bill, so I ripped the whole unit out of the wall, and staggered down to Richmond Bridge with it in my arms. Then I threw it all in the river. It floated for a few yards, then slowly sank.

Next day I rose early with a sense of the catastrophic hangover that was slowly gathering pace inside my body. I went straight downstairs all the same, avoiding the tiny splinters of glass all around. I stood before the safe, that steely tabernacle in the wall. I knew now why Fordie had abandoned it: because of the way the story ended. Or because of the way it didn't end, not even with Pelham's death. You'd think a man could at least rely on death for a decent terminus. I leaned forward then and, through the blur of my distemper, started carefully turning the dial, having resolved at last to get on with my work, and this time finish it.

When Lord Chilford finally drilled into the cranium of the corpse on the table before him, he briefly held his breath. The sheer absurdity of it, he thought, but still he held it. No malignant shadow swooped wildly round the room. No dreadful new stench assaulted their nostrils, though the smell in the underground chamber was bad enough already. Neither he nor his friend Benjamin Franklin fell twitching to the ground. And no sound was emitted from within the calcined chamber of the body before them. So they set about their business, doing that which the law of the realm did not permit them to do, but which intellectual enquiry demanded of them all the same. And when they had finished, they both stepped back, almost in unison.

'The mind of man expands,' Lord Chilford said, wiping the blood from his hands and leather apron, both stained from the hacking and sawing, 'but none too quickly, eh Ben?' Then Chilford walked over to the nearest cask, and taking the wooden mallet which hung on its bristling string, he thwacked out the bung. He filled the two half-pint tin pots to the brim with claret, and carried them across to his companion, sweating gently now on his stool at the other side of the makeshift autopsy table. Then he raised his cup in a toast.

'So much work,' he said, 'so much work in medicine and natural philosophy, merely to establish the parameters of the great void that is superstition. Half the time we labour so fiercely only to establish what's not even there.'

'The body?' Franklin asked, getting his breath back slowly. Chilford pointed a finger down towards the shiny stone slabs beneath their feet.

'Jacob will inter the remains of Richard Pelham later tonight. The man has already disappeared into obscurity. He passed beyond the reach of legality or legitimate inquest some time back. To all intents and purposes, the body before us is anonymous. It belongs to no one. Our little posthumous enquiry has made no difference to that.'

Franklin nodded, and they both drank deeply for a while in silence, before rousing themselves finally to collect up the dismembered remains of the poet Richard Pelham, which lay between them.

In 1998 renovation work began on 36 Craven Street near Trafalgar Square, the house in which Benjamin Franklin lived from 1757 to 1772, when he was in London as agent for the Pennsylvania Assembly, and the very years in which he did his crucial work on electricity. The men digging out the old basement found the bones of four adults and a minimum of six children. The bones had been sawn and drilled. It was probably Dr William Hewson, Fellow of the Royal Society, and a pioneer of modern surgery (also husband to the daughter of Franklin's landlady) who performed the operations. These appeared to be anatomical experiments, either on Hewson's patients or possibly on bodies stolen from graveyards. It is now assumed that Franklin probably knew all about these activities, for it is thought that his scientific interest would have weighed more strongly in his mind than his fear of the illegality of the operation. Before the 1832 Anatomy Act, it was illegal to dissect a human body at a private home. Doctors frequently bought their specimens from grave-robbers.

Some of the Craven Street remains showed evidence of trepanning – the drilling of holes in the skull to lessen the pressure on the brain, or even to release evil spirits. The normal assumption has always been that it would be pointless to carry out this operation on a corpse.